Reign of the Dead
Apocalypse End

Len Barnhart

Dedication

To Carol

I have looked across majestic mountain ranges in awe.

I have marveled at the stars in the night sky and the secrets they hold.

In the simplest of things in nature I see complexity.

But dearest to me is when I look to my side and know you will always be there.

Part 1

TANGIER

1

Leon Baltimore walked into the storeroom of the makeshift armory on Tangier Island and stopped dead in his tracks.

Jacob DuBois, a recent immigrant from Louisiana, was swaying back and forth on his knees, chanting a rhythmic cadence. His face was upturned and his arms were outstretched, palms up.

"You think that'll conjure up some big miracle?" Leon asked. "That those bastards will just drop dead again and go away with a little Who-do Voodoo?"

Jacob stopped swaying and looked up at Leon's black face. "It's powerful stuff. If it can raise de dead, it can work de udder way, too," he said with a heavy Cajun accent.

"Well, how about keeping your little rituals at home, Swamp Man?"

Leon pushed past the kneeling man. "Jesus Christ, just what we need here, another freak!"

Jacob got to his feet and stormed from the room. A loud echo reverberated throughout the building as the door slammed shut behind him. Leon shook his head ruefully and set about the task that had brought him there; another recon mission. He hated them. They always ended the same, with dead air, dead cities, and wasted time. Washington, D.C. and all of its suburbs had been that way for over a year. For the life of him, he couldn't figure out why they still bothered to look. It was just something to do, he figured, something to give them hope, to keep them busy day to day and stave off insanity. But across the water there was no hope and no sanity, only death and more death.

Leon pushed aside the images of the mainland and of the Cajun's swaying prayer and unlocked the gun cabinet positioned against the back wall of the dank, cinderblock building.

Wafting from the open cabinet, the sweet smell of gun oil filled his nostrils and he breathed it in. He liked the smell of it. It meant the weapons were being properly cared for. Like everything on the island, the armory was damp. A misfiring weapon would not be his undoing.

"I'll put my faith in you," he cooed, stroking the barrel of his favorite weapon before slinging it over his shoulder. After all, it was the only tangible item that stood between himself, death, and more death. Wits and weapons—fail at either and you were in for a very bad day.

The March sunlight was warm as Leon stepped outside and he tilted his face upward to meet it. He turned his head to one side and rubbed the tense muscles on the back of his neck, hoping to relieve the tension that was building there again. What he really needed was a pair of pretty, black hands to massage his troubled thoughts away. How long had it been since he'd actually touched a woman in an intimate way? He couldn't remember, certainly it was before the plague, before the world went to shit.

The past two years had nearly destroyed humanity. But with good management and the Chesapeake Bay as a buffer zone, they had managed to survive. They were safe from the walking death that invaded a thriving world and turned it into an animated graveyard—safe and isolated.

Leon's favorite place to waste away the unused hours of the day was only three doors down the street from the armory and he still had time to get a glass of Julio's apple wine before the trip. Maybe it would be enough to ease the stiffness in his neck; one, maybe two, but certainly not three. Three could cloud his judgment. It could dull his wit. Wits and weapons…death and more death. He couldn't think of one without the other and while his contribution to the island community allowed him to eat and drink more than most at the little pub, Julio would certainly curb his ability to get falling down drunk, especially before a scheduled search. "You have to save some for the others," he would say, "and drinking too much will make you look like one of those dead-heads across the bay, staggering this way and that. And you drool when you're drunk. Someone is liable to shoot you by mistake."

Leon would usually smile at the little man's funny words, but he was well aware of the price of over-indulgence at the wrong time. He would have one or two, but certainly not three.

The bright blue sign over the door proudly declared Julio's to be Tangier's social club of choice. That description was likely true since it was the only place on the island that served alcohol. The other shops and stores were dedicated to keeping the population fed and sheltered. Julio was thankful for what his place did for a community that had little in the way of lifting spirits. His was a gathering place, a place to forget the world outside. It was perhaps the most important of all the shops and barter styled businesses on Tangier, and of all of them, it was positively the most popular.

The door was locked when Leon tugged on it and the anticipated tang of Julio's apple wine teased the back of his tongue even more now as he realized he would get none this morning. Julio was late again and Leon had no time to wait. He was leaving for the mainland in less than an hour.

***

The helicopter was readied for flight on the pad in front of the airport's main building. It was a modest airport, too small to handle anything but single or twin engine aircraft. Two hundred yards away, the tides of the Chesapeake Bay licked the sandy shoreline. The chopper's rotating blades created a strong, steady wind that tore at Leon's clothing with a ferocity equal to that of the tropical storm they had experienced a week before. Its military green skin was dull, but clean. Great care was taken with the equipment on the island. It was too difficult to replace.

Leon noticed Hal Davidson and Jack Lewis standing in the doorway of the main structure. They would be going on this futile expedition with him. Hal would fly the big green bird and as usual, he and Jack would do the grunt work.

Leon tried to shake off his aversion to the trip and smiled at the approaching men.

2

Jim Workman stared hopelessly at the guts of the communication console in front of him. He had devoted countless hours to get it operational again. It was ironic that the most powerful and advanced communication setup within fifty miles had failed shortly after their arrival at the Mount Weather Underground.

For more than a year he had pulled, poked, and pounded on it. He had finally succumbed to the reality that it would never work again. The simple truth was that vital parts had burned out and there were no replacements to be found.

Jim reclined in his chair and glanced up at the video monitors that lined the wall in front of him. Four of the screens were dead and blank. Two were still live. One had a clear view of downtown Moscow, a desolate place, void of life, the only movement—walking corpses.

The other monitor was of Washington, D.C. and that scene was no better than Moscow's. The other four screens had ceased to function, one at a time, months before. More than likely, the satellites had spun out of their orbits or had simply stopped working. In any case, they were cut off from anyone who might still be alive in the world above.

Dr. Sharon Darney, their resident expert on the plague, had once said the walking dead could remain mobile for ten years, maybe more, before decomposition made movement impossible. Two years had passed and Jim couldn't wait another eight to find out if anyone else was alive. They had survived, so others must have survived as well.

He needed to do something. Complacency had set in and it had become too easy to shut everything out and hope for the best. Surely there were survivors out there banding together to regain control of the situation. It was time to go find them. Amanda would be against the idea. After all the horrors they had been through, she would be content to stay right where she was and say to hell with it all. As they had all learned, it was not just the well-intentioned kind and honest people who had survived the plague. They'd all had more than their fill of the other kind. But being cooped up in the massive hole in the ground was finally catching up to him. It was time to make a move. Surviving was not living.

Amanda sat at the corner table in the cafeteria, pushing powdered eggs around on her plate. She had forgotten what real food tasted like. She had forgotten much in the past two years— her life before the plague, old friends, and old loves. She thought it was better that way, at least for now. Dwelling on the past only brought sadness with it and a desire for the way things were. But life would never be as it had been. The world was different now. It was dying.

When Amanda looked up from her plate, she noticed Jim standing in the doorway and motioned for him.

He sat down across from her in the familiar manner of old lovers. She couldn't help but notice that his mood had not changed. Lately he had become jaded, at times distant and isolated. He would hide away in the war room for hours without so much as an appearance for food or water. She was becoming worried about him. This sullen behavior stood in stark contrast to the ways of the man she had fallen in love with. The caring and compassionate leader that he was only months ago had become reticent and even a bit callous. She feared not only for him, but also for herself. She loved him and now she feared losing him. The worst part of it was that she didn't know why.

Amanda finished chewing her forkful of bland eggs and hoped that a little small talk might coax him into a meaningful conversation. "Anything new?" she asked, expecting the usual answer.

Jim squirmed in his seat and then replied the same as always—"No."

He fell silent again, leaving Amanda to think up a new topic to keep him talking. Anything was better than another silent meal, she thought, stirring her eggs once again.

"That radio's never going to work," she said finally. "Have you thought about looking for other survivors? There hasn't been a creature near the complex in months. It might be safe to—."

Jim's eyes widened and an exhilarated look washed over his face as he interrupted her. "Yes, I've thought a lot about it. Tangier Island," he said. "I want to go to Tangier Island."

Amanda's jaw dropped. This was not the conversation she had hoped for when she began asking questions. She had opened a big can of smelly, walking-dead worms.

"That's not what I meant. Not Tangier Island, Jim. It's too far." How quickly he had turned this around. "It's too dangerous and besides, it's been a year since you got that message. How do you even know that the person who sent it is still alive? For God's sake…"

"I *don't* know. That's the point. They never acknowledged our reply. I don't think the radio was sending, even then."

Amanda dropped her fork with a clatter that mirrored her jangled nerves. She had suddenly lost what little appetite she had. Her head was spinning and now she had to win an argument with one of the most headstrong men she'd ever known.

"So that's it? You want to risk your life and what little happiness may be left to us because you're stir crazy? Jesus, Jim, why?"

"If there's someone alive there, I have to know," he said. "We all do. We can't go on forever here. Eventually, we will run out of supplies. Tangier Island would be the ideal place. If there are survivors, there's a good chance they'd be there, maybe even hundreds of them. We have to know. This is important."

"No, goddamn it." Her voice quivered as she stood up. "*We* don't have to know anything—*you* do!"

She stormed away and left a perplexed Jim Workman sitting alone.

3

The helicopter rose in the crisp spring air and Leon felt the familiar churning in his gut that returned every time the bird took off.

There was no approval or clearance for takeoff. The sky was free of traffic. Not so much as a single airplane had been seen flying over the island since the first couple of months. No planes, cars, or people were where they were going. No living ones, anyway. They were going into the pits of hell once again.

The airport grew smaller beneath them as they rose higher. Leon stared out the window, hoping the scenery would relieve his upset stomach. The churning did finally settle down after the chopper leveled out for their flight to the mainland. Leon watched the island as it dropped away behind them, noticing for the first time how green everything had become since winter. The blue-green waves of Chesapeake Bay glimmered in the sunlight and occasionally a wave caught the sunlight just right and sent flashes of brilliant, blinding light up to him.

"Where today?" Hal asked, glancing at Jack who was seated next to him, a pen clenched between his teeth, reading some maps.

"Go up by Crisfield," Jack said, "then turn west toward St. Mary's County and follow the coast north for a while. We'll see from there." His eyes never left his maps. He turned them to the left, then to the right, as though trying to find the best angle to view them. He flipped from page to page trying to find the right one.

Leon rolled his eyes in disgust. He'd seen this same scene play out many times before. No wonder they hadn't found anyone yet. They were lucky to find their way home.

Jack finally threw the papers aside and drank from the cup of coffee hanging in a cup holder next to him. His creased face and graying hair showed every bit of his fifty-two years. He had become hard like a rock since the plague, but his strength didn't lie in calculations. He was a soldier, an unstoppable force once he got started. If there was anyone he'd want in a foxhole next to him, it would be Jack.

The chopper continued to fly north along the path Jack had laid out until they reached Crisfield. The familiar sight of the Mormon temple came into view, its tall golden steeple, still as pristine as it had been two years before. The rest of the building was in shambles. When things fell apart and people were left with nothing else they turned to the churches, temples, synagogues, and mosques, hoping their religion would save them. But doing so only made them easy prey for the bloodthirsty ghouls that surrounded the buildings like dogs herding sheep to be slaughtered.

Yes, religion did make matters worse. Many maintained the outlandish idea that God had somehow willed the dead to rise and attack the living, that it was the resurrection foretold in the Bible. Religious zealots had whipped the easily-led masses into a frenzy of Bible-thumping idiots shouting, "God's will!" Faithful flocks refused to properly incapacitate the bodies of the dead. They saw it as a contradiction to "God's will." Others thought resurrected family members and friends were still, at least on some level, themselves. But nothing was farther from the truth. Those misguided herds of humanity had in large measure caused the downfall of mankind with astonishing speed. It had taken a mere two months for eighty-five percent of the world's population to be annihilated, most of whom then joined the increasing numbers of walking dead. It was a desperate situation. But they were safe on Tangier Island, at least until the walking corpses learned to swim.

Leon shifted in his seat. He didn't want them to set the chopper down. Sometimes they did, sometimes they didn't. He was hoping this was a time when they wouldn't. It was never a good time on the ground. You could never really tell from the air what was below. They had nearly been overwhelmed on two past occasions when a safe landing looked feasible from a thousand feet, only to have the hordes pour from shadows and open doorways to fill the streets. Leon was in no hurry for another adventure.

He breathed a sigh of relief when they flew past Crisfield and turned west toward St Mary's City.

Their flight was now taking them over Smith Island. The view created a sense of normalcy in a world turned upside down. Traffic moved on the island roads below, mainly bicycles. But life moved on with at least some of the past's regularity. People strolled the sidewalks and slipped in and out of trade shops in a manner impossible to imitate anywhere else. Children played stick ball in the street, unafraid. One man stood perched on a ladder, painting the wooden siding on his house. A woman stood below him, her eyes shielded from the sun in an upturned salute.

A group of no-nonsense locals on Tangier Island had been the first to take things in hand and make it safe. Once the situation had been handled, they began broadcasting Ham radio messages in an attempt to locate other survivors. The island's population began to grow as the haggard masses clung to the hope that the island was a safe place and made their way there by boat. One group of twenty made the trip clinging to a half dozen lashed-together inner tubes, kicking and paddling their way across the bay to Tangier.

To make a stand on the mainland would have meant certain death. There were simply too many walking dead cannibals. They needed better odds to survive. The logical answer was Tangier Island. When Tangier became overcrowded, a team was organized to go to Smith Island to repeat their feat.

Smith Island was a bit more complicated to conquer than Tangier. It was much larger, meaning more ghouls to destroy, but eventually it was made safe as well and their little community began to grow and become self-sustaining. Later, they would take the Bloodsworth and Hooper Islands, an area totaling approximately forty miles in length located between Virginia and Maryland in the Chesapeake Bay.

Things were still far from normal as Leon could attest to, but from fifteen hundred feet in the air, it looked much better than where they were going.

The chopper flew along the coastline toward St. Mary's City. Leon's stomach began to churn as his anxiety mounted. This was not the coastline of an island, but the state of Maryland. Real danger lurked below. If they set down there, they'd be putting their lives in serious danger. Hal turned west and the chopper moved inland.

St. Mary's City was a typical town on the bay, with lots of seafood restaurants, shopping centers, and buildings on stilts. Before the plague, tourism had flourished. Families and friends arrived by the hundreds each week during the summer months for the sites of the bay, deep-sea fishing, and vacation bliss.

Gleeful tourists had been replaced with uncaring monsters that aimlessly roved about in large numbers, not sure of where to go or what they were there for until some unfortunate person happened to stray into their field of vision. If there were survivors there, they were hidden well. A simple flyover would not bring them out. The easy task of extracting survivors from rooftops had long since vanished. If the truth be known, they hadn't found anyone to save in more than a year.

Jack pointed to a cloud of gray smoke that billowed into the sky several miles ahead. It was coming from an area just south of Lexington Park. Hal tilted the stick and the chopper increased its speed. Leon knew what they were thinking, that someone needing assistance had set the fire—a smoke signal for help.

Leon began checking his gear in the event that they would have to get out of the craft and set out in a ground fight. Adrenaline spiked his chest as though liquid steel ran through his veins. His breathing quickened and perspiration beaded his forehead. He found himself not so much afraid as exhilarated at the thought of making the trip meaningful. Finding just one person still alive would make all the fruitless trips worthwhile. He was getting his hopes up again.

Hal flew the chopper counterclockwise about three hundred feet above and outside of the column of smoke above a strip mall that housed several small businesses. One of the businesses in the middle of the mall had caught fire. In a few minutes, the whole mall would be burning.

Leon watched closely, waiting for someone to flee from the flames, their arms flailing about so the saviors in the helicopter would see them. Anytime now they would rush to the ground and lay to waste the ghouls that were smart enough to stay away from the fire and wait for their prey to come out, then load the chopper with grateful occupants and give them a new home, a home that was safe. Anytime now it would happen…

Hal kept the chopper in a circular path around the building. All eyes were focused on the ground as they waited for someone—anyone to make their whereabouts known. They waited until the flames spread from business to business and consumed the entire mall. The roof caved in from the center out, and sprays of sparks shot upward. The heat was intense and could be felt now even in the chopper.

A burst of heated air exploded above the inferno and the chopper rose fifty feet in a matter of seconds. For a moment it seemed the aircraft would spin out of control and crash to the ground as the sudden rush of heated air pushed them upward too fast for Hal to maintain control. He fought with the stick for what seemed like an eternity as the chopper swung left to right, then dived forward and backward, all the while bouncing its occupants around in their seats as they pondered their fate. Then he regained control and it settled again. Hal turned the stick and pulled the chopper further away from the blasting heat and hovered there.

Hope dwindled as the building burned and the ghouls moved in. Seeing no one to attack, they dispersed and moved on, ignoring the green bird overhead. The occupants of the chopper watched silently, then moved on themselves.

Leon's stomach churned again.

4

Jim Workman spread the maps across the top of the conference room table.

He was looking for the fastest and safest route to Tangier Island. Staying away from the more populated areas whenever possible was a given, but as he stared at the maps, it was becoming all too clear that there would be no safe way to get to his destination. From this particular map, he couldn't even tell if there was a bridge that led to the island or if he'd have to use a boat to cross the bay.

Route 17 would take him most of the way, but it would also take him through several small towns. The fact that it was such a straight shot outweighed the danger of crossing through populated areas—time versus safety.

He could follow Seventeen as far as Tappahannock. From there he would have to take 360 and rely on stealth to get him through heavily inhabited areas and to the coast.

Tangier Island was twelve miles offshore. If there wasn't a bridge, and that seemed to be the case as far as he could tell, it seemed logical that there would be boats docked in or around Smith's Point. Smith's Point was the closest tip of land to the Island.

Jim studied the small island on the map and searched his mind for details from the static-filled message he had received a year before: *This is Tangier Island, off the coast of Virginia. Is anyone there?* The message repeated several times before it stopped. He would have missed it completely if not for the fact that he'd forgotten to turn off the radio when he left the room and had returned to do so.

He had tried for weeks to get a response to no avail. In the pit of his gut he knew they were still there. Somehow, he knew. Though they never received the message again after that one time, it remained in the back of his mind until he had become obsessed with finding out once and for all.

The total trip was over one hundred and sixty miles. If he was careful, he would make it there in one piece, but he would do it alone. If by chance something did go wrong, he would not be responsible for another person's injury.

***

In the outer lobby, floor-to-ceiling windows gave Felicia an excellent view of the front lawn and the Easter lilies that were now in full bloom. It was a beautiful day and happy thoughts flooded her mind. She enjoyed the green foliage and the leaves that gently blew in the breeze. She enjoyed it so much, even from the inside looking out. If she could only step through the door and stand outside she'd let the fragrance of those flowers and spring air fill her senses. But she knew better than that. It was important to stay hidden away. They'd learned from past mistakes that it was vital to remain unseen and unheard. One blunder could bring a world of trouble upon them.

They had been safe at the Mount Weather complex since arriving a year before, tucked away underground in the seven-story city built by the government to maintain control in the event of a national crisis. When the crisis finally arrived in the form of an Armageddon of walking-dead cannibals, the tenants had been done in by their own selfish desire for power and ill-advised procedures. But their failure had a silver lining…it left the way open for the sixty-eight survivors, counting Felicia, to find a new and safer refuge.

How long they would have to stay hidden didn't matter to her now. She had become comfortable with her surroundings and most importantly, they were safe as long as no one stepped outside. She could not smell those flowers, but she was content to look at them from her chair and dream.

Felicia turned at the sound of the elevator door sliding open.

A year ago, a sudden noise that broke the silence like that would have made her jump from her skin, but not now. The premonitions had left her, and calmness reigned. But the grimace on Amanda's face made it clear that she did not feel the same. Amanda walked over to the window and stood beside Felicia.

"It's pretty outside, isn't it?" Amanda said.

"Yes."

"It looks so peaceful, so calm. Do you think it's this peaceful out there beyond the safety of the mountain?" She turned to face Felicia and a lone tear slid down her cheek.

"I don't know, maybe."

Amanda brushed the tear away and focused on the lawn outside. "I hope so," she said, then fell silent.

"He's going out there, isn't he?" Felicia asked. "Jim, I mean. He's going on a search for others to Tangier Island?"

Felicia knew it would come to this, even if Amanda didn't. Jim Workman was not one to sit idle. She was surprised that he had stayed cooped up this long. Everyone in the complex knew of the message from Tangier Island the previous year.

"Yes, he is," Amanda said.

Felicia tried to think of a way to console her friend. She felt Amanda's pain. If Mick came to her and announced a plan like this, she wouldn't take it too well, either. She would quickly lose the contented feeling she had been experiencing. A terrible thought suddenly came to her.

"Mick's not going with him, is he?"

"No. Jim's going alone."

Amanda's answer eased Felicia's mind and she released a long sigh. Mick wasn't the adventurous type. He was a coordinator, a layer of plans. He would be perfectly happy to make sure everything was just as it should be at home. Felicia was glad for that.

"Amanda," Felicia said, "Jim has a purpose. If it weren't for him, we would have all perished long ago. He saved us all. God— or whatever is controlling this world gone crazy—has things in store for him. That's what I believe. Who's to say his purpose isn't helping someone else to survive now?"

"That's a lovely little scenario, but we don't know that. All I know is the man I love is leaving me on a very dangerous whim. I may never see him again and I think I'm beginning to hate him for it."

"What if you're right, Amanda? What if you never see him again? Do you really want to spend your last moments with him full of hate? Go to him. Let him take your love on this journey with him to keep him company. It will help to keep him safe.

You'd be surprised how much something like that can serve to keep one's wits sharp. If you don't, you'll regret it forever if something does happen."

Amanda fell into Felicia's arms and sobbed. Once again it seemed her world was falling apart. It had fallen apart when the walking dead stripped her of everything she held dear and now with Jim leaving, once again her life was being turned upside down.

She felt helpless and afraid.

5

Mick was tightening the last bolt on the access panel to the backup generator when Jim found him.

Mick hadn't seen Jim enter, but he sensed him there and turned. He brushed his blond hair away from his face and huffed a sigh of completeness upon finishing his job. Matthew Ford was clearing the tools away from the work area.

"All done." He wiped his hands on a towel draped over his shoulder. "That's the last one. This equipment is still in good condition. We may never need to use the backup stuff, but it's good to know it will work should we need it to."

Jim nodded his agreement as he watched Matt put the tools they had been using back into the cabinet on the far wall of the utility room.

Mick leaned over, picked up a forgotten tool from the floor, and tossed it to Matt. "You don't know what's out there, Jim," Mick said.

Here we go again, Jim thought, another sermon on the dangers outside. Word of his planned trip had obviously traveled fast.

"That's the point isn't it, Mick? None of us do. No one's been out there since we got here."

"Yes, we do know. Have you been ignoring those monitors in the war room? One satellite is still pointed at Washington, D.C. It looks to me like those things are still out in full force."

"I'll stay away from D.C."

"They're everywhere. And in case you've forgotten, one bite and you're infected. And you know what that means."

"I know what it means. I'll be fine."

Matt, who had been listening, said, "I'll go, too. It'll be—"

"No!" Jim snapped, cutting him off. "I go alone."

"But—"

"No buts! I won't risk another life."

"There," Mick said, "You see? You do realize the danger. Why risk it at all? Let those people take care of their own."

"And us ours?" Jim asked. "We're fine here. Those things couldn't get down here even if they had the brains God gave a chimp, and they don't. What if there are people there and they need help? It would be selfish not to try. Besides, eventually we'll need a new place."

Mick had discussed this topic with Jim before, and he had yet to come out the winner. Jim was going to do what Jim wanted to do and that was that. Still, he felt it necessary to try to convince him of what he thought was the most prudent decision.

"I've got it all figured out," Jim said.

For the first time, Mick noticed the satchel Jim had been holding.

"Let me show you," Jim said. "It may make you feel more at ease."

Jim pulled some papers from the bag, selected the map he intended to use for the trip and laid it out on a nearby workbench. He had used a yellow hi-liter to trace the route he would take from their location all the way to Tangier Island.

Mick studied the map. He was familiar with the route Jim had outlined. "It should be smooth sailing until you get to Fredericksburg," he said, pointing out the spot. "You'll have to be very careful there, and again once you get to Tappahannock." He traced his finger along the yellow line as he spoke. "From there on, you'll have your hands full all the way to Smith's Point."

Mick turned to Jim. "How do you figure to get there?"

"The Humvee up top."

"What if it breaks down?"

"I'll throw a motorcycle in the back. If the Humvee has problems, I'll use the motorcycle."

"Where are you going to find a motorcycle?"

"There are several in the warehouse at the far end of the property."

"You've been up there?" Mick asked.

"I have."

Mick's eyebrow rose in surprise. Even he had not ventured up top for fear of attracting unwanted guests.

"It seems like you've got it all figured out.

"I do."

"Well, I guess the only thing left to say is good luck."

Jim smiled and they shook hands.

Matt formulated a plan of his own.

***

Sharon Darney was the resident expert in the field of virology. When the dead phenomenon began she had been sent to the Mount Weather Underground to assist in finding an answer for the sudden plague of living-dead.

Her work had been in vain.

Before she could unravel the mystery, war broke out between the two differing military factions running the complex. They finally killed each other in the final moments before her escape amid a flurry of gunfire.

One hundred soldiers and staff members lay dead, though they hadn't remained that way for long. Before she left the compound, they had reanimated, forcing her to leave through the ventilation system. It was later that she found Jim Workman and the rest of the survivors who now occupied the underground complex with her. They had briefly taken control of a prison for asylum from the marauding dead until that too had proven unsafe.

Ironically, she was back where she had started, along with the sixty-eight survivors from the prison. But on her return, there were new questions to be answered. The hundred soldiers who had reanimated before she left were found to be once again dead on their arrival, sprawled motionless on the floors of the compound. She had hoped to solve the undead puzzle by now, but she was still without answers. Complicating matters further was the fact that her private lab specimen still functioned. She did have one clue. The reanimated soldiers had never gotten to ground level. They had never had the light of day fall on their shoulders. Given the amount of decay, Sharon figured they had ceased to function soon after her escape. The dead soldiers' bodies had decayed as normal, dead flesh. But a reanimate's flesh was different. What normally took days or weeks to decay took months or years once the body was mobile again. Those infected early in the plague decomposed at a slower rate than those infected later, and no two reanimates were exactly alike. This made it difficult to be sure exactly how long they would remain mobile.

Once again she had spent the majority of the day pouring over old data, hoping to suddenly see something she had missed the first hundred times. In her thirty-seven years of life, she had never been so frustrated. Sometimes she felt like packing up her lab equipment and simply riding the whole thing out without even trying anymore. It would ease the headaches, but not the desire. She was passionate for answers.

Why did the world's dead suddenly begin to come back? How could they continue without the slightest sign of blood flow, need for nourishment, oxygen, or water? Then there was the strangest question of all…Why did they feel the urge to consume living, human flesh? It was definitely not for sustenance; it was more like a primal urge that drove them. Somewhere in the back of their malfunctioning brains lurked a very dark and evil desire—a cannibalistic urge. It was the only motivation in a brain that lacked the ability to reason.

Sharon suspected a virus from the beginning—something they'd never seen before. And maybe a new virus or bacteria *was* responsible for the agonizing death one suffered from even the slightest bite, but she was beginning to think something else was responsible for their return from the immobile state of death. Lately she had wondered if God himself hadn't put the whole thing into motion after all. If a human died for any reason they would without fail, revive. Contact with the unknown virus was not needed. A bite was not necessary. The inactive state of death was simply a bridge from life to walking death.

It was beginning to seem like a greater power was indeed at work.

Sharon removed her lab coat and hung it on a metal hook close to the door leading from the lab. She passed a mirror on the way and pulled at her wilted strands of shoulder-length, blond hair. She needed an Oprah makeover. To her surprise, there were gray streaks hiding beneath. Her oval face was smooth, but the stress of her job showed under her blue eyes, now hollow and tired looking.

Sharon turned away from the mirror.

Her research day had come to an end. Maybe she should just give up her work altogether and sit down with a good book for a while. At least take a break. In seven or eight years, the problem would take care of itself. The decomposition rate, though slowed, would eventually take its toll on the reanimates by refusing to allow their brains to function at all. The state of their bodies would become so decayed that they would no longer be able to move. They were literally rotting on their feet.

Sharon opened the door and stood face to face with Jim Workman. The sudden encounter startled her and she stumbled backward into the room, clutching her chest as though to calm her pounding heart.

Jim grabbed her by the shoulders. Sharon raised her hand to show she was able-bodied and Jim released her.

"I didn't mean to scare you like that," he said.

Sharon straightened her disheveled hair. "It's okay, Jim. What can I do for you?"

"I'm going on a little trip and I need your advice."

Sharon wasn't aware of any planned trips to the outside. It wasn't any of her business, but still, to her it seemed a little bold.

"Where are you going?" she asked.

"Tangier Island."

"Ah, yes, the message. Did you get another one?"

"No."

"A little risky, isn't it?"

"If I'm not careful it could get hairy."

"Indeed. What is it you want to know?"

Jim wrinkled his brow as if trying to think of specifics. "Is there a way to not attract attention to ourselves as far as those things are concerned? What I mean is—is there a way to keep them from noticing us as prey?"

"You mean like dressing up as one of them? Maybe smear some rotten intestines over your body and blend in?" Sharon allowed a chuckle to escape her lips, but Jim simply stood in front of her as if it was what he had meant when he asked the question.

When he didn't reply to her attempt at humor, she said, "Silence is key. Movement, too. Don't let them hear you or see you. Maybe they *can* smell us. For all I know, we might give off a bright glow to them, like a lit up Christmas tree. They can tell us from one of their own, so I wouldn't try to play Halloween dress up. That could be very dangerous."

Jim nodded. "So that's it? No real secrets revealed yet?"

"I'm sorry, Jim. I wish there were, but the truth is that I just don't know. The safest way to go is not to go."

6

Leon sipped from his glass of apple wine, letting it trickle down his throat to savor each drop. He was belly up at Julio's bar, enjoying the company of friends and the sounds of music. A song by Credence Clearwater Revival spewed from the small stereo in the corner:

I see, the bad moon risin' I see, trouble's on the way.
I hear earthquakes and lightnin' I see, a bad time today.
Well don't come 'round tonight
Cause it's bound to take your life.
There's a bad moon on the rise.

The words echoed in Leon's ears amid the room's background noise. He was preoccupied with the apple wine and with Julio, who was talking rather harshly to his wife in his native tongue. She threw her arms up, screamed something back at him, and then stormed off into the restaurant kitchen.

Julio was five-foot-two, a scrawny man with big ears and a pot belly. Leon was amazed that his wife, who towered a good six inches over him, and outweighed him by at least fifty pounds, had yet to retaliate for his constant tongue-lashings. It was a safe bet that one day she would pick up something and beat him over the head with it, putting an end to his verbal barrages, once and for all.

Julio finally calmed down, but still spewed his displeasure by flailing his arms about in a comic fashion behind the bar. Leon chuckled at the little man's tantrum. "Julio, I swear, she's going to get you one day," he said, with a laugh.

"She gets me now!" Julio howled. "Right here!" He patted his rear. "She's a pain in my ass!" He released a stream of Latin curses, waving his arms once more.

"It's impolite to speak anything but English when in the company of others who can't understand you. Don't you know that?" Leon teased.

"I'll tell you what is impolite, my friend," Julio fumed. "It is impolite for me to say what I say to her so that you do understand. That would be impolite."

Leon laughed, then downed the last of his wine and pushed it toward Julio for a refill. Julio filled the glass and went back to wiping the bar clean of the cracker crumbs and peanut shells that littered its surface.

Leon took a sip and rolled his eyes in pleasure. "This is some good shit here, Julio. You damn sure can make some tasty apple wine."

"You like it so much because it is all there is, but I can make good wine from lots of things." Julio dumped the peanut shells and crumbs he had gathered with his rag into a trashcan behind the bar. "I could make good wine from the dirty water in this dishrag if it was all I had to work with, my friend. And even if it wasn't good, you'd like it because it is all there is."

Leon grunted. He doubted it, but he smiled, and took another sip.

Hal Davidson walked through the door and took a seat beside Leon. He removed his baseball cap and laid it on the bar in front of him, exposing the shiny dome of his bald head and then motioned for Julio to bring him the usual. In a flash, a glass of apple wine was placed beside his cap.

"I thought we had something out there today," Hal told Leon, and took a sip from his glass.

Leon remained silent, swirling his wine around in his glass, ignoring Hal without so much as a look to acknowledge his presence.

Hal tried again. "One day we're gonna find someone. It's just a matter of time."

"That's bullshit!" Leon snapped back, and then looked around to see how much attention his outburst had drawn. "That's bullshit," he repeated, lowering his voice. "There ain't no one out there to find. They're all dead and you know it. If there are people alive, they sure ain't gonna be anywhere around that city over there. If there's someone left alive, they're not in our flying range. You can bet your ass on that. You know what I think? I think we're wasting our time and the fuel it takes for you to fly that bird, that's what I think. Besides, what the hell do you know? You don't get out of the chopper long enough to let it get to you."

Hal was agitated and it showed on his face. Leon was well aware that Hal wasn't particularly fond of making the weekly trips over to the mainland either, but he justified the danger with the possibility of saving lives. Something they had not achieved in a long time.

"You're just trying to get out of work. That's what I think," Hal said. "If the kitchen is too hot for you, then get the hell out."

"The kitchen's fine. It's the cause that's lost. We're putting our own lives in danger for something that doesn't exist anymore. There is no one left over there to save. It's a waste of my time and the risk far outweighs the payoff."

"Fine, Leon," Hal said. "Then don't go anymore. You just keep your ass right here on this island, on that barstool, for that matter. Jack and I will go it alone."

"Whatever," Leon said with a grunt, and marched out of the bar leaving his glass half full of wine.

Leon walked down the street toward his house, half mad at Hal and half mad at himself for saying what he had said. He should've kept his mouth shut, but he could no longer cope with what he saw on to the mainland. The city was in decay. The walking corpses were in decay. Hideously mangled and disfigured, they roamed about in groups, searching for prey. On one occasion in particular, they had put down near Waldorf, Maryland. There was a commotion below. It could have been survivors needing their help.

What they found was a pack of wild dogs that had dragged one of the ghouls to the ground and were tearing at it as it squirmed to break free. The dogs quickly dismembered it and moved off with the appendages to gorge on the rotted meat. Head and torso were left lying in the middle of the street, alive and writhing in its own rotten stew. He would've put a bullet through its brain and ended its miserable existence if not for the fact that they had drawn a lot of attention to themselves.

Remembering that day made Leon shiver, and he turned up the collar on his jacket.

A bullet to the brain did it. Kill the brain, kill the ghoul. It was elementary school education these days. His life would be so much better if he could just stay on Tangier and not have to look at that sort of thing. Maybe then the nightmares would stop.

It was a new moon and the walk to his house was a dark one. Unlit streetlights watched him as he walked past, their dark eyes pointing downward on the ends of curved necks. It was a bit unsettling. Like in the old War of the Worlds movie he expected them to glow green or gold at anytime and incinerate him with a death ray. Of course he was just letting the night get to him, or was he? The street lights were creepy to say the least. Who designed them to look that way? Someone with a morbid sense of humor to be sure.

It wasn't hard to figure out why Julio bothered to open the bar and make his apple wine. He did it for the company of friends and for some sense of normalcy. It was hard to preserve one's sanity in a world gone mad. The Islands gave them their own little niche away from that madness. The fact that it could all come crashing down was never far from anyone's thoughts. How'd the old saying go? *A running man in the night can slit a thousand throats?* The same applied here. One quiet deadie could create a hundred more in one night. One makes two, two makes four, and so on. Yes, it could all come crashing right down, he thought. Still, it was the safest place to be. If there was a death, the body was quickly disposed of by fire. The trick was to stay on top of things. They could not afford to let even one ghoul go unnoticed.

Leon pressed the button on the side of his watch and a green light flashed on. It was 11:15. It would feel good to crawl into his king-size bed and stretch out for the night. He had lots of nice things now, his house—the big screen that he watched old movies on—the state-of-the-art stereo that would cost ten thousand dollars in the real world. He had those things now because the population living on the islands was much less than it had been before the plague of flesh-eaters. The ones lucky enough to survive got to pick where they wanted to live. His choice was a large, three-story Victorian home with an octagonal tower attached to one side. It was white with a wraparound porch and plenty of shade trees in the front yard. It was the kind of house he'd always dreamed of having, but his delight was diminished by the small detail that it was obtained at someone else's expense. It was his residence, but not his home.

Leon turned down Appleway Avenue, obviously named so for the abundance of apple trees that lined both sides of the street. The hard heels of his boots clicked on the asphalt as he walked, echoing off the houses as he passed them. Each echoing step was drawing him closer to his warm bed. Each step drew him closer to the safety of his own house.

Then there a loud crash and Leon stopped.

His heart thudded heavily in his chest as he drew his pistol from its holster and pointed it in the direction of the sound. He squinted to find a target. He couldn't see more than thirty feet. The noise had been twice that far.

His mind raced as he turned around, fearing an attack from behind.

Then another crash, even louder than the first and Leon whirled back toward the noise.

"Who's there?" he demanded.

His request was met with silence.

Leon waited, pointing his weapon nervously into the dark void.

"Who's there?" he demanded, louder this time.

When again there was no response, he eased forward into the darkness, adrenaline spiking his chest.

The sound had come from the side of old man Grady's house. He lived four houses down from him in a two-story home with green trim. Old man Grady was in his seventies and the possibility that the old man had died in his sleep crossed Leon's mind.

Leon reached the corner of the house and peered around the corner. There were two trashcans so close to where he stood that he had almost tripped over them. One of the can's lids was lying on the ground beside it and some of the garbage from the can was scattered at his feet.

He suddenly felt very foolish. An animal had been digging in the old man's trash. It had knocked off the lid and then probably scampered away as he approached.

Leon relaxed his grip on the weapon and lightly kicked the lid at his feet. It clanged against the side of the can and a flash of movement streaked across his foot.

Leon fell backward into the trashcans and sent them both rolling out into the street with what sounded like thunder. He quickly got to his feet and pointed his gun at the culprit now sitting on old man Grady's front porch licking its front paws—a small black and tan cat.

Leon exhaled the breath he'd been holding as the porch light flashed on and ole man Grady opened the front door. He was holding a double-barreled shotgun in his hands and it was pointed right at him.

"What the hell is going on out here?" he shouted when he saw Leon. "Sounds like you're tearing up the neighborhood." The old man cocked his head to one side. "You drunk or something, boy?"

Leon put his gun back in its holster, thankful he hadn't fired off a shot. He imagined himself being forced to carry bullets in his shirt pocket like Barney Fife to avoid further accidents. "Sorry, Mr. Grady. I heard something and thought it could be trouble. It turned out to be just a cat."

The old man looked down at the cat, then picked it up and tossed it inside the door. "Don't you go shootin' my cat now, ya hear? I've had that mangy thing for thirteen years. Keeps the mice away, and what the hell are you going to do about my trash cans?—seems you've made a hell of a mess out here tonight."

Embarrassed, Leon said, "I'll take care of it first thing in the morning, Mr. Grady," and started to walk up the street toward his house.

The old man's voice echoed behind him. "See that you do, ya hear?"

It would take Leon a while to get in the mood to sleep again.

7

Jim Workman selected the motorcycle he wanted to use and parked it in the middle of the warehouse floor to give himself room to work. It was small, easy to load, and should the need arise, get him out of a tight situation or blocked roadway.

Matt walked down the long isles of equipment in awe of what he was seeing. The aisles seemed to stretch on to eternity in the largest warehouse he'd ever seen. Everything was neatly parked in straight lines like tin soldiers primed and ready for battle.

"Why the hell didn't you tell us what was up here, Jim? Christ, this place is an armory!" Matt said, pointing to a line of large army tanks. He counted twelve. Besides the tanks, there were also trucks, Jeeps, armored personnel vehicles, and an assortment of heavy weapons.

Matt jumped onto the tracks of one of the tanks and climbed up to open the hatch. He peered down into the dark compartment, then turned back to Jim, who had already removed the battery from the motorcycle.

"Man, we could kill a lot of those things with this stuff—blow 'em right back to hell." He jumped from the tank, then walked around the vehicles, touching each one like a child in a toy store, not sure of which toy to buy. "How long were you going to wait before you broke out the heavy stuff? Holy shit, Jim, we could have our own army."

Jim put the battery on the floor. "And what would we do with it, Matt?"

The question caught Matt by surprise. What else would they do with the stuff? There was only one answer to that question…

"Kill those son of a bitches, that's what. Go out there and hunt 'em down," he said, matter-of-factly.

Jim walked over and eyed the tanks. "You mean like the U.S. army did? Like every well-equipped military on Earth didn't try? It didn't work for them and they were a lot better trained and equipped than we are. What makes you think it will work for us?" he said, and resumed his work on the motorcycle.

Matt shrugged and continued to explore.

Jim had scouted out every inch of the compound property. He knew what was there. There was something else he knew, but had decided not to share with anyone, and that was the location of missile silos over the hill. Not just any missile silos, these contained nuclear missiles—three to be exact.

He had used a Geiger counter to check the missiles for possible radiation leaks but had found none. There was no reason to inform anyone of their presence. It would cause too much uneasiness.

"Well, it seemed like a good idea." Matt pulled himself away from the tanks and joined Jim by the bike. "I suppose using one of those tanks to go down to Tangier is out of the question then?"

Jim placed a pan under the bike to catch the old oil, and laughed. "They use too much fuel and are too slow. More trouble than they're worth."

"How's Amanda taking this?"

"Not too well, but she's accepted it." The old oil emptied and Jim replaced the plug. "There's some oil for these bikes over there on that shelf," he said, pointing. "Get it for me."

Matt grabbed some and brought it to him. Jim cracked the seal and dumped it in as Matt watched. "No, she didn't take it well at all," Jim said. "Like I said, she accepted it; she doesn't like it."

Matt listened. He was a good listener. He learned from just listening. He was still alive because he had listened to Jim and had learned to keep his head in bad situations. Jim had saved him from starvation when he had come to clear the way for the others to move into the prison. Matt had been on the verge of joining the rest of his prison mates, who had all perished and were pacing their cells as undead cannibals. They had been left to die by a prison staff who had either died themselves, or abandoned their post. Another day or so and he would have died too.

Matt was trying to remember how long it had been. Was it a year? Yes, more than a year. More than even a year and a half.

"You can't blame her for that," Matt said, wiping his forehead. In doing so he left a smear of black grease over his eyes. Jim noticed it and was about to tell him, but thought better of it and chuckled quietly to himself. "I don't. I feel for her," Jim explained, "I really do, but I don't plan on going out and getting myself killed."

Jim tossed the empty oil bottle to Matt, who turned around and pitched it into a trashcan made from a fifty-five gallon, metal drum. "Two points," he said, as it bounced around the rim and fell inside.

Jim smiled, wiped the excess oil from the bike's motor, and picked up the battery charger. "Get that battery and let's go see if we can get the Humvee started."

Jim and Matt walked up the hill toward the main gate where the Humvee was parked. Matt was getting his first good look at the sprawling lawns, now grown thick with tall grass and rows of office buildings. A high fence surrounded the mountaintop complex.

"FEMA was here before all hell broke loose," Matt said. "Up top, anyway. Look at it, Jim. They're gone and we're still here. It didn't do 'em one damned bit of good to have the inside track."

Jim took a sweeping glance of the area, more to check for unwelcome guests than to speculate how FEMA had fallen. A thick forest bordered the fence in all directions which made advanced warning, nearly impossible.

"I imagine that the personnel working up top deserted their posts when things got bad," Jim said. "They weren't part of the station below. I doubt many of them ever saw the underground or knew much about it. It was a secured area. They would have probably been shot if they tried to get in."

"You mean to tell me that if atomic bombs were about to fall on their heads, they wouldn't be allowed to get to safety down there?"

"That's right."

"Well, I gotta tell ya, that blows!"

"Keep it down," Jim cautioned. "We have neighbors we don't want to invite to dinner."

"That blows," Matt repeated quietly. "Those shits downstairs deserve what they got."

Jim switched hands to carry the heavy charger and picked up his pace. "Whether they deserved it or not, they got it because they were stupid. They had it made and blew it because they couldn't agree on what to do. They split into two factions; one who thought nuking the cities was the best solution and another who didn't. They went to war and killed each other."

"I'm glad they didn't nuke the cities."

"Me, too," Jim said.

***

The Humvee was a wide, squatty-looking thing, larger than a Jeep and more rugged in appearance. This one was outfitted with reinforced windows and heavy bumpers to deflect objects from its path.

Matt admired the hard, powerful exterior. It was the perfect vehicle to take on the trip. Not too large to get through a tight squeeze and not too small to plow over a crowd.

Jim placed the charger beside the Humvee and walked into the guard shack at the main gate as Matt followed.

Documents and fax sheets littered the floor of the tiny room. A calendar on the wall displayed a date of almost two years before. Jim pulled it from the wall.

"Look at that," he said, and passed it to Matt. "According to the date, this post was abandoned a couple of months after it all started."

Matt gave it a quick glance and let it fall from his hand. "Yeah, either that or they just didn't bother to turn the page. I know the last thing on my mind, with everything happening, would be to keep that calendar up-to-date."

Jim picked up a fax sheet from the floor. "The fax machine panicked, too," he said.

Matt took the paper from him, read it, and crumbled it into a ball when he saw the same month dated near the header.

"Didn't waste any time, did they?" Matt grumbled.

"Would you?" Jim asked. "Stuck up here, away from your family and not allowed to go below ground where it was truly safe? I'm surprised they stayed that long. There wasn't much left for them to go back to at that point. They'd have been better off staying put. They're probably dead now."

Matt nodded, acknowledging their probable fate.

"Check that cabinet over there and see if you can find the keys to that Humvee," Jim said. "I'll look in the desk drawer."

Matt rummaged through the cabinet, slinging items to the floor to break or clang when they hit the concrete. He winced each time, peeking over his shoulder, expecting a scolding from Jim for making too much noise. When he found two walkie-talkies he held them up by their straps for Jim to see.

Jim held a ring of keys and jingled them. Matt lowered the radios.

"Are they the right ones?" Matt asked.

Jim flipped the keys around and gripped them in his palm. "I won't know that until I try them," he said, and walked out to the Humvee.

Matt considered the radios, then surreptitiously pocketed a set of handcuffs and their key from the desktop, and followed.

Jim studied the key ring. There were about forty keys on the hoop and he didn't feel much like trying each and every one before finding the one that fit, if it was on the ring at all, so he thumbed through them all before deciding on one in particular. It was a perfect fit as he inserted it into the ignition and the engine roared magnificently to life.

Jim smiled, and reclined in the seat, pleased with his choice.

"Put the charger in the back," he said. "I'm going to take this thing down to the warehouse so I can load up the motorcycle."

Matt opened the back door and tossed the two radios in before getting the charger.

"What do I need the radios for?" Jim asked.

Matt bit his lip. "You never know."

8

"I have sworn to uphold the Constitution of the United States and oppose tyranny," George Bates reminded the young officer. "The situation changes nothing. We will continue as our forefathers intended and wipe clean the moral decay that caused this great nation to fall asunder and rebuild."

His tall stature and no-nonsense style made Lieutenant Colonel George Bates the practical successor to Col. Hart, who had been killed three months earlier. Rugged and strong, Bates never gave up and fought for what he believed to be right.

The Virginia Freedom Fighters had been around long before the end of society. For years they had trained for a racial war, a civil war, or perhaps the day the United States government handed supreme governing power over to a world leadership, the so-called New World Order. What that really meant was an end to personal freedom. Their organization stood as a bulwark against such tyranny at home. They had trained for many such scenarios, but nothing could have prepared them for what had happened. Still, it changed nothing. Their goal remained the same. They would continue to uphold the Constitution the way it was intended to be—unchanged.

Bates handed the orders to the young officer.

"Take these to Lieutenant Hathaway. Tell him to meet me here in my office ASAP. I have something else to discuss with him."

The young officer saluted and walked out.

Pressure had been mounting lately. The former commander had procrastinated, possibly for too long. The time was ripe for a move. If they didn't do something soon, the state of affairs could revert to what it had been before the plague, and once again they might be on the verge of totalitarianism. More recruits were needed. To take back the nation, they needed many, many more.

If they could unite all the Militias spread across the country it would be easy, but long distance communications were out. Attempts to contact them with scouts had been met with failure. They had most likely found their fate at the hands of the flesh-eaters. There were just too many pockets of humanity left. Once the plague was over, they would reunite and return to that post-Cold War style of thinking of a one-world government and in turn abolish the Constitution. It was unimaginable that they could have such a golden opportunity as this to set things right and then fail to take advantage of it.

Lieutenant Robert Hathaway straightened his disheveled attire and knocked lightly on the Colonel's door, quickly running a hand through his hair.

"Come in!" the weighty voice on the other side boomed.

Hathaway entered the room trying to not look like he had just dragged himself out of bed and stood at attention in front of George Bates' desk.

"At ease, Lieutenant," Bates said, motioning for him to sit.

Hathaway slipped into the black leather chair, eyes forward, trying to appear alert. His shift started in an hour, but he hadn't had time to properly get himself together.

"There's a matter of importance I need to discuss with you. It requires that you leave camp and go east, toward the coast."

Hathaway's eyes narrowed.

"We've received several communication signals from the coast and the radar onboard the carrier we commandeered in Norfolk last year has picked up air traffic in the region."

Hathaway leaned forward.

"I need you to put together a party of about ten men," Bates continued, "and find out if it's our own flying around up there or if it's a foreign, possibly hostile, aircraft."

Hathaway studied the Colonel. It was odd that he'd send his second in command on such a dangerous mission. Could it be that he wanted him out of the way? Maybe his presence threatened the good Colonel's command. That must be it, he thought. He would have to be very, very careful with this 'new' man in charge.

"Sir, going on these missions is at best, risky," Hathaway said, in his most respectful voice. "Do you think it wise to do this?"

"I *think* it's necessary," Bates said, with a raised eyebrow. "I want answers. You know what we're here for and more than ever we all know what's at risk—"

"But, sir," he interrupted, "the coastal areas were heavily populated and are surely overrun with those putrid monsters. May I remind you that not one of our search parties has returned from their assignments?"

"Those search parties had to travel over twenty-two hundred miles to reach their destination in Montana. You'll be going less than two hundred. I've looked over the map and laid out the route I want you to take."

Hathaway's lower jaw began to hurt and he realized he'd been gritting his teeth. He didn't fear the trip; his years in the army had made him strong and fearless. It was the audacity of Bates that upset him. Who was he to put him in such danger? He couldn't quite figure out why Bates was so highly regarded. Bates had served in Vietnam, but that was a lifetime ago. Where was this great leader when he was inhaling poisonous gas and sweating the Middle Eastern heat in Iraq? Here in Virginia, that's where, playing army with a bunch of over-the-hill wannabes. In their small minds they were saving the United States of America from the bleeding-heart liberals who wanted to give it all away. Hathaway sucked in a jagged breath at the thought. But it was nothing more than war games.

"Yes, sir," Hathaway said.

"You have the specifics in the orders you received," he said, then stood and opened the door. "I want no contact made. This is to identify only. Is that understood?"

Hathaway felt a surge of anger. Not only was this mission unworthy of his talents but, now he was being ordered to do it half-assed.

"Yes, sir!" he replied and forced a halfhearted salute.

He could certainly remedy part of the problem. The Colonel wanted him to lead a dangerous mission into the bowels of hell on some wild goose chase for invading armies. Well, that was fine and dandy, but he'd do it his way, with men he chose to take. If the Colonel wanted to play hardball, then he could do that, too. He'd show him by executing those orders with complete success and return in one piece. Then where would the Colonel be? He'd be right back where he started, that's where. Bates outranked him, but he sure couldn't out think him. He'd have to find another way to do away with him. Bates would be wise to watch his back from now on.

Hathaway continued to fume as he walked down the corridor. Two guards by the door saluted him as he walked past. Hathaway ignored their salute and stepped out into the brisk, morning air.

Morning drills had already begun and well-trained units exercised in groups of forty. A row of eight wide and five deep did jumping jacks on the main lawn to his left. Another unit did squats on his right. A third unit jogged the perimeter, singing silly rhymes as they ran.

Hathaway watched in wonder. A year ago they had been on the verge of total defeat. The Virginia Freedom Fighters had been low on morale, food, and personnel. Throngs of the undead had besieged their ranch at Roanoke. They'd lost many good men in that battle. Then they joined up with another militia from West Virginia there at Big Meadows, on the Blue Ridge mountain range in the Shenandoah National Park, where they had remained ever since. Now they were strong again. They were more organized then ever and boasted almost twice their original numbers.

Big Meadows had been a good choice for holding camp. The top of the mountain was more than twenty-five hundred feet above sea level and adequately equipped with cabins for shelter, stores of food, and other things. Wildlife thrived. Deer, bear, squirrels, and rabbits were plentiful, total seclusion from the catastrophe miles away.

Hathaway followed a gravel walkway back to his office to prepare. There were so many things to be ironed out before the mission could begin—so many decisions to be made. Bates would need to be taken care of once and for all. The only question that remained was how to do it.

***

As the sun sank low in the western sky, Lieutenant Hathaway inspected his troops. He shook each one of the ten men's hands as he made his way down the line. Most of them were his men, his friends, handpicked specifically for this mission. They would follow him to the ends of the Earth if so asked; the ends of the Earth, in this case, being Norfolk, Virginia, a large urban area on the Atlantic Ocean, also home to the country's largest East Coast naval base.

Their destination was an aircraft carrier. They had been using its radar dishes to watch for hostile forces that might deem the current situation a good one in which to invade America. There were no known facts as to who created the plague, whether it was God-sent, or merely a creation of man. If a creation of man, then it seemed likely that war had indeed taken place and the United States was on the losing side. With no information available regarding the state of foreign countries, the Communists could be sitting pretty, just waiting for the right time to move in and take over. Or perhaps it was the radical extremists in the Middle East who had started it all—a new kind of germ warfare.

Hathaway began to fume again. The towel-headed bastards had no respect for human life. Everyone knew that. They should've kept right on going in the Gulf War and wiped out the whole lot of them. They should've nuked the entire region, turned it all into a giant sand pit.

Hathaway shook the hand of the last man in line, his closest friend, Jake Peters. He'd known Jake for many years. He'd served with him, gotten drunk with him, and generally gotten in and out of trouble with him. It had been Hathaway who had first acquainted Jake with the Ku Klux Klan several years before. They had profited together and killed together. They had been inseparable ever since.

Hathaway turned on his right heel and spun about face, then walked three steps and turned again to face his men in military fashion.

"Dismissed!" he barked, and the men began to disperse.

"Not you, Jake."

Jake turned.

"I've got some things I want to talk to you about."

Jake walked confidently toward him, his muscles rippling beneath his tight, green T-shirt. His hair, shaved tight to his scalp, made him look fresh out of boot camp. A wad of tobacco filled one side of his mouth, and he spit frequently.

Hathaway lit a cigar and inspected it as though appreciating its fine flavor. He savored the smoke for a moment before letting it escape through his nostrils. "I'm almost out of these things. Maybe we can get some more while we're out."

Jake spit, then nodded. "What'd you wanna talk to me about, Bobby?"

Hathaway turned, and watched a group of men as they marched around the compound, hoping none of them had heard Jake address him so informally.

"You see those men over there?" he said, pointing. "They are oblivious to what's going on around here. They'll live or die by whatever Bates says, without question."

Jake glanced toward the marching men, feeling disdain for his comrades without really knowing why. But if Bobby Hathaway said so, then it must be true. "What are they oblivious to?" Jake asked.

Hathaway went eye to eye with Jake. "That we're doing nothing here. We do drills, we march, and we sit and wait. Now we're expected to go out and wait again. Sit back and watch, don't make contact. Risk our asses, mind you, but don't take action. We're no more living than those walking piles of rot out there in the Valley." Hathaway flicked away the ashes hanging on the end of his cigar and then pushed the burning end into the palm of his hand, twisting it until it was out. He didn't flinch.

"You see that?" Hathaway said. "That's the reaction of a man who's lost all sensitivity to his surroundings. A man who doesn't care anymore—the man I've become." He pocketed what was left of the cigar. "But not anymore, Jake, not anymore. From now on we do things our way. Eventually, everyone will do things our way."

Jake spit again, leaving a brown smudge hanging from the corner of his bottom lip. Jake wasn't sure what Hathaway meant, but he nodded his agreement just the same. If Bobby Hathaway said it, then it must be true.

"We'll go on this little mission," Hathaway said, "but when we get back, we'll do things our way."

***

It was nearly three-thirty in the morning before Hathaway finally attached the timer to his crude bomb. A simple relay would send an electrical impulse from the battery to the four sticks of dynamite at the chosen time and then detonate. It was beneath his skills, but given the available material and the short notice, it was all he could come up with. It would be perfect timing and more than adequate for his needs.

Hathaway took a small knife, turned the screw in the back of the timer, and set it for eleven that night, eighteen hours after he was scheduled to leave on his mission. He wouldn't be a likely suspect; he would be miles away when it happened and Bates would be asleep.

With a roll of duct tape, he wrapped everything tightly together and slipped it into a satchel, then cleared away the evidence by putting the leftover material into the satchel with the bomb. He would wait another hour before placing it.

***

Minutes passed like hours as Hathaway waited. He double-checked his plans as the hands of the clock inched from one minute to the next. It was a simple plan. What could go wrong? He'd be miles away when it happened. No one would be the wiser. It was clever of him to think of it so quickly.

His mind drifted. Lack of sleep had made him unsure of his own ingenuity. He shook his head to clear away the cobwebs. He had to appear fresh for the day ahead. What's more, he had to be alert. It would be dangerous after they left the safety of the mountain. It would not be clever to finish this task only to go out and get himself killed. He wanted to tell Jake of his plan earlier that day so they could both share in his brilliance and ingenuity, but the fewer people who knew about it, the better.

Finally, the clock's hand hit the magical number: 4:30 A.M. It was time. Bates' room would be empty now.

Hathaway's adrenaline pumped as he slinked down the hall to George Bates' quarters to place the bomb beneath his bed.

9

Matt dashed through the underground street past the cafeteria, past the park bench by the underground lake, and across to Sharon Darney's lab. He was running late. There were so many things to do and so little time in which to do them. Jim was leaving shortly and he had to be ready.

Sharon was waiting when he burst through the door out of breath. "Are you ready?" he huffed.

Sharon held up the needle. "Yes. Take off your shirt."

Matt fought to tear off his shirt and then bared his arm.

"What the hell is it, anyway?"

"It's a mega dose of antibiotics." She cleared the air from the syringe.

"What the hell good will that do? I thought there wasn't a cure for a bite from one of those things."

"There's not. Not that I know of, anyway, but it may help to have it in your system beforehand."

Matt flinched as the needle pierced his skin. After Sharon removed it, his arm began to ache and he rubbed it.

"Has Jim had his yet?"

"He got his an hour ago," she said, and trashed the empty syringe. "Does he know yet?"

"No, and I'm not going to tell him until the last minute. You know how he is. He'll try to talk me out of it if I give him the chance."

"Wear these," Sharon said and tossed two midnight blue jackets to him with the letters FEMA embroidered on the backs in yellow.

"Why?"

"Most people get bitten in the arm when they're attacked. If you're wearing a jacket, it will make it more difficult for their teeth to penetrate through to the skin."

Matt bundled them under his arm. "Just what we need. Jackets in seventy degree weather."

"Wear them!"

Jim walked arm in arm with Amanda to the elevator. She had reconciled to the fact that he was going to go, no matter what. She held on to him as they stepped inside and the door closed behind them.

The elevator rose swiftly to the ground floor, leaving Amanda's queasy stomach several stories below ground.

When the door slid open, Mick was standing there. He smiled as Jim and Amanda stepped out. At his side stood Felicia and the small golden-haired child they had come to call their own. Isabelle had been mute for almost two years, but lately she had begun to speak a little. Jim figured the shock of losing her family and witnessing the ghastly sights she must have seen at such an early age caused her to temporarily lose that ability, but he couldn't be sure. She had never been able to tell them before and no one asked her now in fear it would cause her to regress.

Like her newfound mother, Felicia, Isabelle had a strange gift. Sometimes they saw, or knew things, that no one else did. This gift had somehow brought them together. A year before, their intuitions had helped to save them all from doom. But lately, there had been no such foresight as an eerie calm fell over the occupants of the underground compound.

Mick shook Jim's hand. "Good luck and don't take any chances. We need you here," he said. "If it gets too dangerous, turn around and come back home."

Jim nodded. "I will."

Jim turned to Felicia, who held back her tears as she hugged him, waiting for that flash of insight into danger to sting her body. She almost wished for it to come so she could tell him he mustn't go, that she sensed perils in his journey, but nothing happened. Maybe it was a good thing, she thought as she pulled away.

Jim reached out for Isabelle, but she stepped away from him and hid behind Felicia. He gave her a wink and took Amanda's hand, then walked to the door. Isabel fidgeted for a moment, then dashed after him. Jim stooped down and she ran into his arms.

"God helps you," she said, then pulled away.

Amanda bent over and put a hand on the little girl's shoulder. "Yes, we know. God will watch over him."

Isabelle shook her head. "No-o-o," she answered, and stroked the hand Amanda had placed on her shoulder. "God helps, touches you. You have his light on you." She took a step away from him and smiled. "I see it."

"Thank you, Isabelle," he said, standing up.

Jim waved to Mick and Felicia across the room and then gave Amanda a lingering kiss.

"Come back to me," she whispered, "or I'll come looking for you."

Jim cracked a smile.

"I'm serious," she said with a scowl.

***

Jim stopped short of the vehicle and stared at Matt, who was sitting in the passenger seat.

"What are you doing here, Matt? I told you nobody else goes."

"You need me to go. You might need the help."

"I won't need the help. Now get out."

Matt pointed to a grab bar attached to the dash and Jim groaned when he saw that Matt had handcuffed himself to it.

"Where the hell did you get those things?"

"From the guard shack the other day."

Jim considered walking back up the hill until Matt got hungry enough to give up his plan, but instead he slid behind the steering wheel with a grunt and a moan.

"Does Mick know you're here?"

"He does. He wants me to go, too."

"I'll not be responsible for you if something happens."

"Okay," Matt said. He unlocked the handcuffs from his wrist and let them dangle from the bar.

Jim grinned. "I thought you'd had enough of those before the plague."

"Yeah, well it's sure the first time I put them on willingly," he said with a grin.

Jim started the engine and drove up the hill. He was still shaking his head ruefully as he drove through the main gate.

10

Leon was waiting by the chopper when Hal and Jack arrived at the airport. Jack disappeared into the terminal as Hal walked up to Leon. For a moment they only studied one another, trying to weigh what the other was thinking. Then Leon gave Hal a light tap on the arm, a silent apology that without a word, mended the rift between them.

Leon threw his gear into the back of the chopper and climbed into his seat behind the cockpit, and as if nothing had happened, said, "Where to this morning?"

"West," Hal said. "We're going to follow Route 17 north for a while and just see what we see—maybe as far as Fredericksburg."

Leon was usually indifferent when it came to where they went, one place being as bad as the next. But this trip would be longer than most. Today they would be taking the chopper to its limit. Even so, his dread of the trip was less today than it had been in the past. He had finally come to view the excursions as something he had to deal with regardless of how he felt about them. This was his duty, his place in this new life—his role to play.

***

As the sun rose higher, they approached Fredericksburg, a town of more than fifty thousand before the plague of flesh eaters. Now the streets and parking lots were dotted with the slow-moving figures of the dearly departed in search of live prey. It wasn't clear if they held the mental capacity to actually form thought, something needed to conduct a search. It was more likely that they simply roamed about, mostly unaware of their surroundings until some unfortunate soul happened along, thus triggering the instinct that motivated them.

Even from this altitude, Leon could see the town's utter decay. Staggering, lurching, living dead peppered the landscape. Trash blew in the streets like newspaper tumbleweeds. Trees felled by storms over the past two years were still on rooftops, their branches like giant, skeletal hands gripping the sides of their bearers. Broken windows and smashed doors were abundant in a sea of now-precarious dwellings.

Leon's thoughts went back to the first few days of the plague. He had doubted, as many had, the validity of the details released to the public. *The unburied dead were returning to life.* It had happened so quickly that there was hardly time to let it all sink in. Most had only begun to understand how bad the situation was before it was all over. Leon had survived run-ins with the living corpses many times before finding safety on Tangier Island. Some of those run-ins had been with friends and family. But they were actually only the *bodies* of his friends and family, vehicles that harbored a dark and evil presence. There was no detectable spirit of its former resident—no soul or personality. Whatever they were, they were not the people he had known.

Television broadcasts had been full of news reports and talk shows. Government officials and religious-oriented shows all gave their opinions and theories on what was happening. *It's a virus! It's God's doing! It's Mother Nature rebelling for mankind's destruction of the planet*, they had cried. All had been blabbering idiots as the dead multiplied at an alarming rate.

A month, if he remembered correctly. That's how long it took for civilization to collapse. That's how long it took for mankind to lose its foothold as the dominant species on Earth. Now, two years later, only a small percent of the world's population remained alive. There were others out there somewhere, there had to be, but try as they might, they could not find them. Living people had basically become extinct, at least from the cities and populated areas. That's why he thought it was unproductive to search in the cities. Only a fool would venture into heavily populated places.

A warning buzzer sounded and a red light blinked on the instrument panel. Then the chopper's motor began to sound labored.

Jack dropped the maps he'd been studying and tapped the blinking light in a vain attempt to make it stop, his face white with trepidation.

Hal fought with the stick to keep the chopper level and Leon could see beads of perspiration began to dot his forehead as he turned to him. "Look out the side window and tell me what you see, Leon—hurry." His voice trembled. And now Leon could feel his own body begin to tremble as well. If Hal was afraid then they were in serious trouble.

Leon pasted his face to the glass in an attempt to do as Hal had asked. "Black smoke, Hal. I see black smoke. Is that bad?"

Sweat dripped into Hal's eyes. "I've gotta set us down— Jesus, I've gotta set us down!" he screamed. "We're losing oil pressure!"

Leon jumped into his seat, buckled the safety straps, and moved his weapons closer. His heart was pounding now, about to leap out of his chest. If he could take deep breathes, maybe he would calm down. He had to calm down. He should calm down. Hal and Jack knew what they were doing. They would figure this out.

"There's a field ahead," Hal said. "I'm going to try to make it!"

The chopper moved forward even as it lost altitude and then the motor suddenly quit.

The sweeping sound of the rotors filled Leon's mind and he clutched the arms of his seat as the sound of the moving rotors slowed to silence. They floated in a deafening silence for what seemed like an eternity, waiting for the ultimate end of their flight. Then the chopper tilted to the right and clipped a tree. The tree broke away, and slammed backward into the tail fin. Leon found himself facing downward as the chopper plummeted nose first to the ground. It was the last thing he remembered.

***

A cloud of pain engulfed Leon when he opened his eyes.

When the chopper slammed into the ground, the force had flung him forward against the safety belts. He was hanging there, looking down toward the front of the chopper, which sat on its nose. There was a sharp pain in his chest, broken ribs, at least.

Hal and Jack were crushed between the front panel and their seats. There was blood, and they were not moving.

Leon fought to release the straps that held him in mid-air, dangling beneath his seat. After fidgeting with the buckle, it released and he fell six feet into the back of the cockpit seats with a thud and coughing blood.

His nostrils were burning. The fuel tank had ruptured and there was gas flowing into the compartment, pooling around the two men trapped below him.

He did his best to balance himself by placing one foot on the dash panel and the other on the wrecked metal above the windshield. He faced Hal first and pulled his head away from the twisted metal in front of him.

The sight made Leon pull back in revulsion.

Hal's face was gone—crushed and torn away by the impact. He was dead.

Leon's breath was jagged, his face flushed. Bile rose in his throat until stomach acid burned in his mouth. He closed his eyes to fight the panic that threatened to consume him. Then he put his hands over his face to blot out what he'd just seen.

As his heart rate steadied, he removed his hands and opened his eyes. The instrument panel had broken in such a way that a large metal shard had pierced Jack's chest. His dead eyes stared blindly ahead.

Leon stood there for a moment against the inside of the roof, dazed and confused. He tried to convince himself that he was dreaming and that none of this was real. The moment took on a surreal quality. He watched from outside of his body, but he was not emotionally involved in the terror. The surroundings became vague and out of focus.

Then the moans came and Leon snapped back.

He had forgotten about the monsters outside. His friends were dead and he was stranded. He did not know how many cannibal corpses were closing in on him. How long had he been unconscious?

Leon found his rifle and the bag of necessities that he always carried with him lying against the back of Jack's seat. He slung the bag over his shoulder and snatched up the rifle.

There was a thud against the side of the downed chopper.

Another thud—more moans—the unmistakable sound of hands pawing at the green bird for entrance.

Leon searched for a way to escape.

The chopper was wedged in between two trees. Escape through the side door was impossible. The front of the chopper was tight against the ground. To escape, he would have to climb back up to his seat and try to get out through the window beside it, and the gas fumes—they were getting worse. At any moment the whole thing could go up in a ball of fire.

Leon grabbed the safety harness and pulled himself to his seat, wrapping his legs around it for a better grip, then pulled himself up and stood on its back where he watched through the window.

His heart sank. Hordes of ghouls were moving in from every direction. He would have to do battle to get past them.

As Leon glanced back at Hal and Jack he realized that Jack's death had not been caused by a head injury and he briefly considered putting a bullet through his brain to prevent his transformation, but there was not enough time and if the shot created a spark, it could ignite the pooling fuel. "I'm sorry old friend. There's nothing I can do for you," he said, and positioned himself.

Leon leaned back and kicked at the window until it shattered.

As soon as he hit the ground, two creatures were on him. He kicked one away and held the other at arm's length until he could bring it down to the grass beside him.

The first ghoul moved in as he sprang to his feet and he snatched his pistol from his hip and shot it in the head. He shot the second ghoul before it could regain its footing and started to run.

Leon spotted an opening in the fence at the edge of the field and ran for it. Sharp pains engulfed his chest as he ran. His ribs popped and moved painfully with each stride. His left foot would hit the ground and a rib on his right would pop. When his right foot hit the ground, a rib on his left would pop. It was painful, but he ran through the pain.

When he reached the road, he stopped to catch his breath and plan his next move. The largest mob of ghouls was still behind him, a crowd of fifty, crossing the field as fast as their decrepit bodies would allow them. Still more chose to stay with the downed chopper and were searching for a way into it. Along the streets around him, others were taking notice now as he stood hunched over on the road with his hands on his knees.

Their moans and cries rose together, creating an eerie wail of hunger and excitement that reached his ears in stereo. A large blackbird sat perched on a telephone wire above him. It cocked its head to the side and watched as the crowds closed in.

11

It was almost an hour before Jim and Matt got their first look at a ghoul in nearly a year. It wore military fatigues and was slumped over a barbed wire fence beside the road. It remained so motionless that at first it appeared to be truly dead.

Jim brought the Humvee to a stop fifteen feet away from where the ghoul dangled over the barbed wire. Normally he would have driven on without a second look, but this one garnered his interest. Maybe it was because the ghoul had been an enlisted man before his death. Jim had been in the military. He knew the risks a soldier took. To allow a soldier who might have fought gallantly in life to have his body used in such an obscene manner was in his mind, immoral. Or maybe he was just curious. In any event, the area was clear and he could do that soldier a favor without much danger to Matt, or himself.

They stared at the ghoul from the safety of the vehicle for several minutes before it moved. It raised its head in short jerks and strained to gain solid footing without the aid of the fence. It staggered backward before moving toward them and bounced off the fence, unaware that its path was impeded by the barbed wire.

It stood confused, and stared at the wire barrier, unsure of how to get past it. After a moment it released an exasperated howl that gargled in its throat with what must have been the last bit of moisture remaining in its desiccated body. Its lower jaw dropped and hung open, disconnected from the upper portion in a disturbing way. The jaw swung freely as it thrashed against the fence.

"Look at that thing," Matt said. "What the hell happened to it? It looks like it's been out here rotting away. It's not like the others we've seen. I thought they weren't supposed to rot like that—so fast."

Jim opened his door and went to the back of the Humvee and pulled out a tire iron, then went to the fence where the ghoul thrashed.

It was a putrid thing with exposed ribs and three missing fingers. Jim watched it as it pushed against the fence before he covered his nose and mouth with a handkerchief and donned a pair of plastic goggles. Holding the tire iron high in his right hand, he brought it down hard on the creature's head. After a nauseating thud that sounded like a hammer smashing into a ripe melon, fragments of skull and brain matter spewed from the opened cavity and the creature dropped to the ground.

Jim wiped the tire iron clean in the grass and then returned it to the back of the Humvee. He was still swabbing away foul smelling bits of the creature's cranial contents when he sat in the driver's seat.

"That one wouldn't have lasted much longer anyway," Jim said.

"What do you mean?"

"I mean, in a little while his brain would've been too severely decayed to have sustained it. It would've simply dropped dead on its own. I'm going by something Sharon Darney told me. The people who died, or were infected and died when this all first happened, have a lifespan of at least ten years, maybe more. But from the information she's gathered, she believes that one reviving now, or recently, wouldn't survive nearly as long. Their decomposition rate is much faster; they rot faster. Once the brain becomes unable to function, the creature will die. That poor soldier must've survived for quite a while before finally meeting his doom because there wasn't much left of him, assuming Sharon's hypothesis is correct."

"Damn," Matt said, looking at the dead soldier. "Hey! If they're all like that, this could be a cakewalk. I could handle twenty of those things in that condition. Beat 'em right down to the ground easy. That poor bastard looked too rotted to even bite you."

"Don't bet your life on it, Matt," Jim said.

***

Ten miles later, Jim had to stop again to move a fallen tree that blocked their way. Nearby, a country ghost town that had fallen victim to the elements was half hidden in an overgrowth of vegetation. It beckoned for companionship to revive its once quaint beauty and once again become a place with white picket fences, porches with rocking chairs, and flower gardens of yellow and red.

Jim visualized the past splendor of the small community, how it might have been, with children playing ball in the narrow streets, laughing and having fun. The vision faded away in the face of the weed-filled yards and houses with peeling paint and broken windows.

Jim checked his rifle for ammunition before leaving the confines of the Humvee. He motioned for Matt to do the same, then removed the chainsaw from the back of the vehicle and went to the fallen tree.

Blue smoke jetted from the chainsaw in steady streams as he cut through the thick trunk. Matt watched for trouble, his eyes darting this way and that as Jim sliced through the tree with the expertise of a Montana woodsman. When a twelve-foot piece of the tree's trunk was removed and rolled from their path, Jim put the chainsaw back into the vehicle and brushed the sawdust from his clothes.

An unnatural calmness, empty of life, filled the country air. Even birds refused to make known their presence in the trees around them. It was never more evident to Jim that the passage of days had little meaning anymore outside the boundaries of the mountain. There was no bustling Wall Street, no air traffic in the sky above them, and no moving vehicles other than their own on the roads. They were in a dead world now.

Jim removed a small canteen from his belt and filled his mouth with water. He would waste no more time than needed. They still had quite a journey before they arrived at their destination. They'd be hard pressed to go to Tangier and, if it proved to be in vain, turn around and get back to Mount Weather before dark. Spending the night in the unprotected wild was not at the top of his list of preferences. There was nowhere he could think of that would offer the needed security through the night. Weapons, food, extra gas, and even a small generator were loaded into the back of the Humvee, all squeezed in around a motorcycle, but they were not equipped for a prolonged trip. A person could not go to sleep, no matter how safe, and expect to wake in the same condition. Not out here. Not in this new world. He'd learned from past experience that perceived security was not something to be taken for granted.

Jim and Matt turned upon hearing cries of anguish behind them. Seven grotesque bodies staggered from the small village beside the road, attracted by the noise of the chainsaw. Their ragged clothes and deteriorated features were visible proof of what they were.

Matt ran to Jim's side and raised his weapon. Jim put his hand on the weapon and pushed it away. "No," he said. "We don't have the time for it. No use wasting the ammo. We're not here to kill every one we see. Let's just move on."

Matt lowered the gun and wasted no time getting back inside the vehicle.

Jim drove through the opening he had cut out and watched in the rearview mirror as the gaggle of flesh eaters faded into the distance.

Matt was humming a tune from an old song to calm his frayed nerves. "We're gonna be okay, you know? We're gonna be okay," he reassured himself amid his humming.

Jim nodded. "Yeah, we're gonna be fine." He prayed they were right. He was sure they would encounter situations that were a lot worse than this one. Their journey had only just begun.

12

The small convoy came to a stop on the road two miles outside of Culpeper, Virginia. Hathaway stepped out and spread his maps over the hood of the lead truck.

"We'll follow this road until we get to Fredericksburg. Then we'll take 95 and 64 to Norfolk. We shouldn't run into too much trouble as long as we stay on the highways."

Jake nodded as Hathaway refolded the maps.

Hathaway felt confident as he glanced at his watch. By this time tomorrow, Bates would be dealt with and command would logically fall to him. It shouldn't have come to this. He should've been given the post in the first place, but now it was out of his hands. The plan had been set into motion. He would ride back to camp in a few days and accept his new position. He would finally have the power he so deserved. Power over less than a thousand people would not have meant much before the plague, but now it was *real* power. Now, it could be considered a 'world power'.

An army one thousand strong could go out and effectively take whatever it wanted. There would be alcoves of other survivors who would be dominated and added to their numbers, the undesirables weeded out in the process. Bates was right about one thing, they should be prepared for the possibility that foreign nations might move in and take over. He didn't see this as an immediate threat, but as soon as the plague was over, it was something they would have to be prepared to defend against. It would be a race to see who could get organized first.

"Sir?" a voice called from behind. "Sir?"

Hathaway turned to find Donald Covington, a fresh-faced boy of twenty-two, a kid who looked up to him as a role model. His hand shook as he waved a quick salute.

"What is it?" Hathaway asked.

"There are some coming in from the west, down by a farmhouse. It looks to be about eight or ten of them."

Hathaway's expression hardened. "There's *what* coming, boy?"

The boy fidgeted. "Monsters, sir—dead things."

"The next time you have something to report make sure you clarify what you're reporting. To be efficient, we need facts—hard, accurate facts. Battles are lost because of poor communication. Do you understand?"

"Yes, sir."

"Good," Hathaway beamed, his voice suddenly cheerful. "Now, how far away are they?"

"A couple hundred yards."

"Then there's no reason to worry just yet. It'll take them ten or fifteen minutes to get here as slow as they move. Make sure we keep a good lookout. If any get too close, shoot the goddamned things in the head and be done with it."

"Yes, sir." The boy gave another quick salute and disappeared around the truck.

Hathaway smirked at the young lad's nervousness. He was the least experienced in the group, brought along, basically, to groom as Hathaway saw fit. He was little more than an errand boy, but he'd learn.

Hathaway walked away from the front of the lead truck and into everyone's view.

"Listen up!" he ordered, and everyone moved closer. "I stopped us here before we entered the town of Culpeper for a reason. This will be the first time we pierce a formerly populated area. We will surely encounter the dead in larger numbers than any of you have seen in a while. I expect everyone to keep their wits about them and behave in a manner befitting what you are...trained soldiers. We will proceed through town without stopping unless it is absolutely necessary, then continue until we reach Fredericksburg."

Hathaway glanced toward the pack of ungainly creatures slowly approaching via the field. "Move out."

13

Leon was running.

Groups of decomposing creatures reached for him as he ran past them, grasping only empty air, too slow to catch him as he darted through. The morning breeze carried their cries in waves of high-pitched wails that assaulted his ears to the point of madness. Screams—moans of desire—agitation for their failures. It filled the air around him like a swarm of yellow jackets all riled up and ready to sting.

Leon ran until he was too tired to continue. He needed somewhere to hide, just for a moment to catch his breath. He found such a place behind a truck that had come to rest on its side and slipped in behind it.

He was unfamiliar with Fredericksburg. He knew the general direction of the Interstate from seeing it through the window of the chopper, but with trees, trash, and wrecked cars littering the roads, it would be difficult to reach without motorized transportation. If he could clear the blanketing haze that had suddenly formed around his thoughts—"A car," he whispered, and pounded a clinched fist into his open palm. "Focus, focus!" He had to move, stay ahead of the relentless crowd. But when he got into a crouched position to peek out from behind the wrecked truck, he was blindsided by a heavy blow.

Leon reeled backward, falling into the grass by the roadside. His head throbbed and his ears rang with deafening intensity. A large, shadowy figure grabbed his boot and pulled. Leon was yanked from the grass and heaved back onto the road as the big ghoul dragged him away.

Leon reached for the wrecked truck as he was pulled past it. His grip was broken by the seven-foot specter that was more powerful than him, even in death.

It walked sluggishly, legs bent at the knees, shoulders slumped as it dragged its feet step by plodding step, all the while pulling Leon, who thrashed and twisted against its hold on him. Usually they were weak, attacking in packs to make up for their decrepit and decomposing bodies, but this giant handled Leon with ease. Leon's fingernails dug into the cracked asphalt as he dangled at the end of the big ghoul's grip like the quarry at the end of a woodsman's hunt.

It wasn't attacking. Not once did it try to bite him. Was it carrying him away to feed without interruption from the others? No, Leon thought, they did not have that kind of mental reasoning power. Then he heard the wailing cries again and he realized that he was not being dragged off to a hidden location so the big ghoul could feed alone; he was being dragged right into a waiting crowd, a group, twenty strong, simply waited and in ten seconds, he would be surrounded.

Leon thrashed at his captor again. He fought with all his strength. He kicked as hard as he could at the hand that held him, but the ghoul continued walking, unaffected by the blows.

On his third kick, the giant released its grip and Leon moved, crablike away from it, and clamored to his feet.

The ghoul turned, and lurched forward, but Leon had already moved beyond its reach. Its maw hung open and poisonous slime dripped onto the ground in one continuous green strand. It began to howl in frustration. Its arms flailed wildly, like a child throwing a temper tantrum. The others, who had been waiting patiently, began to writhe and wail in unison with the big ghoul and started to move toward him. Leon turned, and once again found himself on the run through the streets of Fredericksburg.

**

The first prospect for transportation proved to be useless when Leon discovered no key in its ignition and he moved to the next, a silver sedan with a sunroof and leaped inside. There were keys in the ignition, and for a moment his hopes were high until he tried to start it and it only made a clicking sound.

Leon pounded the steering wheel in frustration. Several creatures were exiting the open doorways of buildings that lined the street. More topped the crest in the road behind him. He would have no time for rest—no time to try to hotwire any of the cars. It was vital that he keep moving or he'd find himself stuck inside a dead car, surrounded by dead people with a voracious appetite for human flesh.

Leon tried to maintain an even pace, checking each and every vehicle as he jogged toward the Interstate. All of them either had no keys or wouldn't start after two years of sitting idle. The ghoulish crowd that followed grew larger by the minute. For every city block he passed, a few more creatures joined in the chase. Ghouls were beginning to appear ahead of him now as well. If he was to make it out of the city alive, he would have to endure a sustained run.

The slow-moving horde of walking dead quickly fell behind as Leon increased his pace to a moderate run. Once he lost sight of them, he changed directions and turned down a side street. He kept the same pace through two more intersections and then turned south again onto a four-lane road where he found himself in the commercial sprawl of Fredericksburg.

Where cornfields once stretched across the land, new structures now clogged each side of the four-lane highway on which he was standing. There were strip malls, fast food joints, gas stations and convenience stores. For the first time since leaving the downed chopper, it was quiet.

Leon turned to face every direction several times before feeling secure enough to settle down on the curb beside the thruway.

A green van rested precariously against a telephone pole in front of an office building, its front wheels three feet off the ground, its front end crushed into a V shape that wrapped around the pole like a hotdog bun.

A pickup at the gas pumps of a nearby service station was probably abandoned when its user found the station closed and his truck out of gas. He'd check it anyway, but not before he'd had a short rest on the curb.

He was beginning to think he'd been better off dying in the crash with his friends. At least their deaths were quick and painless. It was a preferred option to what might be in store for him. This was the world outside their island safe-haven, an abandoned, overrun wasteland.

Leon fell exhausted into a patch of grass and fixed his eyes on a white fluffy cloud in the blue sky above him. It would be easy to fall asleep. Just closing his eyes would do it. But through the soft, steady breeze, he could hear a faint sound. Slight as it was, it was familiar to him. It was the cries of the dead.

The mobs were getting closer.

PART 2

UN-CAGED HATE

14

"Our best bet is to follow that road through town and get on the Interstate headed south," Jim said. He lowered the binoculars and handed them to Matt.

Matt looked over the scene below. They had taken a small detour from their path to the top of a hill to gain a better perspective of what lay ahead. Until now, their trip had been uneventful. They had stayed on back roads and away from towns whenever possible. This would be the most dangerous leg of their journey until they reached the coast.

Matt scanned the area from left to right with the binoculars. He almost missed the small finger of flame and black smoke barely visible behind a stand of trees in the distance. He refocused the lens. It was a mile or so north of the direction they were headed.

"I've got something here, Jim," Matt said, handing the binoculars back to him. "There's smoke down there, but I can't make out what's causing it."

Jim studied the oddity through the binoculars. "It could be caused by lightning. It looks like maybe a tree was struck or something."

"Do we check it out?"

"Absolutely," Jim replied.

***

The Humvee came to a stop beside a large field on the outskirts of Fredericksburg.

At its far edge, a burning mass was wedged in between several rows of trees. The trees, and even the grass around the burning object, were ablaze.

Jim shifted to four-wheel drive and barreled into the field, ignoring the rolls and dips of the terrain as the Humvee plowed its way through with ease. They got as close as one hundred feet before the burning grass forced him to come to a stop.

At first they watched the object burn without speaking. The question that followed Jim even into sleep was finally answered. There were other survivors. The helicopter before them had crashed recently, very recently in fact. Even if no one had survived the crash, it had to have come from somewhere, and that's where the others would be.

"What now?" Matt asked, as he watched a crowd of dead things that had been maintaining a circular path around the chopper change their dance to a unified march toward them.

Jim gave a quick glance to the approaching figures, still a safe distance away. "Nothing changes. We do what we came to do. We move on."

"Yeah, but what about this, shouldn't we try to find out where it came from? I mean, we did come looking for survivors and it would seem this is pretty good proof that there are others who have survived. We can't just leave now without knowing."

"And how would you suggest we find the answers to your questions, Matt? Shall we go over there and ask some of those friendly folk on their way to greet us right now? Maybe they will know."

"Maybe they will, or maybe they used to know, but don't now. Jim…what if one of those walking corpses coming at us was in that bird when it crashed? He could still have something on him to tell us where he came from."

In an instant, Jim was out of the Humvee and pawing through the back of the vehicle until he found the climbing rope he had packed. "I've got an idea," he said, as he slipped back into his seat.

Jim worked with the rope for a moment, then threw it between the seats and drove the Humvee toward the approaching mob of ghouls.

"What the hell are you doing?" Matt yelled. "This is the wrong way, man! We want to go that way!" Matt pointed toward the outer perimeter of the field, away from the crowd. "We can pick out who we think was in that thing from a distance. Why are we driving into them?"

"Just calm down. I'm not going to get too close. Lock your door."

Matt pushed the lock down, hard. "Hell, man, we are already too close!"

Jim slowed as he approached the army of walking corpses and began driving between them. Bloodied fists and severed limbs thumped and pounded at the Humvee. Rotted faces pressed toward the reinforced windows, their eyes glazed with a milky film.

Matt sank down in his seat. "Not too close huh? This is pretty goddamned close!"

"I'm looking for something in particular," Jim said. "Pay attention!"

Matt sat up higher.

"I'm looking for a fresh kill. Someone who looks like they haven't been dead too long. Keep your eyes peeled."

Matt did his best to do as Jim requested, but it was difficult to look at the ghouls up close. He wanted to shut his eyes until it was over. Worst case scenarios filled his thoughts. What if the vehicle broke down? What if they got stuck in the bumpy field? He couldn't shake the dread.

Then he saw it.

"There!" Matt pointed.

One of the creatures had been burned beyond recognition. His smoldering clothes hung in scorched strands from his blackened body. He staggered along the outer edges of the pack.

"Maybe he was in it when it crashed and caught fire."

Jim steered toward it.

Once he got near the chosen ghoul, Jim pulled a safe distance ahead of the pack and stopped. With the rope in hand, he jumped out and loosened the knot he had made, then started to twirl it high over his head. When his lasso formed, he tossed it at the ghoul.

The rope landed below its shoulders and Jim pulled the hoop tighter around the ghoul's arms. He wrapped the other end of the rope around his door handle and got back into the driver's seat.

The Humvee's tires spit dirt as he drove away from the pack, dragging the ghoul along behind. After he had driven a safe distance, he stopped the vehicle and grabbed his rifle. Jim aimed for its head and squeezed the trigger.

"Keep a lookout while I check this thing out," he told Matt.

Matt leaned against the door; his rifle propped on his thigh, and watched as the mob inched closer. They could only afford to stay for a few minutes before the mob became a danger again. They had attracted a lot of unwanted attention and soon others would arrive as well.

Matt glanced at Jim, who was rummaging through the dead man's pockets. "Hurry up, man!" Matt yelled, his voice cracking. "We're gonna have company real soon."

Jim stood and walked away from the smoldering creature.

"Did you find anything?"

"No—nothing. Everything on him was too badly burned." Jim sighed. "Maybe he was on that chopper, maybe he wasn't. He could've gotten too close after the crash and then caught on fire in the burning grass. There was something in his inner jacket pocket that looked like a map or something, but I couldn't make it out. It just crumbled in my hand. We'd better move on before they get any closer."

"We've done all we can do here," Matt said, noticing Jim's mood. "There's no use in feeling guilty."

"I don't feel guilty," Jim said. "Disappointed, but not guilty."

"Yeah, me too. It would've been nice to find someone already. It would've saved us the trip to Tangier."

"No, it wouldn't have saved us the trip to Tangier," Jim said. "Even if we had found someone here, we'd still go to Tangier. That's where the signal came from. But it would've been a nice bonus to find others here. I'm hoping there are a lot more people out here than we thought. In any event, it's time to go," he said, eyeing the approaching mob.

Jim couldn't help but think had they arrived sooner they may have been able to save one or more of the chopper's occupants. He knew it wasn't his fault, but from the beginning of the plague it always seemed to be too little, too late. He hoped things would change once they found their way to Tangier Island.

On their way again, Matt opened the map of Fredericksburg he had taken from the Mount Weather complex and traced the route Jim had decided to take. He was telling him what streets to take for the safest passage through the city to the Interstate as Jim drove.

"Turn here," he said, just in time for Jim to make a hard turn, tires screaming on the paved street.

There was another near miss when Matt yelled, "LEFT HERE!"

Jim made another quick turn onto a larger road, and then another quick swerve to miss a large crowd of ghouls clustered together, unseen until the Humvee was practically on top of them.

Jim sped through the crowd and drove on before finding a place to stop in the road.

His hands gripped the steering wheel and his jaw muscle twitched. "Damn it, Matt! Will you please give me a little more warning on where to go than before we're in the middle of the goddamned intersection?"

Matt held his hands up, the lighter palms toward Jim. "Sorry, sorry! I'm doing my best. Maybe if you slow down a bit…"

Matt's words trailed off as three camouflage-painted trucks, two of them with mounted machine guns, came to a halt in front of them. Armed men in fatigues assumed positions around the trucks and trained their weapons on them.

A man stepped forward and stood in front of them. He looked beyond Jim and Matt to the creatures a half mile or so down the road before focusing his attention to them.

He was a strong-looking man, bulked up in his upper body, probably mid to late-thirties, with short brownish red hair and a thin mustache that ended at the corners of his mouth. For a moment he simply glared at them, as though contemplating his next move. Then he said, "Get out—slowly."

Jim and Matt moved in even steps to the front of the Humvee and assumed an unthreatening posture there.

"I'm Lieutenant Robert Hathaway. I am in charge of this unit of the Virginia Freedom Fighters. Who are you?"

Matt drew a breath to speak, but Jim placed a hand on his chest to stop him.

Hathaway walked closer. "I won't waste time with you," he sneered, casting a quick glance toward the advancing horde. "What unit are you with? Why are you here?"

Jim and Matt remained silent.

Hathaway moved in closer to Matt; their noses were two inches apart. Hathaway sniffed, then wrinkled his nose. "You stink, boy. Didn't your mamma teach you how to take a bath?"

Matt felt his anger begin to rise and he fought the urge to say something—anything to the redneck-looking bastard in front of him. He had just called him boy. It was a term with definite racial overtones, and he was about to do just that when the man stepped away from him to stand in front of Jim.

"What are you, some kinda nigger lover? Are you with our nigger-lovin' government? Maybe you're this nigger's master." Then he glanced at Matt for a second, and said, "I'm sorry. You'll have to pardon my manners. I meant Nigga. That's the non-offensive use of the word these days isn't it?" And with a chuckle, he returned his attention once again to Jim. "I can't keep up with kid's slang these days. All that rap shit and ghetto talk. It's a bad influence on our youth. Kids…what are you gonna do?"

"I know who *you* are," Jim growled through clenched teeth. "I know your kind. You're a disease, like those walking piles of filth back there. You should've been wiped out with the rest of the garbage in this world."

Hathaway snickered. "Disease?—filth? That's pretty good. That's pretty damned good, comparing us to those things like that. You've got no idea who you're messing with or what we're capable of. How about I show you?"

Hathaway stepped away, snapped his finger at one of his subordinates, and pointed to Matt. Before Jim could react, the other man placed a well-aimed bullet into Matt's heart.

Matt was dead before he fell to the ground.

Jim growled, and lunged at Hathaway. He was met by the butt of a pistol to the side of his skull. The blow knocked him from his feet and nearly rendered him unconscious. By the time he regained his wits, he was on his knees, held by two militia soldiers.

"You son of a bitch," Jim cursed as he fought to remain awake. "I'll kill you for that—YOU MURDERERED HIM!"

Hathaway grabbed him by the hair and tilted his face upward to meet his hardened gaze. The pain from the blow to his head and the fact that his hair was being pulled from that very spot sent him in and out of blackness.

"Now, you tell me where you're from," Hathaway barked. "That vehicle you're driving has government issue plates. Where's your home base and how many of you are there?"

Jim spat in Hathaway's face. It dripped from his cheek until he wiped it away with his sleeve.

Again the butt of the pistol came, and so did the blackness.

15

When Jim came to, he was bound with rope and lying face-down in the back of one of the trucks. His mouth and lips were dry, peppered with dirt and debris from the bottom of the truck bed. His head ached from the pistol whipping and his hands were tied tightly together behind him.

He tried to clear his head of the painful cobwebs that clouded his mind before giving an outward indication that he had regained consciousness. Matt's cold-blooded murder replayed over and over as if acted out on a nightmarish stage for his inner eye. The bullet wound to his chest, an explosion of life-giving blood in a spray of red mist as the bullet exited between his shoulder blades. His lifeless body falling to the asphalt. It was murder—cold-blooded, and calculated.

Jim was twisting his hands back and forth, testing the bonds. After several tries he surrendered to his predicament for the time being, then rolled over onto his back and sat up, pushing himself into a corner of the truck bed with his feet.

A single militia soldier sat guard on one of the wheel wells. As Jim situated himself for a better view of his predicament, the soldier trained his weapon on him.

The barrel of a mounted machine gun that was bolted to the center of the truck bed swayed slightly as the vehicle roared down the highway. It moved with the motion of the truck, until it came to a stop with its ported barrel aiming directly at Jim.

It was an M2 .50 caliber weapon. He was familiar with it. The M2s were used on multipurpose-wheeled vehicles in Iraq. It had been jury rigged and attached to the bed on a tripod. It was as if an unseen force had directed it to move and was daring Jim to resist his predicament.

The soldier watched, and a wide smile formed on his grizzled face, a face that had seen a thousands deaths—a face scared with countless battles and the hatred of a lifetime of learned behavior. This was a man who could be unpredictable and capable of great violence. The warnings were there in his scared face, behind his deep set eyes. He was where he belonged, with others like him.

Jim pushed himself into the corner of the truck bed with his legs bent at the knees and leaned his head back against the cab. The sky was blue with only a few fluffy white clouds moving slowing overhead. He could hear the men inside the truck talking to each other, but he couldn't understand what they were saying over the roar of the truck. If he could hear them, find out where they were taking him—that information could be useful.

They were moving south. That much he did know. It was the direction he wanted to go, but not the way he wanted to get there, not with these people. He knew of the Freedom Fighters. They were little more than a militarized Ku Klux Klan, their beliefs founded in white supremacy and anti-government rhetoric. They were an old group, dating back to the days prior to the Civil War. This militia gave militias in general, a bad name.

Jim eyed the machine gun that was still pointing at him. If he could break free from his bindings, he could use the gun to kill his captors and jump from the speeding truck into the grass along the road. Three men rode in the cab. The other trucks were in front of them. For the time being the men in the cab paid no attention to the goings on in the back.

Jim wrestled with the ropes, twisting his wrists behind his back. It felt like they were loosening up a little. Just a little more and—

"You get those off and I'll have to shoot ya," the soldier said, watching him closely.

Jim said, "You're going to shoot me anyway, aren't you?"

"That's not up to me," he snickered, "unless you make me. Then I'll put a bullet in your brain. I don't want ya gettin' back up while we're going down the road at seventy miles an hour. Quarters are too close. I might fall outta here trying to fight your biting ass off of me. Nah, fuck all that. One to the brain…that's the way to go."

Jim looked at the sun again. His best guess put the time at about two o'clock. He had been unconscious for at least two hours.

"Where are we going?"

"You'll see when we get there."

"Why? Are you afraid to tell me?"

The soldier roared with laughter, revealing a jack-o-lantern grin framed in swollen, pyorrhea gums. If Jim had to make a guess, he'd figure that this man's bite might be almost as deadly as one inflicted by the dead walkers.

When his laughter had settled a bit, he cocked his head, and said, "Now why the hell should I be afraid of you? Are you someone to be afraid of?"

Jim lowered his gaze. "No, I guess I'm just along for the ride," he said, trying his best to prevent the hatred he was feeling from surfacing in his voice.

"That's what I thought. You didn't seem like much back there—you or your nigger friend."

Jim's jaw twitched with anger. He fought the urge to explode onto the man, tied hands and all.

"His name was Matt and he was a better man then you will ever be." Jim stared through the hair hanging over his eyes to catch the man's reaction.

"He's a dead man," the soldier said. "And you will be too if you don't shut that filthy mouth of yours."

Jim lowered his gaze and purposely allowed the hard knot of hatred to rise in him as he reclined in the corner of the truck bed. He had felt red-hot anger at various times in his life, but never before had he experienced the swell of malignant emotion that now threatened to overcome him.

"You could all be dead men real soon," he whispered. "The whole damned lot of you, and that would be a good thing."

16

This isn't working out, Leon thought as he stepped onto the Interstate. He was still a long way from home, without the benefit of motorized transportation. At least he'd left the hordes of creatures behind. He was alone now on a long stretch of highway heading south. It would take several days to walk all the way to the coast. The thought of closing his eyes for sleep terrified him. He would surely wake to meet his fate at the hands of rotting corpses.

What were the odds? Pretty good, he thought. Each week they took their lives into their own unprepared hands by getting into that chopper, all the while making half-assed repairs and safety checks. None of them were experienced enough to ensure a safe trip each and every time. Hal could fly the chopper, but he knew only enough about the mechanics to fix the most obvious problems. It was a bad idea with good intentions. That was the trouble with good intentions. The road to Hell was paved with them. And this was certainly the road to hell—two dead and another hopelessly stranded and soon to join them.

But now he was considering making the rest of the trip in his sock feet. His boot heels were clicking on the asphalt as he walked. In his mind any noise was too much and the tapping sound with each step seemed to amplify around him in hammering, mammoth thumps. It would surely draw attention to him. In a world where stealth was the key to survival, he was not being very stealthy.

Leon moved to the side of the road and walked in the soft grass.

Occasionally, Leon could see through the trees that lined the interstate. There were abandoned subdivisions and quickie marts,

Seven Elevens and gas stations, schools and police stations. And along with it all…the living dead. At times he caught glimpses of them wandering around exit ramps and under bridges. Most took no notice of him as he quietly crept by. But now he was squatting beside the road, eying a car in the middle of the Interstate ahead. A lone figure stood at its side, staring into the direction of the evening sun. It was too far to determine if it was a living corpse, or a living, breathing, person, but Leon took no chances as he watched motionless and low to the ground.

If he used his gun, the noise would bring others down on him. His journey would change from a leisurely stroll, to a hurried escape down the four-lane highway. He could simply run past it, but it would tag along and attract others along the way. Besides, he needed to check that car for keys. He would not survive the trip on foot.

Leon slithered to the other side of the road and down the embankment between lanes. It offered him better cover and at the same time put him in a better position to come up from behind the strange figure, unnoticed.

Halfway there he stopped to contemplate his course of action. He needed another weapon, something that didn't make as much noise as a gun, something solid for smashing in the thing's skull.

Leon searched the ground around him, picking up one rock after another, looking for one that was big enough to do the job of smashing its brain. Then he caught a glimmer of light reflecting off an object in the gully ahead. It was an iron pipe, three feet long and crooked in the middle, just right for swinging and killing. Leon reached out and pulled it to him, then climbed the embankment just behind the lone figure.

Standing on the shoulder of the road, he studied it for signs of life. Its clothes were ragged and covered with filth. It stood perfectly still as it leaned awkwardly over the roof of the car with its head tilted up. No, this was not a living person. It was one of *them*. He was certain of it.

Leon raised the pipe and in three running steps, he was close enough to strike…

The creature twirled around as its body collapsed to the ground. The head flew away with the swing and bounced, rat-a-tat-tat, down the road. Leon jumped away, surprised by the ease of his attack and by what he now realized was a mannequin, a plastic clothing store dummy. Someone had wired it to the roof of the car, for what purpose, he couldn't imagine, but when he hit it, the wire that had been wrapped around its neck broke and its body fell to the asphalt.

He let loose a sigh of relief, but his bewilderment lingered as he stared down at the dummy on the ground.

"Bizarre," was all he could whisper.

Leon jumped into the driver's seat, and released a yelp of excitement when he saw keys in the ignition. "Come on, come on," he cooed, patting his hand on the cracked, vinyl dash and turned the key.

The engine sputtered, and Leon pumped the gas pedal as the starter cranked the engine.

It finally steadied into an even thrum and Leon gleefully pounded the steering wheel, and howled.

He had found a way home.

17

The imposing aircraft carrier towered above every other ship in the port. Over a thousand feet from bow to stern, the other ships around it paled in comparison.

A thick haze hung over the bay, contrasting the clarity of the vessels close to shore against the miasma that surrounded the giant carrier almost a mile out into the bay. It was a vessel of might and absolute power, yet it had been powerless to prevent the total collapse of humanity. A multi-million dollar joke left to one day rust and sink to the bottom.

Jim turned his face away from the great ship and back to his immediate predicament.

They were moving slowly now that they had entered Newport News. The ever-narrowing street on which they were driving was littered with abandoned cars and other debris. Jim watched as they passed less-than-capable ghouls who crawled or staggered from alleys and doorways. They were now mostly rotting piles of stinking flesh due to the elements and passage of time, or perhaps the salt air of the bay had taken its toll on their fragile bodies.

For a few moments the massive carrier fell from view as the caravan of trucks wound its way down the forgotten street toward the bay through the old section of town. It appeared again a few minutes later, even more impressive as they negotiated the road leading into the harbor. Larger than life, it gleamed in the evening sun. Its weighty presence commanded respect and awe from all who beheld its majesty. *U.S.S. Nimitz*, it proudly proclaimed.

Jim found his footing in the moving vehicle and stood up behind the cab. His wrists were raw from the bindings that he yearned to rip free.

They were almost there. A few hundred yards and they'd be along the shore. In spite of his situation, he felt a spike of excitement. The ship mesmerized him. It was such a magnificent creation that he found it hard to divert his eyes.

"Sit down or I'll knock you down!" his captor bellowed, infringing upon his momentary break from reality and reverence for the carrier.

Jim turned. "What are we doing here?"

The man moved forward. "What do you think we're doing? We're saving the world, or what's left of it, anyway."

"Really?" Jim said. "How's that?"

The man didn't answer. His attention was focused on the harbor.

"By killing innocent people?" Jim asked. "Is that how you'll save the world? What kind of insanity are you people living out here?"

The militiaman delivered a vicious kick to Jim's stomach, sending him sprawling to the bottom of the truck bed. The force of the blow sent the air from his lungs.

"Insanity? You want insanity? How's six thousand years of war for insanity?" He kicked Jim again. "People living in fear every day of what's to come next. How about working your ass off for every little portion of shit that's dished out to you while others get it handed to them so they can sit on their lazy asses and collect welfare, then spend our hard-earned money buying crack and heroin. How about fucking dead people walking? How's that for insanity?" Drool hung from the man's lower lip. "You just lay there and keep quiet. I don't need to explain myself to you. You just shut the fuck up!"

Jim gulped oxygen back into his lungs, then settled back into his corner. His determination hardened and his hatred for these people grew darker, to a shade he was not accustomed to. It was not in his nature to feel so much hatred for anything or anyone. It would be easy to lose control and in so doing, lose rationality. It would be his downfall. If he was to escape, he had to keep his wits.

The trucks stopped and militiamen spilled from them, taking protective positions around the caravan. They aimed their weapons in a way that covered a full three hundred and sixty degree swathe.

As Hathaway barked orders, several of the men boarded a small yacht anchored close to where they were parked. The yacht was a Languard Nelson 113, about forty feet long, with an aft cabin. The flags of both the United States and the Confederacy waved in the breeze as the men disappeared below deck.

Jim watched, cataloguing his surroundings, until the guard forced him from the back of the truck and pushed him toward the yacht, and Hathaway.

Hathaway watched as the men carried out his orders without question. His eyes gleamed, drunk with the fix of power he possessed—and like a junkie, it seemed he craved more.

The boat's diesel motors growled in unison as the men finished their task of prepping it for the trip. Jim watched, as one by one, the men who had taken positions around them moved close to the boat and once again took up a defensive posture.

Ghouls began to move in from every direction, but Hathaway's men refrained from firing their weapons. They were well trained. It would be a waste of ammo to fire on them unless they were in immediate danger.

Hathaway pushed Jim toward the boat. "Get on!" he barked.

Hathaway was the last man to come aboard, flanked by Jake, his second in command.

A simple nod from Hathaway and the boat began to move. Once it was away from the dock, it turned and headed in the direction of the Nimitz.

Jim looked over his shoulder at Hathaway, who returned the look with a smug grin. He was indeed in power of these men, but was he the leading figure of the larger group? How many more were willing to carry out the dastardly deeds of these few?

He had to know.

18

Sharon Darney marveled at the sight.

For only the second time in two years, she had caught a glimpse of it. Black and featureless, it darted back and forth on the screen, unsure of where to go now that it was separated from its host. There was nowhere for it to hide this time, nowhere to escape her study. Trapped between the microscope slides and exposed, it still remained very active. It was the same organism she had discovered two years before. She would learn from it this time and find out why the dead walk.

The tiny organism's host, a reanimated corpse of a man in his thirties, was strapped to an examination table separated from the main room of Sharon's laboratory by Plexiglas walls. The reanimate had been in her custody for the full two years, except during her brief stay with the other survivors at the prison. He was the only corpse still animated upon their reoccupation of the Mount Weather Underground and that presented her with another puzzle to unravel. It could also be key to understanding the cause. More than a hundred bodies had littered the corridors throughout the facility, but only this one remained active. The others were dead and rotting on their arrival.

Study showed them to have a lifespan of ten or more years, but that had not been the case with the ones reanimated in the underground. Why did every corpse in the underground cease to function after only two months except her original specimen? Now that she had a major piece of the puzzle trapped on the glass slide, she would find out more. The logical place to begin would be to match the organism to something already cataloged. They had tried this before, with no success. If she could find a close similarity in another organism, she might have a point of reference, somewhere to begin.

Sharon considered the image of the tiny life form on the computer screen. Dark and unremarkable, it resembled nothing she had ever seen. She would go through the records again. The computer banks held information on every microbe, germ, and disease known to man. She would go through them one by one until she had covered them all.

***

Felicia sipped her tea at the kitchen table. Oddly enough, the drink had flavor. That was odd because Felicia knew she was dreaming. There should be no sensation of flavor in her dream. She could also smell the honeysuckle that grew heavy against the backyard fence, entwining the pickets so thickly that it formed a privacy barrier between her grandmother's house and the one next door. The sight of the honeysuckle in full bloom through the kitchen window brought to mind memories of her childhood, of afternoons running about and greedily sucking the nectar from the flowering thicket one tiny drop at a time.

Since her last night at the prison, her sleep had been devoid of the pleasant dreams that had carried her away from a dead world to the company of her beloved grandmother. In those dreams, her grandmother had warned her of the impending doom that was to fall upon their sanctuary. She had also warned her of "the wolf."

The wolf had arrived in the form of a deranged preacher with thoughts of godhood and a band of devoted followers intent upon destroying them all. That had been their last night at the prison. That was the night the wolf and his followers met their fate at the hands of thousands of rotting corpses, the same night Felicia's side lost half its numbers. Felicia had been nearly killed, and she had concluded that her near-death experience had brought about the end of her "gift." That night, less than seventy survivors escaped their prison stronghold and found their way to the place they were now—a seven-story hole in the ground with all the conveniences of home, an underground military complex constructed in anticipation of a nuclear war or other national emergency. It offered a safe haven, a world without sunlight or warm summer breezes. And as much as Felicia tried to inwardly deny it; their safe-haven sucked the life from her a little more each day by depriving her of the barest essentials, like real sunlight that warmed the face and body, and the power of spirit it gave her.

She was becoming depressed. Watching the world from inside the above ground lobby was after all, not enough. If not for Mick, she was sure her sanity would've been lost long ago, but his company kept her mind in check. With him by her side, Mount Weather was bearable.

Felicia took another sip of tea and studied her dream surroundings. Usually her grandmother was there to greet her, but today she was alone. It was daytime in her dream, but surely it was evening in the real world. In the real world, she was nestled close to Mick, his arm wrapped tightly around her, holding her and comforting her during a late evening nap. Mick's presence offered a sense of security, but the nagging reality of the dead world above them was ever present, like waves crashing against the beach, ever eroding her grasp on sanity. Perhaps the dream had come to her again to ease her pain, a gift from her grandmother who felt her building anguish. It was a warming thought and Felicia took comfort in it and drank her tea.

***

Amanda awoke on the floor of her kitchen where she had cried herself to sleep with grief over her dead husband and lost dreams. Today was the day. She would have to make her escape before too many creatures converged on her house. Today she would still have a chance.

She groped around in the semi-darkness, throwing essentials into her backpack and making a mental checklist. She had done this before, she was certain of it—a feeling of déjà vu. Be sure to take all the shotgun shells, and this time, be ready for the weapon's kick, she thought. Yes, now she remembered. The last time it had caught her by surprise and the shot missed its target. What was the target? She fought to remember. Then it all came back to her. The target was her husband, William. She must end his suffering.

Amanda slipped on her backpack and grabbed the gun. Her heart was pounding as she readied herself to do what had to be done.

Amanda turned the lock and swung open the door...

The sunlight blinded her and silhouetted the dark figure of her dead husband in the doorway. He took a stumbling step toward her and she saw the dead visage and milky eyes of not her husband William, but of Jim Workman.

Amanda choked the rising scream in her throat and the strangling sound that emerged from her echoed in the empty lobby as she sat bolt upright in the easy chair she had stationed herself in to await Jim's return. She sucked in gulps of air and then leaned over and vomited into a wastebasket beside the chair.

Amanda paced the floor, her arms folded. She held them tightly against herself to keep away the feeling that she would literally explode with worry. Since Jim had left, the feelings of helplessness had returned until she thought she would burst at the seams—and once again, sleep offered no respite.

She cursed Jim under her breath. It was inconsiderate of him to cause her to worry so. It was uncaring of him to go off and leave her alone like this. "Uncaring, inconsiderate asshole!" she said, out loud.

She regretted the small outburst as soon as it left her lips. What if something *had* happened? That was an awful thing to say. She swore to herself that she would never allow him to leave her alone again. The next time, she would go where he went, do what he did, and stay by his side. Never again would she be the mindful little woman who stays behind to wait and worry.

19

In the holding cell, the sound of metal tumblers brought Jim's mind into focus as the door opened.

Two men stood before him. One of them was a scruffy giant—six-foot-eight with a crooked nose and missing teeth. He grinned at Jim with a jack-o'-lantern smile. The other, smaller man was clean-cut and presented himself with standard military discipline. He stood straight, one arm at his side, the other on his holstered weapon.

"Lieutenant Hathaway wants to see you," the smaller man said. "Stand up and keep your arms to your side, sir. Leave the cell and don't make any quick moves."

Jim stood up, and for the first time he realized his hands were no longer tied together. The smaller man left the cell first and stood in the corridor outside the door. Jim left the cell next and kept an even pace as he walked down the narrow, darkened hallway. The small man walked ahead of him, the large oaf followed behind.

In Jim's mind, he envisioned a deceptive move of bending over in make-believe pain, turning on the oaf behind him, delivering a lethal karate chop to his shoulder, and using the oaf's weapon to shoot them both in the head. Even if the outlandish feat was successful, there was no place to go. Escaping from the ship would be very difficult. No, there was no need for such a desperate measure yet. If they were going to kill him, chances are they would have done so already. Obviously, they wanted information first.

He continued down the corridor trying to think ahead, and would wait for the proper moment should it present itself.

***

Jim found himself standing on the bridge of the mighty ship, a spacious room surrounded by windows. Hathaway stood by the one overlooking the flight deck, peering into the near night darkness.

The oafish giant pushed Jim into a chair.

"Funny, isn't it?" Hathaway said, his attention still focused outside. "One ship like this could quite possibly conquer the world right now." He turned to Jim. "You see, I doubt there's an organized army on Earth in possession of such a thing. We have enough aircraft to lay waste to anyone who opposes us. We can equip them with nukes and destroy entire cities. Of course, those cities are already graveyards, infested with those murderous sons of bitches, aren't they? But my point's made."

Hathaway smiled, and moved to face Jim. "Where's your home base?" he asked pleasantly. "What company are you with?"

"Company? I have no company. I'm unemployed, like most everyone now." Jim turned on a deceptive smile.

"What's your outfit? That's what I mean," Hathaway said. "Don't play games with me."

"I'm not playing, not with you. We were alone. We were loners. We had no home base, no outfit, and no company. We lived from day to day, hand to mouth. We were on a search for food when you found us."

Hathaway moved to a console across the room, picked something up, and then returned to Jim. "I know that to be a lie," he said, "because I have this." He shook the map they had been using to plot their way to Tangier Island.

Jim swallowed hard. The map could lead them to Mount Weather.

"We got this from the vehicle you were driving. It has a travel route traced in yellow." Hathaway unfolded the map and pointed to a particular spot. "We found you here, in Fredericksburg. Where were you going when we found you, or were you just out for a ride about town?"

Jim showed no emotion. "I've never seen that map before in my life. Where'd you say you got it again?"

Annoyance began to surface in Hathaway's voice. "We got it from the government vehicle you were driving. Now I'll repeat the question: Where is your home base?"

Jim remained silent.

Hathaway exhaled loudly. "The route traced has two ending points. One to the north on Route Seven, about twenty miles north of Leesburg, Virginia. The other point ends just north of here at the coast, a place called Smith's Point. We've been picking up a little air traffic in that area." Hathaway pointed to the spot near Tangier Island. "Is that where you're from—Smith's Point? Are your people responsible for the radar contacts we've been receiving?"

"I told you, I'm not from there. I've never seen that map before and I have no home base. It must've been in the Humvee when we found it."

Hathaway folded the map. "You'll tell us what we want to know and you'll tell us now."

The large oaf who had been standing close to Jim handed his weapon to Hathaway and rolled up his sleeves as he walked to where Jim sat. He smiled again, exposing toothless gums, and backhanded Jim across the face.

The blow sent Jim and the chair he was sitting in crashing to the floor. Jim staggered to his feet as the giant moved in for another strike. Jim met him first with a kick to his groin, a kick that hardly fazed the giant. A quiet moan escaped with his breath and then he swung.

Jim ducked and the swing missed. Another blow made contact with the side of Jim's head. He crashed to the floor and the giant stopped.

Jim's head throbbed in pain.

Hathaway looked down at him. "Where's your base?"

Jim spat as he lay face down on the cold metal floor. His spit was red. "No base."

The giant grabbed Jim from the back, lifted him to his feet, and swung at his face.

Blood spewed from Jim's nose and his return trip to the floor was stopped by the giant who held him up long enough to slam several more hard punches into his chest and sides.

Jim lay motionless on the floor, barely conscious of anything except the cold metal against his cheek and the blood that now flowed into his eyes. The air had been forced from his lungs and he was on the verge of passing out.

"Last chance, hero."

Hathaway's voice seemed far away to Jim.

"Where's your base? Where are you from? I swear to God, I will kill you and every one of your friends if you don't answer me. If you don't think I can find them on my own, you are wrong. For your friends' sake, you had better tell me something now!"

Jim was too dazed to answer even if he wanted to. It wouldn't have made any difference because nothing they could do to him would make him tell. The startled look on Matt's face as he realized his fate flashed through Jim's mind. —*Nothing they could do to him.*

The giant began to kick him. Kick after kick came until Jim lost consciousness. Then the giant picked Jim up again and slammed a fist into his face before Hathaway ordered him to stop.

Hathaway put a boot against Jim's shoulder and rolled him onto his back. Jim's eyes were open and unfocused. His face was covered in blood. Hathaway leaned down and tried to get a pulse from his wrist.

There was none.

"You've killed him! Jesus Christ, I told you not to do that," Hathaway screamed, and pushed the oaf aside.

The oaf dropped his head in shame. Not for killing the man, but because he had failed to follow Hathaway's order. That was priority number one, pleasing the lieutenant.

Hathaway kicked Jim's chair and it skidded across the floor. "I needed him for information. You were supposed to keep him alive until I had it!"

The rage left Hathaway as quickly as it had come, and he walked back to the window and stared out at the deepening twilight. "Take him outside and throw him over. The fish have to eat too, same as everything else."

20

Leon was laying on the front seat of the car he had found on the interstate too afraid to raise his head. The night was dark, without even the moon to offer light. He was parked by the waterfront at Smith's Point. This was where they docked their boats when a trip to the mainland was necessary by sea. It was close to Tangier and the docks were isolated from the more populated residential and commercial zones around it. A boat could come in, anchor off, and be disembarked unseen by the crowds loitering around the downtown subdivisions only a stone's throw away.

Sleep was not coming easily for Leon. If he had gotten there before nightfall, he could've grabbed one of the boats and been on his way. But without light, he could not see, and without sight, he was not going to budge. He'd simply have to stay still, quiet, and wait out the night.

From time to time he could hear footsteps close by. He held his breath as they passed, afraid to even breathe. The dead's eerie wails did little to comfort him. Some were close, others distant; they reminded him of different things. There were some that sounded like crying infants and some that sounded like a whale song. One sounded like a screech owl, high and shrill, while others sounded like wounded animals. All were lonely sounds, calls of desperation and need as he listened, motionless.

At any time, he expected a thump on one of the car's windows, clawing hands digging in blackened fingernails to gain entrance. They were smart enough to use tools, a rock or stick. They could break the glass. If that happened, he would move the car, if he had the time. But where would he go? At first he thought he'd be safe there at the marina. It was uninhabited, or so he had thought. But after a while they came. They always did. They eventually found you no matter how careful you were.

Maybe they had a sixth sense, a kind of radar or something. Could they detect him there in the car? Were they closing in on him? That certainly seemed to be the case tonight. They were closer now. So close he could smell them—it was the smell of death.

He was sweating now, soaked with it. He could smell it, strong and acidic. He wondered if they could smell it too. "Dumb bastards," he whispered, before realizing he had said it. They were likely too feeble minded to realize what they were actually looking for unless they spotted you. "Stupid things," he whispered again. Stupid was a good thing. Stupid was great. They can keep on being stupid, he thought…stupid tool users.

Leon's eyes grew heavy. They closed without his permission and he quickly opened them again. Lying on the seat was too comfortable. He was physically drained from the day's events. He had survived a helicopter crash, been chased by flesh-eating mobs, and walked for miles before finally finding a car. He had also lost two close friends and now he wanted to sleep. But that would be a mistake, possibly a fatal one. Turning over in his sleep could make the car move ever so slightly. The slightest movement would be enough to reveal his position. He was also known to snore—to be a window rattler, actually. Ghouls would swarm to the car from all around. They would break through the windows and pull him out by his ears. To top it off, he was hungry. His stomach growled at the mere thought of food. He held his hands over his belly in an attempt to quiet it. He wondered if they could hear it. Who knew? Maybe they had the hearing of cats and the eyes of eagles.

Leon's eyes closed again.

21

The sudden impact of Jim's body hitting the water brought the life back into his body and his eyes opened wide. In the few seconds before he sank too far beneath the surface of the cold water, he was able to gain his senses enough to realize where he was and what had happened.

His head and shoulders broke the surface and Jim Workman sucked for air.

That's when he felt the pain.

It was intense and from head to foot. His head throbbed and his chest ached with each breath of air. The big oaf had beaten him until he lost consciousness. But why would they throw him overboard? Did they think they had killed him? Had they? They would never lose their only source of information; never just toss him over the side. He *had* died, if only for a minute, he was dead. The shock of hitting the water must have brought him back, but where was he? Where was the shore? He could just start swimming, but if he swam the wrong way and out to sea, he wouldn't survive, not in his condition. He needed to be certain. It would take all his strength to make it to shore.

Only the outline of the carrier and the light from the deck and windows stood out against the dark background. There were no city lights, no shoreline to see, but he *could* see the carrier and which way it was pointed.

When they brought him there, the starboard side was facing shore.

He was certain.

Jim started to swim.

***

Jim had to stop swimming several times to rest. He could barely make out the shoreline now as he bobbed in the water, but it was there, and it was getting closer. He would make it if he took his time and stopped when the pain got to be too much. What's more, he *had* to survive. He needed to warn the others.

When Jim was finally out of the bay surf, he fell to his knees on the sandy shore at the bottom of an embankment.

His arms and legs felt like throbbing rubber. The salt water had found every open wound on his body and turned them into fiery burns. It hurt to breathe. It hurt to think.

Jim collapsed.

A light rain splashed at his face and Jim opened his mouth to let the clean droplets quench his parched throat. It had been dry. So dry that he couldn't swallow, as if he'd tried to eat a thousand stick pins. But the rain drops were quenching his thirst and the pain was diminishing. He could breathe again now, his mind was clearing. How long had he been lying there? Only a few moments, he was sure, but he had momentarily forgotten about the dangers he faced there on the rain-soaked embankment. He would surely have unwelcome company soon, and he would be without the benefit of a weapon or healthy body to defend himself. Had it only been a moment? Maybe it had been longer.

Jim lurched to his feet and the pain raced through his body, threatening to send him back down to the sand. Every step he took was a chore and he wiped the dripping rain from his eyes as he limped his way to where the trucks were parked. The rain, though cold on his aching body, covered the noise he was making. There were unseen things in the darkness. Things that wanted to harm him.

Amanda would already be worrying herself sick. It saddened him to think about it as the outlines of the militia's covered trucks came into view. He would not leave her to worry again. Once his mission was complete, he would stay put, but first things first. Tangier was on the way home from where he was now. He could still complete his mission.

Jim reached the first truck and fumbled in the dark to find the door handle. The interior light flashed on, and Jim was blinded. His eyes burned, and his sight was blurred. It was the sight of his .44 lying on the seat where his captors had left it that finally caused them to focus, and as he reached for it, movement to his left caught his attention.

A decaying apparition lunged.

It opened its mouth and moaned pitifully as it grabbed Jim by the throat. Jim reacted with a fist to the thing's head and it fell backward. He made a move toward the fallen ghoul to finish it off, then stopped. He was too badly injured to do battle and at anytime he could be surrounded by more of them.

Jim jumped into the truck and locked the doors.

The rotting man that he had knocked to the ground was on his feet again, pawing at the truck window. Jim's hand swiped the side of the steering column and the keys jingled in the ignition.

22

An hour later, Jim Workman had cleared the city limits and was well on his way up Route 64, moving north. The militia commander wanted to know his starting point on the map he had used to trace his journey to Tangier Island. That meant the militia was not stationed on Tangier or Hathaway would have known which starting point was the correct one. That tidbit of information eased his mind a bit and so Tangier was still his destination. But without a map to point the way he would become lost soon.

* * *

It was after midnight when Jim took the exit to Williamsburg. The night was still, except for two deer that were grazing by the road's edge. When the truck's headlights disturbed them, the whitetails leaped up a hill in graceful strides and disappeared into the safety of the woods. They were beautiful creatures, a doe and a buck, healthy and fat. At least the plague had not infected the wildlife. It flourished. It was not the end of everything, just civilization.

A moment later, Jim brought the truck to a stop.

He had driven into the parking lot of an amusement park. The silhouette of one of the roller coasters was directly ahead, its arching tracks blending into the dark sky. The park was dim and uninviting, a sinister looking thing, under the circumstances. Who knew what evil dwelled there hidden in the shadows? Were there crowds of ghoulish children attracted by past memories of pleasure, beckoned by the promise of comfort, maybe even an interlude from their fractured, strange new existence? That was something the dead things did. They clung to things familiar, or places that had given them happiness. Those were places to avoid.

At the far end of the parking lot, a convenience store was positioned so departing park guests could spend their unused vacation cash on the way out and he drove toward it.

Jim stood by the truck with an ear to the wind and listened. The rain had stopped. All was quiet except for a soft breeze. It was devoid of the voices of the dead; no moans or cries from tortured souls, just a gentle breeze brushed his face as he walked to the store with the headlights of the truck showing him the way.

Most places had been looted during the plague's early outbreak, but this one had been spared such turmoil. No broken windows, no ransacked shelves and no walking dead that he could see by the shining headlights. The front door was locked. Someone had taken the time to protect the business. Were they still inside? Such a place would make a good hideout if you stayed out of sight. There was food and drink, enough to last a while for one or two people. The trick would be to remain unseen by the hordes.

Jim's attention was drawn to a smoker's outpost placed beside the double glass entry doors. Its long slender neck would be good for gripping and the round, sand-weighted bottom was perfect for smashing.

Jim swung it at the door and the glass shattered.

Certainly someone or some thing had heard it. But as he listened, it was only the dark night on the gentle wind. If he had invaded someone's sanctuary, he could get a bullet to the brain. Worse, he could get one to the heart like Matt, one that allowed him to come back. That was a fate worse than death, one he did not want as his own.

"Hello? Is anyone here?"

If he could make them understand that he meant no harm…"I'm looking for a map. I don't want any trouble. I just need a map and I'll be on my way." The thought had crossed his mind that if there were people hiding inside the store, they could be very angry now that he had shattered the door. They might shoot him anyway.

When there was no response, Jim started to search the darkness. He found a flashlight and batteries by the register and scanned the shelves.

There were some state maps and a road atlas on a rack by the front window and he grabbed both. He hesitated as his flashlight crossed a stack of yellowed newspapers with the headline, *"Dead Continue to Rise and Multiply."* The date was September 10, two years earlier. The cover photo showed burning bodies piled high as armed troops stood watch. Another story titled, *"President Urges Calm,"* filled out the newspaper's front page.

Jim turned off the flashlight and left the store.

***

On the road again, Jim roared north, certain that the militia would attempt to find his "home base." They would probably start at Tangier, then move north from there. They might even find the compound at Mount Weather. It was secure from the ghouls, but an organized army would have no problem breaking in. From what he'd witnessed, no person of color would have a chance with these men. They were not an ordinary militia, not like the ones that were so vital to the birth of the country, but a splinter group with depraved plans and no conscience—radicals, subversives. He would warn both the island (assuming there were survivors there), and his own people.

Jim drove faster.

***

Leon opened his eyes.

The sun was not up yet, but a faint glow filled the eastern sky. He had fallen asleep, something he'd promised himself not to do. Fortunately, the mistake had done him no harm. He was unmolested and he had gained some much-needed rest. In a few minutes it would be light enough to make a move for the boat.

Leon sat up for a better look, first just a peek with his eyes barely above the passenger side window, then fully, as he slid behind the steering wheel.

The area around the car was devoid of the dead walkers that had moved by him during the night. The roving bands had moved away from the harbor area to cover ground elsewhere in search of prey and he could move about freely now.

Leon stepped out and stretched, leaning against the car with his arms raised behind his head. He was both surprised and pleased that his injuries from the chopper crash were not as painful as they had been the previous day. His ribs were sore, but the pain was bearable. If they were broken, and he thought that likely, it was a clean break and his lungs were not punctured. Punctured lungs could have led to a collapsed lung, something that would have slowed down his escape. But he would not give thanks for small miracles. There were no miracles. Only curses.

Leon breathed in the salt air of the bay and walked toward the boat. He stopped halfway there and turned.

A green, army personnel truck drove into the harbor and stopped beside his car. A tall, battered man with dark hair stepped out and stood beside the canvas covered vehicle.

As the two men squared off, the same thought passed through their minds…

Is this going to be trouble?

23

Amanda picked at her food with fading interest as Felicia and Mick watched. Worry had quelled her appetite and she was no longer interested in what was on her plate.

Izzy piled her grits into a pile in the center of her plate, and then poured syrup around it. She furrowed her brow, unhappy with its appearance. Discontent painted her small face.

Felicia watched as Amanda continued to pick at her food. "You're going to worry yourself to death," she scolded. "He'll be back."

Izzy placed a half-finished string of beads on the table beside her plate, and then fished a small bag of M&Ms from her pocket. She poured them into her hand and separated them by color.

With a huff, Amanda dropped her fork and glared at Felicia. "They should've been back last night," she said.

"That only means that they're late, not dead. If they found people on the island, they probably stayed an extra day to get some rest before the return trip."

Izzy took one of her piles of candy and placed the pieces on her grits, taking special care in their placement.

"He wouldn't do that," Amanda said. "He knows how much I worry."

Izzy finished her work of art and showed her pleasure in the finished project by clapping her hands.

"What's that, Izzy?" Felicia asked, her attention drawn away from Amanda by the child's outburst. "Are you playing with your food again?" she asked with a questioning smile.

Izzy giggled, and said in a child's carefree voice, "It's an island."

Amanda turned her attention to Izzy's creation.

"Why are all the green candies on top?" Felicia asked.

"All the people," she said pointing, laying a finger on each of the little, round candies.

She now had everyone's attention.

Felicia noticed that one of the pieces of candy was red. It was placed in the center of the others. "How about that red one? What's that?"

Izzy's smile widened. "That's Uncle Jim. He's going to help the others."

"Oh, I see," Felicia said. "Where's Matt? I don't see him."

Izzy's smile faded. She fell silent as she removed the pieces of candy from the plate and pocketed the string of beads. "Not there."

"Where is he, Izzy?" Felicia asked, cocking her head at Izzy's troubled expression.

Izzy put the candy on the table and dropped her head and moaned. "Tummy feels funny now. Can I go rest?"

Felicia nodded and Izzy left the table, pale and drawn.

A portent of doom hung in Izzy's wake. A sense of dread was suddenly palpable.

For the remainder of the meal, the three adults were quiet.

Sharon Darney prepared the slide for the addition of blood cells to the organism imprisoned there. If what she suspected were true, she would quickly see the results. If her calculations were correct, it would take no more than thirty minutes for the changes to take place.

The specimen on the slide was rare indeed, a microscopic parasite. But nothing like she had ever seen. It could survive on its own for long periods of time without the aid of a human host. What puzzled her most was that only a fraction of the numbers normally needed to inflict the damage necessary to cause death had been found. That explained why no one had found it before the world fell apart. They simply didn't have time to discover it. Less than a million individual organisms existed in the entire body, living or dead. That meant there were less than ten of these strange organisms per million human cells.

It was unlikely that the organism itself could be responsible. More likely it was a carrier of some kind, or possibly, a microscopic factory living in the body, unnoticed until death.

Only then did it become active. It also didn't explain the reanimation of the body after death, or the desire to consume human flesh.

Sharon took the blood and added it to the slide containing the microbe, then placed the slide into the electron microscope for viewing. At first she saw no changes. The black organism failed to attack the blood she had added. It was alive, there was no doubting that. It shook and quivered on the slide. She was beginning to think that her hypothesis was wrong.

Then it happened.

As the living blood cells began to die, the little black organism sprang into action. The cells that had died first were the first ones to be assaulted. The parasite began to produce organisms resembling mitochondrias and lysosomes that penetrated the cell walls, replacing their counterparts that inhabited the dead cells.

Then something even stranger happened. The dead cells began to show signs of activity. With lightning speed, they each produced one single organism. It was different than the mitochondrias and lysosomes created by the black parasite. To her amazement they looked like chloroplasts, the part of a plant cell responsible for creating energy from sunlight. They in turn attacked the living cells in orderly fashion.

The chloroplasts penetrated the living cell membranes with ease even though the cells should have rejected their advances. The previously living cells began to die once the chloroplast-like organism became part of them. They in turn created an organism of their own to infect other living cells. A chain reaction had occurred. Reproduction was swift and precise. In only seconds, every blood cell had been attacked, changed, and died.

Sharon had witnessed something that no other researcher had discovered. The answers were there all along. They had simply not looked long enough to find them.

24

Jim was the first to make a move. This man was not part of the militia. He was black and that was a death sentence with the bunch he and Matt had encountered. Neither was the man's posture threatening. He simply stood there, as if in shock to see another warm-blooded, living soul.

Jim approached the man cautiously, his hands away from his body as he walked, palms up in a non-aggressive posture. The man appeared shaken and the last thing Jim wanted to do was provoke a defensive action that could lead to an unwanted battle. In his battered state it would certainly be a short one.

Jim stopped several feet in front of him.

In an easy, friendly drawl, he said, "I'm Jim Workman. It sure is good to see a friendly face out here," and then extended his hand.

Leon did not make a move to accept the proffered hand. He took a moment to size up this stranger who was slightly taller than himself, more muscular and well-fed. He was not a drifter. His face was strong, but judging from the myriad of cuts and bruises, a recent encounter had not been a friendly one. But he did recognize one thing—the haunted, anguished eyes of a plague survivor. He relaxed somewhat, a fragment of suspicion lingering.

"Are you bit?" Leon asked.

"No." Jim answered.

"Your injuries…scratched by one of those things?"

"No, a car wreck," he said, hesitant to say too much.

"I'm Leon."

They were still standing a good distance apart.

"I'm trying to get to Tangier Island," Jim said, pointing to the bay.

Leon didn't recall seeing this man before, but then there were a lot of people on the islands. Maybe he was from one of the others. He had met most of them, but not all. But this man would have stuck out in his memory.

"Are you? What island are you from?"

"I'm not," Jim said. "I'm from inland."

Leon doubted that. He was obviously lying. There were no survivors inland; there were too many creatures there. He'd seen with his own eyes on countless occasions the desolation of the mainland.

"We've searched there many times and found no one," Leon said. "How is it that you managed to survive this thing for so long and what brings you here now?"

The fact that Leon had said *we searched the mainland*, and not *I searched the mainland* did not escape Jim's notice. This man was not alone and Jim was not about to reveal anything about the mountain or the other survivors until he knew more.

"I had a good hiding place," Jim said. "About a year ago I received a radio signal from Tangier. I wasn't able to respond to it, but eventually I knew I would have to come here to see for myself. To tell you the truth, I didn't think I'd find anyone still around."

Leon smiled, his distrust was starting to fade now and he came closer to Jim. "Well, you found us," he said, and slowly extended his hand for Jim to shake. "We used to send those messages out all the time. For a while it worked. Then…there were no more replies and no one to try to help anymore. There are a lot of us on the islands. We moved there when this shit first started. It's safe and about as normal as things can be under the circumstances. You're welcome to tag along with me if you like."

Jim nodded, and followed Leon to one of the boats anchored nearby.

Leon placed a wooden plank between the boat and the dock and they boarded the small craft. The deck was darkened with mildew and mold grew around the cabin's doorway and in every visible crack and crevice. It was obvious that it had not been used or maintained much over the last couple of years.

Jim was being cautious and was scanning the harbor area for trouble as Leon went to work. He was surprised that they had been able to stand out in the open, unmolested, for this long. He was not anxious to tempt fate. A lone ghoul lurched about on the deck of a sailboat fifty yards to the north. The boom, sails, and rigging had been shredded by past storms, and the creature awkwardly maneuvered between the tangled cables. After a moment the thing squatted on the deck where it remained motionless, content for the time being.

Leon worked hurriedly. He checked below deck for leakage before removing the covers to the engine compartment to check for deteriorated wiring and fuel lines. When he was satisfied that everything was as it should be, he primed the motor with fuel and took the seat at the controls.

The motor moaned as Leon tested the worthiness of the batteries. Over and over it turned, first slowly, then faster, then slow again with labored gasps. The creature on the other boat stood and took notice of them. It began to howl in what could only be described as a call to arms.

The motor continued to crank... From the morning shadows trudged more of the foul demons, aware of their prey by the sudden noise and the sailor-zombie's calls.

Ghouls in various stages of decay poured through the gates and into the harbor, their bodies hideously mangled, driven by a common desire. Within seconds they were converging on the two desperate survivors.

Jim removed the steel cable looped around a cleat in the dock and kicked the wooden plank away. It dropped into the water only a few feet from the boat. They needed to move the boat away from the dock before the dead things got close enough to board.

Jim gripped the rail that rimmed the edge of the boat and then kicked at the dock, nudging the boat another foot away, but the aft bumped the bow of a sailboat anchored beside them and it stopped, still too close to the dock.

Jim jumped onto the deck of the smaller sailboat, which rode lower in the water than the big cruiser, skidding across the deck as he landed. The masts were split and the rigging was torn and strewn across the deck of the small vessel. With a few hard jerks, Jim broke off two pieces of the splintered masts and threw them onto the deck of the cruiser. "First things first!" he shouted at Leon as he climbed aboard. "Help me out here!" He handed Leon one of the broken masts as he moved past him.

Leon sprang from his seat and followed Jim's lead, using the broken mast as leverage to shove away from the dock. The men heaved and pushed the boat more than twelve feet from shore, out of the reach of the creatures that had already reached the pier, some of which teetered precariously at its edge. They lurched and wobbled like giant, decaying, puss-covered Weebles.

"Drop the anchor before the tide drags us right back to them!" Jim shouted.

Leon ran to the winch and released it, letting the steel cable with the attached anchor drop into the water. Jim pulled his pole in just as the first big wave of creatures reached the edge of the dock. He watched as they reached out toward him, hovering at the dock's edge. In their zeal to reach their quarry, the mob surged forward. A mangled creature in moldering khakis and a shredded navy blazer with the entire right side of his face ripped away, toppled off the edge of the dock and disappeared into the murky water.

The mob drew back in unison.

"They can't get over here," Jim said. "They can't swim. I think they're afraid of the water."

"Yeah, I know, they don't like the water much. I think they're afraid it will wash away some of that stink, but what do we do now?"

"Do you have any side cutters or anything that will cut a battery cable?"

"There's a toolbox over there. I'll look."

Leon removed the top tray from the toolbox and found what Jim wanted underneath. They looked like heavy-duty pliers with a cutting edge on one side of the jaws. They were rusty, but still useable. Leon tossed them to Jim, who placed them in his pocket.

"Stay here," he shouted, and dove his battered body into the water.

Leon watched as Jim swam to a powerboat anchored two piers over. The creatures also watched. Some stumbled down the dock toward the boat Jim had boarded.

Jim worked fast to cut the powerboat's batteries free, leaving as much of the cables intact as possible by loosening the wing nuts that held them in place. In less than a minute he had the two batteries from the other boat resting on the deck.

He found a floating life ring attached to the cabin's outer wall and ripped the lid from a broken cooler, then placed the ring in the water, put the cooler lid on top of it and carefully placed the batteries on the plastic lid. Jim eased into the water beside the makeshift raft and pulled it with him as he swam. When he reached the boat, Leon pulled the batteries aboard first, and then reached down to help Jim climb over the edge. As Leon gripped Jim's slippery hand to pull him up, he felt a sudden hard jerk and nearly lost his tenuous hold on him.

Jim's expression registered shock. "Pull harder!...Pull!"

Jim struggled to help Leon hoist his weight over the side of the boat. As he clung to the railing to keep from being pulled back into the water, Leon leaned over the side of the boat and grabbed the back of Jim's jeans to pull his body out of the water and onto the deck.

Jim felt the drag of the extra weight on his legs. "Whatever that is on me, get it off!"

The panic in Jim's voice pushed Leon into an adrenal burst of energy. He pulled Jim over the side, along with the hideous blue-blazered ghoul who had fallen off the dock. It clung to Jim's leg, gurgling bay water and gnashing its teeth.

Leon grabbed the broken mast pole and brought it down squarely on the top of the creature's head. The ghoul lost its grip on Jim and slid back over the side of the boat and disappeared into the bay.

Jim, breathing heavily and trying to regain his senses, was lying in a wet heap on the deck.

"You okay, man?" Leon asked, offering his hand to help Jim up.

Jim said, "We'll chalk that up to a learning experience. They can't swim but they don't drown either. I wasn't ready for that one...thank you."

"No problem. There aren't many of us left. We gotta stick together, right?"

"Right," Jim replied, but his eyes reflected the deeper and more troubling knowledge that not all survivors were going to stick together. Some had their own agendas.

Jim went to work, cutting away some of the coating to expose the bare wire on the cables attached to the batteries. He loosened the connecters to the boat's batteries enough to force the newly-exposed wire into them and then tightened the terminals. He now had the power of four batteries connected to the boat.

"If these have any charge left in them, it should be enough to start now," Jim said.

"And if it doesn't?"

"Then we have a long swim ahead of us, and as we just witnessed, that might offer more problems than we can deal with."

Leon slid back into the seat. He'd been through this in his search for transportation after the chopper crash. If the motor didn't start this time, they were in trouble. They were cornered by the monsters with no route of escape.

Leon turned the key and pressed his thumb on the black starter button. The motor turned again, this time with much more force. It popped and sputtered, teasing them with bursts of ignition before finally roaring to life.

"Yeah!" Leon whooped. He fired the engine's RPMs as Jim winched the anchor onto the deck.

One of the creatures on the dock made a desperate attempt to reach them and fell into the water, sinking to the bottom as the boat raced away.

25

Sharon Darney left the elevator and broke the thoughtful silence Amanda was enjoying. She sat up from her reclined position in the padded chair by the window and forced a smile.

Amanda had barely left her station in the lobby since Jim's departure. They were in the ground-level room often visited by Felicia when she became depressed from the lack of sunlight in the underground. It was a large room, with floor-to-ceiling windows on one of its walls that brought in the beauty of manicured lawns and flowerbeds now overgrown and thick with weeds from years of neglect. Still, it was a refreshing change since it allowed the sunlight to pour in and brighten one's mood. It was simply called The Sunroom by the inhabitants of Mount Weather.

Sharon walked to the windows, her white lab coat trailing behind her as she went. At the windows she turned her face upward and let the heat of the sun warm it before turning to face Amanda.

Amanda's eyes were bloodshot and lined with dark circles from lack of sleep. The slight smile that greeted Sharon was gone now as she fell back into the chair and resumed her disheartened posture.

With a soft tone of concern, Sharon said, "You're not supposed to be up here alone, you know. What if something happened?"

"I don't care."

"Mick would be mad if he knew."

Amanda stood, and walked to the window and stared out at nothing in particular. "Mick can kiss my ass. I'm a big girl. I can take care of myself and if I wanted to be around other people right now, I would've invited someone up here with me." Amanda's gaze settled on the waist-high weeds as they gently bent beneath the late morning breeze. She imagined what the breeze might feel like if it were blowing through her hair and inhaled deeply, expecting to smell the spring fragrances that were so close, but only dry, re-circulated air filled her lungs.

"You're worried about Jim. We all know that, but that's no reason to turn away from the rest of us. We're worried, too."

Amanda softened her mood. She had drawn inward, even from Felicia.

"He'll be back, Amanda," Sharon said. "Jim's a smart guy. He knows not to take chances."

"He took an unmitigated chance by going out there, so don't tell me he won't take chances. And sometimes I wonder just how smart he really is for making these foolhardy decisions."

Sharon's lips parted to respond with more words of assurance, but her expression suddenly changed to one of alarm. Upon registering Sharon's indrawn gasp, Amanda followed her gaze, turning toward the window as a gray-faced ghoul smashed against it.

The ghoul patted the window with its creased hands and pulled its face along the glass. The action left a slimy trail as fluid oozed from its open maw.

As Amanda withdrew, Sharon moved closer. "Go get Mick, and tell him to bring some help."

Amanda broke free of her stupor and raced to the elevator, disappearing into the underground.

A few moments later, Mick charged from the elevator with a sawn-off shotgun, Griz and Felicia hot on his heels. Griz was a burly man with an unkempt beard and a .357 holstered around his large waist. He followed Mick closely, more for the safety in numbers than any desire for a fight. In spite of his rough-and-tumble appearance, Griz was a gentle soul. He would fight if he had to, but it was not in his nature. But should the need arise; he was in for a penny or a pound.

Mick advanced to where Sharon stood, watching the gray-faced ghoul and with a sigh, she said, "Well, I guess the question's been answered as to whether there are still reanimates out there."

Mick nodded, his eyes studying the danger outside. "We pretty much figured they were."

"Shoot it, Mick!" Felicia cried, her eyes wide with terror. "Shoot it before he breaks in here! Shoot it in the head!"

"Don't worry, he can't get in here. That glass is four inches thick. It would take more than one of those things to get through it."

Sharon touched Mick's shoulder. "No, don't shoot it," she whispered. "Capture it."

Mick jerked away from her touch. "What in God's name for? You have a specimen downstairs already and I've got to tell you, there are a lot of people who would just as soon that one was shot, too, including me. I'm not crazy about having any of those things down there with us."

"That one is cut up. I've dissected it. And, besides, I need a fresh one."

Amanda wrinkled her nose. "It doesn't look too fresh to me. I agree; shoot the ugly bastard."

"No. I need one I can work with and to compare with the other one. I need more than one specimen."

Mick's face tightened. "No!"

"Damn it, Mick, if I don't have what I need to conduct my experiments, I can't guarantee I'll ever find answers."

"Answers? How the hell will it help to find answers now? The world has gone to shit. There's no one left to help and now you want to risk our health and lives to catch that thing so you can keep busy?"

Sharon walked to the window. "Do you ever want to go back out there?" She pointed outside. "How about future generations? If we can't find a solution, there won't *be* any future generations. If we manage to get through this without humanity getting completely wiped out, we need to know what to do if it ever happens again. We need to know so we can prevent it. We need to know because the next time...Well, let's hope there is no next time. I need that one to ensure that it doesn't happen again. Has it crossed your mind that whatever hope we have might be locked away here in this underground? I might be the only one left still trying to solve this."

Mick thought for a moment, then turned to Griz. "You up for it?" His disapproval of Sharon's request notable in his voice.

Griz shrugged. "Yeah, I'll help ya, but I ain't gonna get bit. If there's a chance that's gonna happen, I'll shoot it," he groused, his heavy voice booming louder than he'd intended.

"Fair enough—you heard that didn't you, Sharon? If things don't go right, we destroy the thing and send it on to hell where it belongs."

Sharon nodded. "Fair enough."

Mick paced the floor, trying to form a plan. He understood that Sharon's motives were genuine; he just didn't see the point. This would be the last time he took such a risk for the sake of science.

Unable to formulate a foolproof plan, he turned to Griz. "Go downstairs and get a roll of duct tape from the maintenance room. Do it quickly."

He wondered if there were more of them outside and how this one had gotten inside the fenced-in complex. If they were fortunate, it was a loner.

Griz returned minutes later with the tape. Anxiety mounting, he clenched his jaw until his teeth ground together. He hated those things. He hated the looks of them. He hated how they smelled and the sounds they made. He swallowed hard and fought back his apprehension of the task at hand and offered the tape to Mick, who waved his hand in such a way that Griz understood he was to keep it.

Mick's plan began to form in his mind. They would use it to restrain the creature. It was a simple plan, but an effective one. Duct tape could be used to remedy any situation in his mind. He had first learned that little tidbit more than fifteen years before, while working stage crew for a rock band. They had used rolls of the stuff every weekend to tape everything from wires to midrange speaker cabinets to prevent them from vibrating off the bass bins when the music got so loud that the thump-thump-thump of the kick drum pounded in your chest with a force strong enough to cause heart palpitations. Duct tape was worth its weight in gold to the longhairs, and right now, to him as well.

Mick eyed Sharon. "Once we go through that door, you close it and lock it behind us, understood?"

Sharon nodded.

Mick and Griz walked to the door at the far end of the room, just left of the windows. "Watch us through the glass and don't open it again until I give you the signal, okay?"

Sharon nodded that she understood.

Felicia gnawed at her fingernails. "Be careful, Mick. Don't let it get you," she warned between waves of panic.

Mick forced a smile and gave her a lighthearted wink.

Sharon typed the code into the keypad to unlock the heavy steel door and closed it again after the men went through, then moved to the window to watch the scene unfold.

Mick ran toward the creature and delivered a sound kick to its midsection. The force propelled it backward and off its feet. Then he slammed it over onto its stomach and planted a knee in the middle of its back, pinning it firmly to the ground. Griz wrapped the tape several times around the creature's ankles, binding its legs tightly together. He did the same with the wrists, careful to pull the sleeves of its jumpsuit down over the decomposing skin before wrapping the tape tightly around them as Mick held the creature's arms behind its back.

Keeping the ghoul pinned, Mick reached into his back pocket and removed a neatly-folded bandana and handed it to Griz.

"Wrap this around its face and then use the tape," he said. Mick then rose from his position and grabbed a handful of the creature's mangy hair.

The creature released a muffled moan as Mick planted one foot on its upper back and jerked its head backward to give Griz the needed room to wrap the cloth and tape around its head and mouth. When that was done, the two men stepped away and watched as the creature squirmed on the ground, unable to break free from the bindings.

With Griz's help, he carried the ghoul inside and placed it on the floor in the middle of the room. Felicia and Amanda backed away, but Sharon stooped to examine it more closely.

"All right," she said, rising. "Take it to my lab."

"You got a table or something to strap this thing to?" Mick asked. "It has to be confined, you know."

"Of course I do! You don't think I'm going to let it just run free, do you?"

"It's your pet, Doc, your job to tend to it. I just wanted to be sure."

26

Tangier Island came into view and Jim strained to make out its details.

They were moving in from the west side of the island. As the boat moved closer, piers and stilted buildings appeared through the morning haze. Fishing boats rocked gently as the tide licked the shoreline. A man took a moment to wave to them as he prepared for his daily fishing trip into the bay. Another man kissed a woman who held a baby, then stepped into his own small boat.

Leon turned the wheel and the boat followed the shoreline. People were attending to their morning business. Some rode bicycles, others carried buckets of water. The island was alive and life went on. The sight gave Jim an overwhelming desire to return to Mount Weather and bring the others back to enjoy life in the sunshine with him. But he couldn't let the urgency of the moment get washed away by what he was seeing. Danger still existed for his people, and for the people on Tangier.

As they approached the pier, Leon throttled back and slowed to a coast, letting the waves carry them up against its wooden support posts until they were in position to tie off the boat. Jim stepped onto the pier's planked walkway first.

For the first time in two years he was not looking over his shoulder. The morning sun felt good on his face, the salt air a refreshing change from the underground. His heart was beating faster. He had found what he was looking for and at this moment, he was on vacation from the dead world.

Leon finished tying the boat and Jim offered a hand to help him up onto the walkway beside him.

Hal and Jack were dead and now Leon had to explain what had happened. He glanced at Jim, who stared straight ahead, a smile gracing his face. He had the look of a prisoner who had just been handed his freedom after many years of confinement. He was alive again.

"You've been out in that shit for a long time, haven't you?" Leon asked. "Did you expect to see this after all this time?"

"I've seen a lot of people die." Jim said, "Some good people…some friends."

"We all have," Leon said, thinking of his lost comrades as he walked toward the settlement with Jim. "But there's none of that here. When people die here, it's from natural causes and we're ready for it."

Jim allowed himself the luxury of feeling safe for the moment, but guilt was invading his sense of security. Amanda was surely worrying herself sick by now. That is when he noticed the single landing strip to his left, a small airport with one hangar. It made him stop. Hope of an easy way home washed over him.

"Are there any flyable aircraft in that hangar?"

Leon eyed it with a heavy heart for his lost friends. "Yes, there's a plane in the hangar. We never used it. The chopper was best suited for our purposes."

"You have a helicopter?"

Leon diverted his eyes away from the airport. "Not anymore. We crashed yesterday. I was the only survivor."

"Was that *your* bird burning in Fredericksburg yesterday?"

Leon nodded, "Yes."

"What happened?"

"We started to lose oil pressure and went down. My two friends were killed on impact. I was able to climb out and find my way back to the spot where I met you."

"I'm sorry about your friends. It's hard losing people you care for." He patted Leon on the back. "Can I take a look at that plane?"

"Sure—you fly?"

"I did back in my younger days, but I've not done much lately."

"Yeah?—Military?

"I was a Navy Seal, but that's not where I learned to fly. Just small stuff mainly, a few lessons here and there, but I can fly, and can even land too if I have to," he said with a lopsided grin.

Leon returned the smile, and slid open the heavy hangar door and daylight flooded inside. Jim walked to the small single engine plane parked in the center of the hangar and ran a hand down the fuselage, as though caressing a woman's leg. "Cessna 150M. 1970s—probably 1975," Jim said.

Jim moved to the wingtips. "It has a bit of hangar rash here on the tips. No big deal. It also looks like the tips have had some repairs done to them. Has anyone been flying this thing since the plague?"

Leon walked closer. "You know your planes. Yes, one of the men killed in the crash. Hal would take it up from time to time just to keep it loose. He said it would freeze up if he didn't. I figured he just wanted to do it for the fun of it."

"It was probably a little bit of both," Jim said. "I'd like to take it up for a quick spin myself before I leave to check it out if that's okay."

"Leave? What do you mean, leave? Where would you go?"

Jim turned. "I'm afraid I haven't been totally truthful with you. I lost a good friend myself, yesterday."

Leon's interest peaked. "The shit you say…"

"I've traveled from northern Virginia. Besides myself, there are about sixty other survivors located in an underground military complex."

"There are still military bases in operation? We thought they'd all fallen."

"No. Like everything else, the place fell apart before we arrived. The soldiers stationed there turned on each other and destroyed themselves. We've been there over a year now. Like I told you, I received a radio signal from Tangier about a year ago. That part is true. I was on my way here when I met up with you, but my trip was interrupted and my friend was killed."

"By those ghoulies?"

"No. We were met in Fredericksburg by a militia, a particularly nasty one at that. They killed him."

"*They* killed him? Why?"

Jim looked evenly at Leon. "Because of the color of his skin. This group in particular is more fascist than militia, Neo-Nazis with an agenda. Their idea of a new world is one of racial purity and domination. They took me to an aircraft carrier down at the port in Norfolk. They have at their disposal a lot of firepower, including jet planes armed with nukes. They thought they had killed me and threw me overboard. Now I'm worried they'll find my people—and yours."

"How can they find us? Do they know about Tangier?"

"They found a map I had used to lay out my route. If they follow it, it will lead them right to this island, or to the Mount Weather Underground. Either way, it's bad news."

Leon scratched the top of his head. "Son of a—we have to do something! Do you think there's a chance they'll use those jets to nuke us?"

Jim considered it. "I doubt it. I think they'll be more interested in forcing their way of thinking on you, subduing, rather than destroying you. Your people, I mean, not you in particular. There's no place in their world for you. You, they'll kill."

"You'd think that way of thinking would be gone now, wouldn't you?" He shook his head ruefully. "Militias...why did we allow them to continue? It seems to me that their time has passed, grown men playing games."

"They weren't playing games. Militias have always been a part of our freedom. Most are law-abiding, honest people and an important part of our security. I wouldn't be surprised to find that many state militias survived the apocalypse. They have the knowledge and the know-how to do it. Most of them will give us no problem. But these...Freedom Fighters...they're different. From what I saw, a collection of skinheads and thugs. They're dangerous."

"How many were there? There are a lot of people on the islands and we're well-armed too. They may be in for more trouble than they bargained for."

"Not that many from what I saw, but I had the feeling there were more at another location. But even if their numbers are too small, they do have the planes and the nukes. If they can deliver the payload, then you would have no choice but to submit."

27

Hathaway studied Jim's map as he drank his morning coffee.

He sat at a small table attached to the floor by a single pole screwed into the metal floor of the bridge. It overlooked the flight deck and he glanced up from time to time to watch as several men tried to make two of the A6 bombers flight-ready.

The men scurried about, replacing fuel, checking lines for wear, and resetting their onboard computers. Two years of setting idle had caused most of the aircraft computers to shut down.

Many of the militia's members had served in the United States military, some of them in the Navy. They were accustomed to this type of work; it was second nature to them. But only one of them knew how to pilot a jet aircraft.

Hathaway traced his finger along the yellow line, studying every inch for a clue. He traced the line to its southernmost point. It ended at a small bayside town, called Smith's Point. The area was too close to Washington, D.C. and its suburbs to be safe for human habitation. The ghoul population would be thick there. More than likely he was from the northern point, but where?

Hathaway reclined in his seat and took another sip of his coffee. He wrestled with that thought until Jake stepped onto the bridge and broke his concentration. The manner in which he wandered around the room before finally settling in front of the windows gave the impression that he was simply bored.

Hathaway folded the map and stuffed it into his pocket and stood beside Jake who was watching the men work below on the flight deck, his jaw flexing around a wad of tobacco.

"We'll be heading back soon. Tomorrow, maybe." Hathaway told him. What he really wanted to say was that he had formulated a very clever plan—and about the bomb. He wanted to tell him that soon he would be in complete charge, but it was not yet time. "There's not much else we can do here," Hathaway continued. "This ship is a floating pile of junk. We'll never get those engines back online. We don't have the know-how. About all its good for is its radar capabilities."

Hathaway fell silent and turned his attention to the men on the flight deck.

"And they think they are really doing something down there. All they really are is a bunch of squids! Nothing more than deck grunts. The only man we have who can fly one of those A6 bombers is back at camp anyway, and I'm not sure I can rely on him." Hathaway turned away from the window. "No worries, though. I've got other things to take care of first."

Jake stopped chewing and turned. A brown smudge of tobacco hung from the right corner of his lip. "What do you mean? I thought we had decided not to look for who's been flying around down here."

Hathaway picked up his coffee cup and downed the last drop. He had another plan, one that would reveal the origin of the man, but he would not divulge that information just yet. It was better to keep it to himself.

"Nothing to concern yourself with."

"You wouldn't be trying to cut me out of any good action now, would you?" Jake asked.

Hathaway smiled, and walked away without answering, leaving Jake alone by the window.

Of all the men chosen for this trip, Robert Hathaway trusted Jake most, but Jake wasn't the sharpest knife in the drawer and therefore, not suited for this mission. The stranger was smart and disciplined. He held his secret, even to his death. He was well-trained, a soldier. Of that there was no doubt, and one with a big secret. That made him dangerous, and there was more than just the two of them. He was certain that he was protecting others. How many, he didn't know. If the carrier was in working order his worries would be negligible, but that would not happen anytime soon. The *Nimitz* was nuclear powered, but the fuel had been removed. If he were to command an invasion, he would have to depend on old-fashioned manpower in order to be successful.

Hathaway thought of using Marty Gibson for his secret mission. Marty was smart, but sometimes he went off half-cocked. He had used Marty to guard the man until they arrived at the carrier. Marty would surely slip up. No, it had to be someone smart and disciplined, and someone whose loss wouldn't matter so much should he meet his fate before the mission was complete.

Christopher Smith could possibly do the job to satisfaction. He was a bit young and he was a fine soldier. He had only known him for the two years of the plague and that left a little to be desired when it came to trusting him or knowing his limits, but he was the best available choice. He would have a meeting with him first, tell him what he needed to know, and equip him with the necessities for his mission.

Comfortable with his choice, Hathaway walked to the flight deck to oversee the work he had ordered the men to carry out. There he paused to consider how his clever plan at their mountain base was unfolding. He should've heard something by now. His radio was working just fine. It would pick up the signal from camp even at this distance. The fact that he had received no message worried him. Surely they would radio him such important news and tell him to hurry home and take command. How could they go on without him? If the bomb did its job, the camp would be in a panic. His leadership would certainly be needed.

Hathaway brushed the troubled thoughts away and went about his tasks. Chris Smith was first on his short list of things to do.

Hathaway found Chris in a lifeboat just over the port side with a larger-than-usual fishing rod swinging from his grip. He tossed it out into the bay and waited for a bite, unaware that he was being watched. Hathaway grabbed one of the lines attached to the boat and swung a rope ladder close enough for a good grab. He was over halfway down the seventy-foot drop to the boat before Chris realized that he had company. He reeled in the fishing line and cast it out in a different direction as Hathaway finished his descent.

"You know what the best thing is about getting stuck with the job of watching over this ship?" A smile lightened Chris's face as he spoke.

Hathaway thought for a second, then shook his head.

"Well, I'll tell ya," Chris said. "Fresh seafood, that's what. Crabs, blues, all here for the taking. Just cast a line or a net. This is the life I always wanted but could never afford. It's too bad it took an apocalypse for me to finally enjoy it."

Hathaway smiled. "I'm glad you enjoyed your stay."

Chris stopped in the middle of casting his line. "Enjoyed? You make it sound like I'm going somewhere."

"You are. I've got something I need you to do. Something you need to keep to yourself."

28

"The men who were with you when the chopper crashed, did they have families?" Jim asked.

"Yeah, Hal did. He has a wife here. How do I tell her that he's dead? Like everyone else, she's already lost so much."

"How about you, Leon? Did any of your family make it?"

Leon stared off into the distance. He drew a deep breath into his lungs and released it before he spoke. "I don't know. I was in Virginia Beach with my lady when this shit first started." He rubbed his temples as though remembering hurt his head. "She was gut-shot by some crazy bastard who had lost his mind and was shooting up the streets. He must've killed fourteen or fifteen people before the cops shot him in the face."

Jim noted the weary expression on Leon's face, as though he were trying to draw the strength to go on with his story from some inner well that had nearly run dry.

"But she got back up. They had already covered her body and were about to put her in the back of the ambulance when she started moving again. She just sat right up and took a big bite out of one of the medics."

Leon sucked in the corners of his mouth. His brow was deeply furrowed. "Hell, I didn't know what to do, so I wrapped my arms around her from behind to get her under control. I tried talking her down. I thought that she had just lost it after getting shot, shock or something. I kept telling her, 'Stop, baby, you're hurt. Stop so they can help you.'" A tear escaped the corner of his eye and ran along the side of his nose. "But she was like a wild animal. They finally got her strapped in and took her to the hospital. It took them a day to pronounce her dead." Leon sniffed. His dark brown eyes stared at the dirt at his feet. "She was dead from the get-go. By the time I finally got my shit together, it had gotten too bad to travel home."

"Where's home?

"Pigeon Forge, Tennessee, four hundred miles to the west. My damned car got stolen so I was pretty much stuck. I tried to call home but there was no answer. You ever been to Pigeon Forge?"

"No, can't say that I have."

"It's one giant vacation strip. Like the boardwalk at the beach without the sand and ocean. People roll in there by the thousands every week. It's wall-to-wall people and bumper-to-bumper traffic. They all come to see the Smokey Mountains and Dollywood. I'll bet this thing turned that place into pure Hell. I can just imagine how those people panicked. Bunch of damned, dumb-ass tourists. If my family had any sense, they climbed to the top of one of those mountains to wait this out. I know Pop, though. He probably broke out the ol' shotgun and stuck around." Leon sighed heavily. "I hope not."

***

When Leon stepped through the door to Julio's bar, a broad smile stretched across the little Mexican's face. He dropped his cleaning rag and with his arms in the air, ran toward Leon. "Leon! Leon!" he shouted in his usual animated way. "Where the hell have you been, man? We have been worried about you so much. We thought you may have been dead, man."

Being the bearer of bad news showed plainly on Leon's dark face, but he said nothing.

"Where is Mister Hal and Mister Jack? Not with you?"

"No, Julio, they're not. The chopper crashed." His next words were hard to speak: "They're…dead."

Julio slumped. "Oh, that's very bad, very bad. They were heroes. They saved lots of people and brought them to this island. I liked them very much."

Leon nodded somberly. "They liked you too, Julio."

Julio patted Leon on the back. "You are okay, though, right?"

"Yes, I'm okay." He turned toward Jim. "Julio, this is my new friend, Jim. He's another survivor of our lost world."

Julio took Jim's hand and shook it fervently. "Come, my friends, you have a drink on the house."

Julio steered Leon and Jim toward the bar. It was eleven in the morning and still too early for most of the islanders to find their way to Julio's. It was usually late evening before the room started to fill with thirsty customers looking to vent and forget.

Jim glanced around the empty room as he and Leon took a seat at the bar. It was dimly lit, with high tables lining the walls. The bar was centrally located, with several small tables surrounding it. There was a jukebox against the wall by the door and sports memorabilia lined the walls, mostly Washington Redskin pennants and Capitals hockey sticks.

Jim's perusal of the room was broken when Julio returned with two glasses of wine. Leon nodded his appreciation and drank the wine in one long gulp. His change in posture was immediate, as if he had just drawn strength for the task at hand.

Jim waved his away.

"Have a drink, Jim," Leon said, smacking his lips at the tangy taste. "Julio makes some good apple wine."

Jim smiled. "It clouds my thinking. I need to stay focused. Maybe later."

"Well," Leon said, wiping the last drop of wine from his mouth, "I guess I should go see Hal's wife. Then we'll get you settled in here. But first I have to go check on Milly."

Jim stood up and pushed his stool close under the bar. "Who's Milly?"

"Milly is my Golden Retriever. She's been locked up in my house since I left yesterday morning. She's gotta be getting' pretty hungry by now."

"Okay, but after that I need to get back to Mount Weather. There will be some people who are pretty worried about me by now. Besides, I have my own bad news to pass on to the others."

"Don't you think you should stick around for a while first? I mean, get settled in and plan your trip back?"

"No, there's no need. I'm going to fly back in that plane down in the hangar. That is, if no one here has any objections."

"You're welcome to use it. No one here will need it. No one can fly the damned thing. It'll just sit there and rust if you don't. Are you sure it's safe?"

Jim smiled thinly. "I haven't seen any flying corpses yet, so it's safer than traveling on the ground."

Jim followed Leon through the small town until they arrived at his home. The ground was less sandy there and some of the lawns had grass growing in sporadic areas. Apple trees grew thick along the street to create a shady setting. The ground around them was covered in grass. Obviously, the soil in this area had been brought in to accommodate its growth. It differed drastically from the sandy, rocky shore several blocks away.

Leon opened the front door and Milly met him head on, nearly taking him off his feet. She lunged against his chest and licked his chin, happy to see her master. Leon grabbed the side of her face and wrestled with her, uttering silly nonsense like one would to an infant: "Whatcha doin', girl? Did you miss your Papa?"

Milly jumped down and dashed across the yard in a playful manner. Leon watched until she got to the street. When she didn't stop, he pulled out a small brass whistle that was attached to a chain around his neck, placed it into his mouth, and blew. Jim heard nothing, but Milly stopped dead in her tracks and sat down.

Leon smiled. "Works like a charm," he said, laughing. He held the whistle up. "It's a dog whistle. We can't hear it, but she does."

"You've got her trained pretty well, don't you?"

Leon swelled with pride for his pet. "She's a good girl. I've had her since she was a pup. She wasn't much more than that when this shit started. She's been with me ever since. She keeps me company and she senses things that people miss. She's alerted me to trouble several times when we first came to this island. It wasn't completely safe at that time. If one of those damned things came close, she could sense it. She hates them and barks like hell."

"An animal like that is good to have around—especially now."

Leon smiled again as he watched Milly, who was sitting patiently, waiting for her next command. "She's my best bud. She'd be good to have around anytime."

29

The possibility that his planned coup had failed wasn't what bothered Robert Hathaway most. It was the fact that he had not been able to determine who the man was and where he had come from. If a splinter faction of the United States Military remained, they could be real trouble. They'd be organized and they would have had functional weaponry to survive the plague. They would ruin his plans of righting the wrongs of the world. They wouldn't subscribe to his way of thinking. At this point he doubted he would even have the full support of his own people, the Freedom Fighters. They were, in his opinion, too progressive to follow his lead. Now, one of their trucks was missing too and he had a good idea who might have taken it. It was him, the man thrown overboard. If he had survived the beating, then he might have been able to reach shore. He would warn others about them and that possibility concerned him very much. He should have put a bullet in his brain before tossing him over the side. It was an oversight born from frustration and anger. And so now it was more important than ever to know from where he had come, and how many were with him.

***

It took almost three hours for the caravan to reach Fredericksburg. There, Hathaway ordered them to stop where they had found the man and his black companion. His men had formed a circle around him and were plucking away at an increasing number of living corpses as Hathaway rummaged through the vehicle. Donald Covington, the young boy he had been personally instructing, was the first to be overwhelmed and fell to the ground under the weight of four, grasping attackers. As more covered him, his cries for help turned to screams of agony and a feeding frenzy followed.

Without emotion, they tore into him.

A blue-faced man in a ripped and bloodied wife-beater pulled a handful of entrails from the boy's stomach and was about to stuff them into his open maw, until they were snatched away by another. A small boy with a rat tail emerged from the crowd carrying one of Donald's hands. He gnawed at it in the corner of his mouth; peeling away layers of flesh. Once away from the feeding crowd, he sat cross-legged in the middle of the road to finish his ghastly snack.

Hathaway dug through the glove compartment in his frenzied search. When he found only a pile of papers, and nothing useful, he scattered the papers to the floor and punched the windshield with his fist. A long crack formed, running right to left, the full length of it.

He continued his search, under the seats, over the visor and in the door panel compartments. There were flares, chains, a fire extinguisher and a pair of handcuffs.

He was gritting his teeth now. Uncontrolled anger flooded over him as if the devil himself had possessed his body. He could feel his blood pressure rise with each failed search and the stinging slap of defeat turning his cheeks red. His life was a constant balancing act, a struggle between red-faced rage and cool intellect. Cool intellect usually won out, but when it didn't, mistakes were made.

Another man went to the ground and cried out as he was besieged by the hungry horde. He put a bullet through the roof of his own mouth just as the first ghoul bit into him.

"WE HAVE TO GO NOW!" a soldier screamed. But Hathaway didn't hear him. He was staring into the back of the vehicle, scanning the items stored there.

A single motorcycle took up the bulk of the space. There was a toolbox and a chainsaw to its left and a small generator crammed in on the right.

Hathaway opened the toolbox and spilled its contents.

When he saw only tools, he sighed and leaned against the open tailgate and stared blankly into the vehicle. His anger was cooling again, replaced by good ole intellect. That's when the two jackets lying behind the motorcycle caught his attention. The jackets did not interest him, it was the possibility that there could be something hidden beneath them that made him reach in and toss them to the side.

As a flash of gold lettering caught his eye, he was thankful for his returning intellect. In his rage, he would have never moved the jackets or found what he was looking for.

Hathaway held one of the silky jackets in his hand and smiled as he studied the embroidery on its back. He fingered the raised lettering and couldn't help but to laugh out loud.

He knew of this place. The map—it made sense now. It was somewhere close to the northern point of the yellow line. He didn't know where exactly, but it was there in that area and it shouldn't be difficult to find.

"FEMA!"

30

Hal's wife, Anne, took the news better than Leon had expected.

In spite of their relative safety, the expectation of death had become part of their daily life on Tangier. Hal had placed his life on the line every day since the beginning of the plague. But Leon could see her *inner* pain. It was obvious that she could feel the hole left in her life by his death. In spite of the fact that she had prepared for this day, her sadness overwhelmed her.

She listened quietly as Leon explained what had happened. With her head down, she quietly stared at the wooden planks on the front porch as he spoke, nodding from time to time as he explained the details. When he was finished, she nodded and closed the door without a word.

Jim, waiting by the curb, had found what he was looking for—other survivors. For nearly a year he had been obsessed with leaving Mount Weather to find others, anyone who had made it through the onslaught of walking death, but the only thing he could think of now was getting home to Amanda. He had endangered their safety in the underground. The militia could find them now, and the thought of Amanda and his friends at the mercy of those animals chilled his blood.

***

Later at the hanger, Jim and Leon did a quick test of the Cessna. Fuel lines, hydraulic pressure and gauges were checked for worthiness. Malfunctioning hydraulics could prevent takeoff, or cause a crash. If the gauges didn't work, he could get lost and run out of fuel before reaching his destination. Even a short trip could end in disaster if the little plane was not flight ready.

"You say Hal kept it in good flying condition?" Jim asked.

"He did the best he could. She'll fly. How long she'll fly, I couldn't tell you."

Leon walked to the front of the plane and dug his fingernails into the peeling paint on its nose. Milly followed close behind, her tail wagging happily. Jim watched Leon as he dug at the paint. He was obviously troubled by something. After he inspected his paint-filled fingernails, he patted the nose of the plane and rubbed his hand across the propeller before inspecting the stability of the wings. All the while, his feet shuffled with indecision.

"You know, you can come with me if you like," Jim offered, sensing what might be on Leon's mind.

Nervously, Leon met Jim's gaze. "No, I don't think I could do that. Not after yesterday. I never did like going out there in that mess."

"It's all right, Leon," Jim said. "Don't feel pressured into doing something you're not comfortable doing. I'm fine to do this alone. I just thought you might want to go along. Are you afraid I won't bring it back?"

Leon smiled briefly and dismissed Jim's question. Deep down, he was unsure of his feelings about the other part though. It was the same with Hal and Jack. He dreaded the thought of going on rescue missions, but in the end he always did. Well, not this time. This one he'd sit out.

"I appreciate the offer but no thanks. Maybe next time." And then he added, "You will be back, though, won't you? I mean…you and your people. I'm not worried about the plane."

"Yes," Jim said. "I'll be back."

Leon seemed to calm a bit with Jim's reassurance and allowed himself a cautious smile.

**

Jim gave the plane another once over, checking the fluids and fuel this time. The trip was more than one hundred miles. He didn't want to find himself in a forced landing halfway between the island and home. A small landing strip at the southern end of Mount Weather was long enough to handle small jets. The Cessna would have no trouble landing there. The trip would take less than two hours. Soon he would be back in Amanda's arms, easing the anxiety she must be feeling by now. He gave thought to Matt, who should have stayed put. God knows he had tried to stop him. And the militia…once again, danger was finding its way to them—to their sanctuary.

Jim opened the cockpit door and crawled into the pilot's seat. He wiped the dust from the gauges and started the engine. It roared to life with little effort and he revved the RPMs until it thrummed evenly and without sputters.

Indeed, the little plane was purring like a kitten, smooth and constant. Leon, who stood just behind the craft, was next to Milly when she became frightened by the plane's engine and spinning propeller. She calmed quickly once Leon stooped beside her and held her comfortingly close to him. Her heavy panting gave way to a more relaxed posture and several licks to Leon's face.

Jim's stomach began to churn with pains of hunger. Until now he hadn't given it any thought, but he had not eaten since leaving home. And that's when it hit him. The Mount Weather Underground had become home. How he desired to return now, to Amanda and that home. Suddenly, she was all that mattered.

Leon suddenly grabbed a black satchel from a table in the corner and slid open the large, heavy hanger doors before calling to Milly. When he pushed Milly inside the cockpit of the plane and then climbed in himself, Jim throttled down.

"You don't have to do this, you know?"

"I know, but I can't just sit here and let you go all by yourself. Besides, I need to make sure you bring this airplane back, don't I? I mean…for appearance sake."

Jim smiled, "I guess so, but shouldn't you let someone know where you're going?"

"No one to tell—no one that cares, anyway."

"I see. Well, you'd better strap in. It's been a while."

Leon buckled his seatbelt and the plane began to move forward, out of the hanger and onto the late morning slight.

31

It watched intently, unaware of anything except Sharon's movements at the far end of the room. He was upright, but bound at the feet. The invisible barrier could only be touched with outstretched fingertips. He yearned to be close to her—to touch her. He pulled in vain at the restraints and then lunged at the invisible barrier he could barely reach. Dejectedly, he moved back to the wall behind him. The emptiness hurt somehow, a craving that could not be extinguished.

The other one like himself was close to her. It was of no interest to him, but he could not look at it without disliking it. When she gave her attention to the other *one*, a feeling of contempt flooded his being. It would be good to push that one away until it was out of sight, but bound to the wall as he was, it could not be reached. The other *one* was not standing upright, nor was it moving much.

He couldn't remember what had brought him to this place. Was he searching? He felt as though he had been, and still was. He was different than the woman on the other side of the invisible barrier. He had known this before, but he just now remembered it again as he watched her longingly.

A kind of lust filled his misfiring brain and drool began to flow over his lower lip and drip from his chin. If he could only touch her, taste her. A desire for what she possessed enveloped him. It pulled relentlessly at his fragmented thoughts, a void to fill, a craving unfulfilled until it consumed his entire being. If he could touch her and become one with her, he would become complete—satisfied.

Sharon finished her work at the desk and moved to the door to the left of the Plexiglas wall. She watched the specimen imprisoned there as it tried to break free from its bindings. A confused expression filled its face. It was unable to compute a solution to his dilemma. It watched her between feeble attempts to break free, giving a pitiful glance from time to time to make sure she was still there.

Mick and Griz would arrive shortly to dispose of the reanimate that had been in the lab for the past two years. It was no longer of use to her. Its decomposition rate had accelerated recently and it was literally falling apart. Bound to the examination table, its lower jaw had disconnected from the upper. The creature's mouth hung open and the odor had become rancid, even for one of them.

The new specimen wanted nothing to do with the older, more decomposed reanimate strapped to the table. When she returned it to the Plexiglas enclosure, the newer one would retreat as far as its bindings would allow, most times to the corner where it would mope for hours at a time.

Sharon moved to the workstation and filled a small syringe with a clear liquid just as Mick and Griz entered the room. Mick walked to the Plexiglas wall and stared at the creature lashing out from the darkened corner.

"I thought I told you to leave that damned thing tied to a table," he said.

Sharon picked up three facemasks, handed one to each of the men, and wrapped the other around her own neck by its elastic band. "I've been handling these things for over two years, Mick. I think I know what to do and what not to do. One thing I do know: Don't handle them without gloves."

She tossed two pairs of yellow rubber gloves to them and motioned for them to put them on.

"Well, still, it would've been nice if you had called me for some help. If he'd gotten away from you…"

"Your point's made, Mick," Sharon said. "Now put those masks on or you'll wish you had when you start to handle it close up."

Mick slipped the mask over his mouth and nose and Griz followed his lead.

Sharon moved behind the head of the creature that had been lying on the table for two years. Its body, in a coma-like state, it had been still for several days. From time to time, the fingers of the left hand twitched, the only sign that a life force still inhabited the reanimated corpse.

The creature bound and chained to the wall behind the Plexiglas lunged and Griz jumped away on reflex. Mick stepped forward as if he would enter the glass room and do hand-to-hand combat with the charging monster.

"Don't worry," Sharon said, her hand on Griz's chest, "He can't get loose and he can't reach us from there, so calm down." She tossed Mick a hard look and he relaxed, but he kept a vigilant eye on the ghoul just the same.

Mick watched as Sharon drove her needle into the base of the ghoul's skull and injected the clear liquid into it. "What are you doing?" he asked.

Sharon threw the empty syringe into a nearby wastebasket and straightened her mask. "It's an old trick Doctor Brine taught me before he died. Rather than shooting them, or sawing off their heads to put them down, he would inject acid into the base of the skull. Their blood flow ceases with death but the nervous system remains very active. The acid will work its way in and around the brain and destroy the nerves that keep the body going. This one will die now." She looked at it thoughtfully. "It would've died soon anyway. The ole doctor had more than a good bedside manner. He was smarter than you think…I miss him."

"We all do," Mick said somberly. "It's too bad the ole Doc's heart finally gave out. I'm surprised he didn't give up much sooner. He was a fighter. To bury him up by the park bench and flowers was fitting."

The creature strapped to the gurney flinched, then became still once the acid had done its job. Mick studied the putrid thing for a moment, then said, "I thought you said these things would last ten years. Has that changed?"

"When I said that, it seemed to be the correct hypothesis. But lately I've been seeing something different, at least from this one. It could be because I've been dissecting it. That may have shortened its lifespan. I can't be sure."

Mick checked the creature's bindings and then flipped down the levers on the table legs, freeing the wheels for movement, and rolled it next to the lab door.

"You can just take that thing up top and bury it somewhere," Sharon said.

"Any place in particular?"

"Any place you want as long as it's over the hill and away from us."

Mick shrugged. "I still don't see how keeping these things down here will help us."

Sharon smiled. "You'll see real soon, Mick. I've gotten quite a bit of information from these specimens."

"Anything you want to share?"

"In time. Tomorrow, maybe. I want to go through my findings one last time before I tell everyone what I've learned."

***

Secrecy was key.

If Mick or any of the others knew what she was going to do they would stop her. She had considered the possibility that she could be jumping the gun, so to speak, but she couldn't stay and wait one minute longer.

Amanda stepped out of the elevator and through the door into the knee-high grass near the now-abandoned security gate. Many of the survivors crept to the surface from time to time, in spite of Mick's warnings. His caution bordered on paranoia, as though merely sticking their heads into the sunlight would bring a world of trouble down upon them.

She was shielding her eyes from the glare of the midday sun. After spending so much time underground, her eyes had become unaccustomed to the brilliance of the outdoors. It hurt to look upward. It was unnatural, she thought, to live like that.

Her hair was tied back into a ponytail that had grown nearly halfway down her back over the past two years. The cumbersome backpack she carried weighed heavily on her. It was the same backpack she had worn the day she left her home—the day she put her husband to his final rest. She shifted it to her left shoulder and took a moment to don a pair of sunglasses to shield her eyes from the sun's rays.

The backpack was filled with the essentials she would need on her journey. Two police .45s were holstered to her waist, one on each hip. She carried a sawn-off, double-barreled shotgun in her right hand, though she had no idea what kind of weapon it was. She had simply brought along the shells that were stored with it.

Amanda skulked across the lawn and down the hill toward the warehouse. There, she would get a vehicle for her trip. Without the map Jim had used to plot out his route, she would have to guess which way he had gone. She remembered that he was planning to take Route 7 to 17 until he got to Fredericksburg. From there she wasn't sure, but he would've taken the safest course. The wide-open Interstate heading south seemed logical.

The bay doors to the front of the warehouse were twenty feet high. They did not open from the outside and she entered through the rusty, squeaking door to the left. Once inside, she saw the reasoning behind the large doors: Tanks were parked neatly in a line down the center of the building. Cranes, two of them, were barely visible at the far end of the dimly-lit room.

Amanda removed her sunglasses to better see in the darkness.

Farther down were what looked like rocket launchers. Two of them had rockets loaded, ready to be sent to targets.

Her eyes quickly adjusted to the dark room as she looked for a means by which to travel. There were a few of the wide, squatty looking Humvees like Jim had used, parked near the wall, but they looked awkward to drive and hard to handle. She shied away from them in favor of a green brush truck. It was the same size as a regular pickup truck with tool chests that ran the length of the bed on both sides.

Amanda slid into the driver's seat and pulled the door shut.

The adrenalin pumping through her veins made her heart pound with the intensity of twenty cups of coffee. Was she really going to do this? There were no keys in the ignition. Maybe it was an omen. Maybe she should turn around and just go back to the safety of the underground. She was being foolish.

Amanda flipped down the sun visor and the keys fell into her lap.

32

Jim pulled back on the wheel and the plane eased upward.

It felt good to be flying again. As the small plane went higher, the aspects of piloting came flooding back to him. He was beginning to feel in tune with it and the island shrank beneath them and he turned to the northwest.

Milly was lying between the seats, front paws outstretched, her head resting on them. She had quickly fallen into a light sleep.

Leon watched as Tangier faded away behind them. He'd only just met Jim, but the man had a way of gaining trust quickly. There was something about him that was noble and honest—a born leader. He was leading now and somehow it seemed natural for him to be along for the ride

Leon had never been in the military and often he had wondered how men could go into battle without blinking an eye. They could blindly charge up a hill to take the high point, knowing full well the difficulties and perils. He knew now; they had a good leader. A man they trusted with their lives. Jim was such a man.

After they crossed the bay, Jim brought the plane lower. The sudden move woke Milly and she sat up. Leon watched as ghouls dotted the landscape below.

"Jesus," he said, "it just doesn't get better, does it?"

Jim either ignored his question or didn't hear it. His attention was on the controls and gauges. Then he leveled the plane out at three hundred feet and started to fly northwest.

Can you tell where we are?"

"Yeah. Colonial Beach. We flew over this place several times in search of survivors."

"I need to get to Fredericksburg to find my way back. Without a map, I'm going to have to fly by sight to get home."

"If you want to go to Fredericksburg, you'd better turn this thing more to the west or you'll miss it. It's not that far."

The left side of the plane dipped to the west and Jim took it a bit higher.

"Wiped out, man," Leon said. "We've been wiped out. There's not a living soul down there, just those dead things. God really had it in for us, didn't He?"

Jim mused over Leon's question. "Someone did."

They flew westward, toward Fredericksburg.

33

The caravan of trucks topped the ridge two miles from camp. Gray smoke blended between the thick trees of the mountain, its smoldering odor heavy in the air.

Hathaway leaned forward in his seat. His scheme must've gone as planned. The smoke was obviously from the explosion. He made a motion with his hand and Jake accelerated the truck's speed.

Upon entering the camp, Hathaway's eyes were wide with shock.

He had not anticipated this. Most of the encampment had burned to the ground. Many fires still smoldered. Women and children were huddled together in the center of camp. Around the perimeter, militiamen watched the surrounding woods and road leading south. Others pulled bodies and goods from the burned structures. The ground was littered with the dead. Some were their own people, others were not.

The trucks had barely come to a stop when Hathaway leaped out and ran into the center of the catastrophe. He turned around, taking in every detail of the calamity. His shoulders slumped at the realization of the numbers lost and of the disastrous outcome.

He turned to face George Bates' office. It was completely destroyed, as were several surrounding buildings. His lips parted. "Jesus," was all he could manage to say.

Of the bodies on the ground, some were mutilated and partially decomposed. These were the bodies of the living dead.

The rotten bastards had found them.

"Goddamn it!" he screamed at the top of his lungs, and kicked the head of the corpse that was lying at his feet.

Jake stumbled his way through the carnage to stand at his side. He stood there in stunned disbelief, still chewing his wad and unable to utter a word.

"It's gone!" Hathaway cried. "It's all gone!" His rage burned. "WHO DID THIS!"

A tall, dark-haired man in his thirties with close-set eyes and a scar that ran from his left eye to the bottom of his ear turned toward Hathaway and walked toward him with deliberate steps. The man was Ben Colby.

Seeing him, Hathaway seethed with contempt. It was the way he was walking, the way he was looking at him, in a blaming way. Hathaway did his best to appear completely surprised. Damage control was what he needed now. He could still pull it all together.

Colby dropped his rifle to his side and stuck the butt in the blackened soil. Hathaway gritted his teeth at Colby's total disregard for the weapon. It was the action of an undisciplined mind.

"I'll tell you what happened," Colby said, his eyes narrowing as he spit the words out to Hathaway. "Someone set a bomb in Bates' building. You wouldn't have any idea who did that now, would you?"

"It's as likely to have been you as anyone," Hathaway countered and pushed him aside. He took several steps forward, away from Colby to scan and assess the situation. Colby followed. "The propane tanks outside the building next to Bates' office went up minutes after the initial blast. The explosion set half the camp on fire. By this time many of our people were outside. The gas sent a jet of flames right into the crowd. You should've been here to hear the screaming. Women and children burned like human torches and they died in agony. They died a slow death. There were just too many to help in all the confusion, my wife included. No, sir, it wasn't me. I didn't do it."

Hathaway walked away from him again and Colby followed, close on his heels.

"And that's not all," Colby said. "Oh, no, there's more. Most of the ones who died from the blast came back. You know, it's funny. You'd think that after dealing with this shit for so long we would've expected that and would have been ready, but we weren't. Most of us were still in shock when they started to walk around again. My wife? I had to shoot her in the head. I had to. It was hard, but I did it. Then I shot another—and another." Colby's fury grew as he continued. "Before long it became a little easier to shoot the people I've known for so long. After all, it's really not them anymore, is it?"

Hathaway closed his eyes and his mind to his responsibility for this disaster. It had no bearing on the outcome, but he couldn't look at Colby.

"And it wasn't just our people coming back that we had to worry about. Bart Shockley shot Phil Stanton's wife in the head, so Phil shot Bart. She had gotten up after she'd burned to death and was determined to take a bite out of ol' Bart. Phil went completely loco after that and started shooting up the place. We had to end up shooting the poor bastard in the head."

"There are more than our people on the ground here," Hathaway barked, his voice cracking with desperation.

"Yeah," Colby said balefully, "There are."

To Hathaway, it seemed like he was trying to get under his skin. It was the way he was putting the words together, like he was taunting him, trying to get him all worked up and make a mistake…a confession.

Colby said, "We finally got things under control. We got the fires out and started to clean up the mess. We were physically and mentally exhausted. We'd lost half our people. Many of us were in mourning…lost family and friends. We didn't know."

"Know what?"

"That others were about to find us. They must've heard the explosions and saw the smoke from the valley below. I don't know, maybe the mountains around us. They came in the night. Again we were taken by complete surprise. We lost a lot of people here this week, big shot, not that you give a fuck."

Hathaway tried to get an estimate of how many had survived. It was hard to tell, but it was bad. "This place isn't safe anymore," he finally said.

"Well, you're in charge now, big shot," Colby told him, mockingly. "But not for long. Most of us don't subscribe to your way of thinking. You're a dinosaur, Robert. This is a new world. The old way of doing things won't work anymore. As a species we are on our way out and you are not part of the solution, you're part of the problem."

Hathaway, vexed by what remained of his conscience, strode away. Jake followed, leaving Colby to finish his tirade with a raised voice:

"You're the one with a plan, aren't you, big shot? You figure out what we're going to do, where we're going to go. Meanwhile, we'll be keeping an eye on you. You can bet your ass on that, big shot!"

34

Steam roiled from under the hood of the brush truck as Amanda drove through Fredericksburg and the sweet smell of antifreeze started to fill the cab. The temperature gauge was pegged to the right and a red light in the dash was blinking.

Amanda glided to a stop by the side of the road as the motor sputtered a final coughing gasp and quit.

She had driven onto a wide, duel lane street running south, an area thick with structures. There were dead things around too, and some had taken notice of her. The open highway was several miles behind her and the road ahead was dotted with slow-moving figures. She had missed the interstate, the alternate route that would bypass the city. She was stranded and in a deadly situation.

When she opened the hood, scorching steam billowed into her face and the reality of her situation hit home. A gapping hole, six inches long in the upper radiator hose spewed a jet of stream and antifreeze fumes that quickly enveloped the front of the truck. Amanda took a step away from the sweet-smelling cloud and released a heavy sigh.

She knew enough about what she was seeing to know what it meant. The truck would not go far without water. She had brought some with her, but it was for drinking, not for this unforeseen predicament. Her options were limited to say the least, but a parched throat was preferred to one that had been ripped out by the approaching hordes. Even if the water leaked out again, it might be enough to get her out of town where she would have a fighting chance. Something she would not have now judging by the sheer numbers she was starting to see.

Amanda found an old rag behind the seat and wrapped it around her hand to unscrew the radiator cap.

Her hand was shaking—she was running out of time, she could hear them now, behind her. They were getting close. She could hear their shuffling footsteps and desiccated cries as she hurried to pour the water from the jug into the radiator.

As the last drop poured in from the jug, there was a series of popping sounds from deep inside the engine block and Amanda's eyes were drawn to the pavement under the truck.

She watched in dismay as the modest amount of water she had poured in leaked out again from a crack in the bottom of the motor. She stood there for a moment, swimming in disbelief at the improbability of her misfortune, then gathered what she could and ran down the dual lanes to clear the closing crowds.

She ran until she didn't think she could run anymore, until her legs ached and felt like throbbing rubber bands, but still she pushed on as new crowds discovered her.

Then she saw something that caused her to skid to a stop.

Up ahead sat the vehicle that Jim and Matt had used for their trip. Fear of what she might find caused her heart to feel squeezed. Palpitations fluttered inside her chest as if a bird had found its way there and was flapping its wings to free itself.

She breathed in deeply and ran again, even faster this time toward the vehicle still fifty yards away.

When she got to it, the rear door was open. A FEMA jacket with its gold letters facing up was lying on the cracked pavement behind it. Jim and Matt were missing and her hope in finding them alive sank. She lost track of how long she had been standing there trying to think of scenarios in which Jim could have survived. Was he nearby? Was he safe, or was he walking around with flesh lust driving his every step, now part of the pursuing crowd? She was taken by surprise when she suddenly felt a hard tug on her backpack.

Amanda turned with a startled scream.

A gray-faced man growled at her and reached a claw-like hand toward her face. She shoved him away and like an old western gunfighter, drew one of the .45s strapped to her side and shot it in the head. Another ghoul reached for her as she slipped to the side to avoid its grasp. It moaned when its stump of an arm missed. She pulled the trigger again just as she stumbled backward and fell against the side of the Humvee. The creature's head disappeared in a cloud of flying gore and it dropped to the ground at her feet.

The street was now filled with the lurching dead. They reeled and swayed toward her in their usual mindless manner, clutching and moaning as they came.

Something had gotten them stirred up recently. It took time for them to come together in one place, and in the great numbers she was seeing. Jim and Matt must have had an encounter there. But where were they now?

"Jim?" She cried out, spinning on her heels and searching the crowd and surrounding area. But there was no answer from him, only the horde's now deafening screams. She released a scream of her own and fired off two more shots, then spun back toward the brush truck only to find that direction filled with disfigured corpses. Horrid things; putrid, disgusting remnants of a lost civilization; the sight of them was maddening to her. She swallowed the urge to scream again for fear that once she started, she would never be able to stop.

There were less of them to the south. She could possibly fight her way through the ghastly cannibals in a blaze of gunfire and so she ran in that direction as fast as her tiring legs would carry her.

As adrenaline coursed through her body; blood pounded in her ears. She tried to think clearly. What was that sound she was hearing now even over the crowd? Was it a motor? Yes…it was the sound of a motor—an airplane, she thought. Was she imagining it? How could it be an airplane and where was it?

Amanda searched the sky.

***

Jim brought the plane down as he passed over Fredericksburg. He wanted to get a better look at the area where they had left the Humvee. Matt was still down there somewhere. He was hoping his body would still be crumpled on the ground in front of it and not walking around in undead limbo. If it was not, he would come back one day and allow him to rest in eternal peace.

Jim swooped down just two hundred feet above an unusually large crowd of creatures that appeared to be gathering. Leon watched as they made the pass. He had seen this kind of gathering in the early days. It usually meant that they had found living prey and that he would have to watch someone die at the hands of hungry ghouls. They rarely got to the ground in time to save them.

Jim turned the plane around to make another pass.

Amanda watched the plane as it turned and started waving her arms and shouting at it. Three creatures moved in quickly to cover her. She fell to the ground under their weight. Two undead corpses were directly on top of her as the third fought for an opening to her right. She held one ghoul under the neck with her left arm to prevent it from biting her as it snapped and clawed. The other ghoul dropped down with its maw gaped—a rotted, swollen tongue lolling out as its grossly disfigured face came closer.

Amanda forced the tip of her pistol into the creature's mouth. She squinted and pulled the trigger. Most of its brain exploded from the rear of the skull, but some of its foul spillage rained down onto her face and hair. Even the creature's blood or body fluids once introduced into her own body could infect her and she spit and coughed.

Amanda pushed the creature's limp body to the side using the pistol still hanging from its now still jaws. The third creature saw this as an opportunity and latched on to her hair. Amanda jerked away from it and it lost its balance. She shoved the one she had been holding away and dragged the other along with her as she backpedaled down the street, her head bowed from the weight of the hair puller. It released its grip finally and she gave it a swift kick in the face before pulling the other pistol and shooting them both.

Jim swooped down closer this time, much lower than the first pass. The plane swished past, close enough to blow the hair on the woman's head and his throat tightened. "Jesus!—It's Amanda!"

Leon caught a glimpse of the woman on the ground as they passed. "What? You know her?"

"We've gotta put this thing down, fast!"

Jim came back again. He could see Amanda, moving erratically to keep from being surrounded and lowered the flaps for a landing.

"You'd better brace yourself, Leon. This is not going to be easy."

There was no time for Leon to voice an objection. The plane bounced against the street several times, throwing him forward against the dash as he attempted to buckle himself in. Amanda saw it rushing toward her and dove to get out of the way.

The plane slammed into a pack of walking dead as it skidded down the street. One creature made contact with the spinning propeller. Blood and body parts splattered the plane and the windshield as it exploded into a thousand pieces. One of the propeller blades broke off, slammed though the windshield between Jim and Leon, and lodged in the ceiling behind them. The right wing crashed into the crowd and tore off, bouncing down the street beside them at equal speed. Then it splintered into several pieces and Leon lost sight of it. The plane started to skid sideways, throwing the bodies of living ghouls into the air as it teetered on the verge of flipping over onto its top. Then the tail crashed into the Humvee and ripped away with a loud crash.

The plane spun around several times before it finally came to a stop.

"You all right, Leon?" Jim asked. He could barely spit out the words. His breathing was fast and he on the verge of hyper-ventilating.

Leon raised his head from the dash and rubbed at the knot that was already forming. "Yeah, are you?"

A creature was already pounding on Jim's door. He kicked the fiend away and raced toward Amanda with Leon and Milly close behind.

Amanda had scrambled to safety down a narrow side street and watched the scene unfold as the plane came down. She couldn't believe her eyes when she saw Jim get out of it. She thought she must be dreaming. He couldn't have possibly been in that plane—at this moment. It was simply too amazing to believe. It had to be divine intervention. There was no other explanation.

Amanda started to walk to him. Her walk became a jog, which became an all-out run. She crashed into him without slowing and wrapped her arms around him.

Jim allowed himself a moment of release as he kissed her head, then her upturned face before she pushed him away.

"I've got some of their blood on me. Don't kiss me. You could get infected."

"Are you okay?"

"I'm fine," she told him, "No bites."

"We've got to get out of here," he said.

Amanda glanced at Leon and realized with a jolt that *this* black man was not Matt.

Jim did a quick study of the Humvee. The impact of the plane had flattened two of its tires and slammed it into a telephone pole. Hundreds of ghoulish cannibals were filling the street around it.

Amanda pointed to the narrow street and said, "This way," and led them into the entrance of the darkened alley. Leon turned when he heard Milly barking behind them. She had stopped and was standing her ground against the approaching army of undead, many were already within a few feet of the dog and reached for her. Milly evaded their efforts and snapped at the ones closest to her, snarling with bared teeth. She backed away as the horde of monsters followed. They crowded around her, momentarily distracted from the three humans in the alley. Leon pulled the dog whistle from under his shirt and blew hard.

In unison, the creatures turned their attention to the fugitives in the alley and away from the dog. Leon looked suspiciously at the whistle between his fingers and then back to Milly, who continued to hold her ground.

He blew on it again. This time Milly came running. The dead began to wail and fling their arms about wildly. They crowded into the alley, stumbling over each other as though they were being driven by an unseen herder.

"We have to move, now!" Jim yelled, taking Amanda by the arm. The three of them ran down the alley and around a sharp left turn at its end.

Jim was the first one to turn the corner and to stop running.

All three stared at a dead end less than twenty yards away.

The alley, sandwiched between two buildings, had turned to the left about three hundred feet in and came to an end where the building on the right L'd in to meet the building on the left. There was nowhere for them to go.

"Get out your guns!" Jim shouted.

Leon patted his pockets. "Mine's in the plane—Shit!"

Amanda tossed her shotgun to Leon and realized that she had no other weapon in hand.

She pulled the remaining pistol from its holster and slung off her backpack. Leon caught the box of shotgun shells in mid-air when she tossed them to him.

"We can't do this! There are too many!" Amanda screamed.

"We've don't have a choice," Jim answered, and soothed her with a hand on her shoulder. "Just shoot out a hole for us to run through," he said. "You can do it."

Jim looked back at Leon, who had moved all the way to the dead end, searching for a way to climb up the walls.

The creatures were closer, about two hundred feet away now. They needed something more to get through the advancing wall of undead. It would be nearly impossible to make it through by simply shooting some of them.

Milly sat next to Leon. She had quit barking, but a steady snarl reverberated through her bared teeth. "Does she sic 'em?" Jim asked.

"What?"

"Will she go after them if you tell her to? It may give us the extra time to get through."

Leon looked thoughtfully at Milly. "Yeah, she'll—" His eyes widened in surprise. "Sweet Jesus!" he screamed and pushed Milly to one side.

Milly had been sitting on a manhole cover. Leon fell to his knees and stuck his fingertips into the indentation in the lid and tried in vain to lift it.

Jim bent down and both men pulled at the cover.

"No, this can't be happening," Leon said, noting the quirk of fate when the cover still wouldn't budge.

Jim searched the alley around them for something to pry open the lid. Milly began to growl louder and Amanda had to grab her by the collar to keep her at bay.

"The shotgun….Give me the shotgun,"

Jim stuck the end of the barrel into the notch and pried. The lid lifted enough for Leon to get a grip under the rim and pull. "Just lay it to one side of the hole," Jim said. "We'll need to put it back on from inside to keep them out." Jim reached over and grabbed Amanda's pack. "You first."

Amanda didn't move.

"Now, sweetheart! We'll follow."

Amanda shoved Milly toward Jim and sat down beside the hole, her legs dangling into it, then leaned forward to the ladder on the inside and crawled down into the blackness.

Jim motioned for Leon to do the same. After Leon crawled inside, Jim handed Milly to him and shot two of the closest ghouls before slinging Amanda's pack over his shoulder and climbing in himself. Then he reached up and pulled the lid back into place. It slammed down just as one creature's fingers reached in under it. The creature, not knowing any better, pulled his fingers out and the lid popped into place. Jim could hear them banging on it as he descended.

At the bottom, they were in total darkness. A trickle of moving water swished around their feet. They held their breath, waiting to hear a noise, a movement of any kind other than their own.

Amanda spoke first. "There's a flashlight in my bag."

Jim fumbled in the darkness until he found the zipper and plunged his hand inside until he felt its cylindrical shape.

The sewer drain was about six feet wide and twice as high. The ledges along each side were a little more than a foot wide and two feet above where the water trickled past.

They stood on one ledge, listening to the commotion above them as Jim formulated a plan of action.

They would go north.

35

"Amanda's gone!" Felicia proclaimed as she bounded into the maintenance room.

Mick laid the generator part he was holding on the table. "What are you talking about?"

"I can't find her anywhere. I've looked all over. She's gone."

"She can't be. Where would she go?"

Felicia bit her lower lip. "I don't know. We've got to look for her."

"She's around somewhere. Where did you look?"

"Everywhere—down here, anyway. I didn't think she'd go back up top after our last encounter there."

Felicia was almost unable to breathe when an unimaginable thought struck her: "Mick, what if she went looking for Jim?"

"She wouldn't do that. She knows better. Jim hasn't been gone that long. There's no reason for her to worry yet. It would be lunacy for her to go out there alone. I can't believe that."

"I *can* believe it. You don't know how desperate she's been the last day or so to know if he's safe."

"He's only been gone for two days. There's no reason for her to flip out yet."

"He told her he would be back the night he left. When that came and went, she started worrying and she was mad as hell. I have to tell you, I'm worried, too. It's not like him to promise one thing and do another. Something's wrong. I feel it."

Mick stood in front of her, looking deep into worried eyes that were swimming with unshed tears. Her premonitions were returning and if he had learned anything, it was not to second-guess her when she was like this.

"Okay, I'll go look up top. She's around here somewhere," he said comfortingly, then drew her close to him.

Felicia was a worrier, but unlike Amanda, who was more independent, Felicia needed comfort and love. She soaked it up like a dry sponge. He had always thought that her closeness with Izzy stemmed from more than the psychic link they enjoyed. She needed love and she needed to express love to others. The young child was the perfect medicine for her in a world dead of most everything.

Mick squeezed her hand before walking away. "Go find Griz and tell him to meet me in the lobby upstairs."

***

The sky was overcast and clouds blew swiftly past as a spring wind gusted over the mountain. The two men stood in front of the gatehouse building as Mick peered into the dark room through a small, dirt-glazed window. After a moment of deliberation, he opened the door wide.

Everything was as it should be. Nothing seemed disturbed or out of place since the last time he was there. Printouts and fax papers still littered the floor. When Mick stepped inside, bullets rolled around like loose marbles under his feet. Griz held the door open while Mick conducted a cursory search of the room.

"I don't know why I'm doing this," Mick muttered. "She's down there somewhere." He spiked a finger toward the ground. Mick closed the door and walked to the main gate.

The gate didn't swing; it slid on a track to the right to allow entrance to, or exit from, the compound. A heavy chain and lock kept it from doing so when they were in lockdown, which they had been in since arriving. The only exception was when Jim left and the gate was locked again behind him. Mick jerked on the heavy chain without thinking. The lock fell open. Without a word, he ran to the guard shack. There were two known keys to the gate. Jim had one with him and the other was kept in the top drawer of the desk in the shack.

Mick yanked open the drawer and found nothing. He rubbed his forehead to ward off an approaching headache. Amanda knew about the key. She was one of the few people who did know.

"What's wrong?" Griz asked.

"Felicia was right."

36

Jim led the way as Amanda, Leon, and Milly followed.

The odor in the sewer was unpleasant, but not in the way one would expect a sewer to smell. It wasn't the smell of human feces and urine. It was more akin to an old, mildewed coat and rat droppings. It was overpowering; the smell of ammonia in particular burned their nostrils as they forged ahead.

Jim stopped and turned. "Shhhh!" He held his finger up to his lips. They stood motionless and listened. The rustling sound came again and Jim shined the light upward.

Several rats watched them from a pipe overhead. They were hunched down, their long snouts bent over the pipe, whiskers twitching.

Jim said, "How far do you think we've come?"

"I don't know," Amanda said.

"About a half a mile or so," Leon whispered.

"Yeah, that would be my guess, too," Jim said.

"What's wrong, Jim?" Amanda asked, moving closer to him.

Leon did the same, but was facing the direction behind them, staring nervously into the darkness.

"We need to find a way out of here as soon as we can," Jim said. "This may not be a good place to be."

"Worse than up there?" Leon asked, peering into the dark void. Another sound startled him and he jumped. "There's not more of those things down here, are there?"

Jim flashed the light in that direction. "I don't think it's any of our undead friends." He glided the light back and forth over the sewer walls and ceiling.

Amanda grew more nervous. "Jim, what's wrong?" she demanded.

"Rats…" he hissed.

Then they heard it. The sound was like that of an approaching wave, the thrumming of hundreds of running, little feet, like someone thrumming fingers on a bass drum, anxious and hungry—screeching. The rhythmic sound grew louder behind them as it grew closer.

"Ah, man!" Leon groaned. "What's the deal with everything wanting to eat us?"

Jim grabbed Amanda by the hand and yelled, "RUN!"

He pulled Amanda along behind him as he ran splashing through the sewer tunnel. Leon stayed close behind, tugging at Milly's collar whenever she stopped to growl at the threat in the darkness behind them.

Leon could hear the running rats in the darkness, even over the sound of their own splashing footsteps. He shook off visions of thousands of them chewing at him, covering his body until he collapsed in the tunnel to be left behind, bleeding out a slow death as they filled their little bellies with his flesh.

How he hated rats.

Rats, mice, squirrels—they were all sharp-toothed, nasty little rodents full of lice and crawly things. *No, no, no,* he whispered as he ran. *No, no, no…*

They made a turn in the darkness and Leon felt a small thud as a rat fell onto his shoulder from the pipe above. Then a piercing pain when it bit him. He slapped it away, and it splashed into the water.

He didn't think it was possible to run any faster, but he did. He ran so fast that he slammed into the backs of Jim and Amanda, who had come to a sudden stop. The impact almost knocked all three of them into the foul, ankle-deep water.

"There!" Jim pointed to the ceiling. A ladder hung on the wall that led to a manhole. "When we get up there, be prepared for anything. We don't know how many of those things will be hanging around, so be ready to run again."

Leon was already breathing heavy and fast. He wasn't sure if he could go another step, much less run again should they need to. The sound of the rats had faded. Maybe they had outrun them.

"I can't do it. I can't take another step," Leon gasped.

Jim shined the light in the direction from which they had come. They were safe for the moment. "Okay, we'll wait here for a second and catch our breath. But we can't stay long."

Amanda supported herself with her hands on her knees to regain strength for another possible sprint. "Why are they chasing us? Rats don't eat people."

"They do if they're hungry enough," Jim said, watching the tunnel behind them. "And I'd say they're pretty hungry. There's been nothing for them to eat, no garbage left by people for two years. There hasn't even been sewage for them to pick through."

"That's disgusting!" Leon said, repulsed. "One of those foul things bit me on the shoulder." He rubbed at it. "You don't think they're dead rats, do you…like the people above? That's not why they're chasing us, is it? Because if it is, there ain't no antibiotic that's going to cure me."

Jim shook his head. "No, they're just rats—hungry rats. I've never seen anything but humans come back."

"Well, just the same, it would be my luck to get the bubonic plague from those dirty little bastards."

Leon's tirade was broken by the soft pattering of the scurrying rats somewhere down the tunnel as they continued their chase. In his mind's eye he saw them, fur matted to mangy hides, crowding the tunnel six deep on their quest for food, their whiskers twitching in anticipation of a meal—"Squeak, squeak!"

Leon flexed his jaw and grinded his teeth at the thought.

Jim handed the flashlight to Amanda and climbed up the ladder. Before he lifted the lid, he looked over his shoulder to her and said, "If the rats get too close, climb this ladder behind me and get off the floor as far as you can."

"You bet I will," Amanda said.

Jim shoved his shoulder under the manhole lid and pushed. It was tight, just like the other one after two years of neglect, but after a few thrusts, it broke free and popped out of the hole and he laid it quietly to the side.

It was still daylight and he had come up on a side street in a residential area. It was a pleasant-looking neighborhood in spite of the unkempt yards and peeling paint. Missing was the lumbering death from which they had escaped through the sewer system.

Jim hushed them with a finger to his mouth. "Come on," he whispered, waving them up with a hand.

Amanda came up first and Jim helped her out. Leon climbed out next, pushing Milly ahead of himself into the sunlight. Below, the rats noisily made their way to where the three of them had been standing only a few moments before. Jim placed the lid back on the manhole and said, "We need a car."

"Good luck with that," Leon said. "I had a hell of a time finding one that would start. All the batteries are dead."

"Did you look in any of the garages of the houses you passed?"

"No, I didn't. I didn't have much time to take that sort of a detour. I had a ton of deadheads on my ass every step of the way."

"That's where you'll find a car that starts. It will have been kept from the elements. Some of them should have good batteries." Jim turned to Amanda. "Why are you here? Has something happened at Mount Weather?"

A rueful smile raised one corner of her mouth. "No. I came looking for you. I was worried, and from the looks of things I had a right to be. What happened to you? You look like you've been put through the wringer."

"There was no reason to be worried. As you can see, I'm fine. I just had a little run-in."

"A run-in, huh? Well, that's better than dead." Amanda's relief was tempered with irritation. "I won't let you do this to me again, Jim. I'm not going to wait behind while you go on some insanely dangerous mission to save the world. I won't."

"Okay," he sighed.

"Good," she said, matter-of-factly.

They rested while Jim scanned the area.

Once it had been a nice neighborhood with upscale homes. Many of them had attached garages and some of those garages were likely to have cars in them. Jim hoped that his theory was correct and one of them would start.

"We'd better get started," he said. "And we need to get out of plain sight. We need rest. Have you eaten, Amanda?"

"I've got food," she said, rummaging through her backpack and then she stopped. "Where's Matt, Jim?"

The sudden question took him by surprise. In all the turmoil of crash landing the plane, fighting off the cannibals, and running from a teeming army of voracious rodents, he had pushed it aside. He wasn't prepared to explain everything in detail yet.

"He's gone, Amanda. Some men killed him."

"What?—Who?" she asked, handing a sandwich to each of them. She broke hers in half and gave half to Milly.

Jim pulled her to her feet. "I'll explain it all later. Right now we need to get out of here."

Amanda glanced at Leon, who had been running by her side through their escape. He had a masculine look similar to Matt's, but he was leaner, less muscular and with a stronger jaw line. He was not as tall, either. Leon was less than six feet tall. Matt was at least six-one, and Leon's skin was darker.

"I'm Leonard, but everyone calls me Leon," he said with a slight smile, noticing her questioning scrutiny.

Amanda tried to smile back, but found it difficult, so she simply nodded.

"We'll try there first," Jim said, pointing to a large brick home with a three-car garage. "We've gotta get out of the city before dark." He watched the sun disappear behind a line of trees to the west. "If we get stuck here after dark with no means of transportation…"

Amanda and Leon knew what that meant.

***

The house was still in good condition. No windows were broken and the doors were all in one piece. Jim walked across the wraparound porch and jiggled the knob on the front door. It was locked.

Next he tried the window beside the door. When it failed to open, he walked out of sight to the rear of the house as Amanda and Leon waited anxiously at the end of the sidewalk.

In a few moments they heard the locks being turned on the front door. It opened to reveal Jim standing on the other side and they hurriedly moved inside and out of sight.

The foyer was large, with hardwood floors and a giant chandelier that hung from a cathedral ceiling. It opened into a formal living room with a centrally-located fireplace. Bookshelves covered two walls and a thick layer of dust covered the furnishings and floor. The air was damp, with a musty, stale odor and a hint of spoiled meat.

Jim went to the fireplace, pulled a poker from the caddy, then pulled Amanda and Leon to the center of the room. "Stay here," he told them and walked away.

"What's wrong, Jim?" Amanda whispered. "Why do you need that poker?"

Jim pointed to the floor. "Look."

In the settled dust were footprints that led to a closed door at the end of the room.

Jim crept toward it.

"Use your gun, Jim," Amanda suggested, looking dubiously at the iron poker.

Leon laid a restraining hand on her shoulder. "It would be too loud and attract unwanted attention. Just be calm. He'll be okay."

Jim opened the door and drew the poker back to strike. When he found it empty, he relaxed his grip, a puzzled expression forming on his face. He studied the footprints again. They went to the closet, but they stopped there. The dust was disturbed in front of the door, as though someone had collapsed to the floor.

There were blood stains on the door trim close to the knob and near the floor. To his right, the dust was scuffed off the floor in two tracks, as though the person no longer lifted his or her feet to walk. The scuffs went through an arched doorway and into the kitchen. The tracks ended there on the tiled flooring.

The only other door in the kitchen would certainly lead to the garage on the side of the house. The footprints were fresh, maybe left as recently as the past month. Whatever had made them was possibly still there lurking about.

Jim drew a deep breath, pulled open the garage door, and came face to face with it.

Amanda gasped in sudden surprise as Milly exploded into a rage of barks and growls. Leon reacted by wrapping his hands around her snout to stifle the noise she was making.

It fell forward onto Jim.

He pushed it away and it fell against the open door and slid to the floor. Its skin was wrinkled and dark—a man, but not hulking, with matted hair and a missing eye. It moved at a snail's pace in an attempt to regain its footing. The ghoul wore jeans but no shirt. His ribs were showing through torn flesh and there was a knife buried deep into its left side.

Unlike any of the others Jim had seen, this one was purple from waist to neck on its left side. It had probably been lying on its side for a period of time and blood had pooled there. It functioned poorly, even for one of *them*.

Jim searched the garage for more trouble before turning again to the pitiful specimen on the floor in front of him. It reached out for his shoe and Jim kicked its fingerless hand away before driving the poker into its empty eye socket.

Amanda turned her head and closed her eyes as Jim rolled it onto its belly, face down.

"We have a minivan," Jim said with a crooked smile. "And if it starts, we have a ride home."

Leon moved closer. "A minivan sounds good to me. As long as it moves; I don't care what it is."

Jim opened the door to the van and checked for keys. When he found none in the ignition, he checked the visor and the console between the seats before turning to Leon. "Go check the house for keys. Check that stiff's pockets too. Be careful. There may be more like him in there somewhere."

As Leon jumped all three steps leading from the garage to the kitchen, Milly tagged along. When Amanda attempted to follow, Jim yelled, "No—I want you here. He can handle it."

Jim opened the hood of the van and pulled two caps off the top of the battery.

The acid was full and as he replaced the caps he noticed a small generator under a table on the wall to his left. His mind was racing…

Did the generator have gas?—did the van?

If the battery was dead—then what?

Jim rummaged through the garage in a frantic search for a battery charger. It could be a lifesaver if the battery in the van lacked the juice to start the motor.

It was nearly dark when Leon returned to the garage and Jim gave up his search for the charger. The light filtering through the garage door windows was barely enough to guide his efforts. Soon he would be working in darkness with only a flashlight to help him work. The light could also give away their position to any dead roamers outside.

Leon said, "No keys, man. I looked everywhere, but I can hotwire it if you need me to."

Jim grabbed some tools that were lying on the table and crawled under the dash without answering.

"I guess he can do it," Leon said to Amanda.

With a sly grin, Amanda said, "He's done it before."

Jim pounded the steering column several times until the casing broke free. With a screwdriver and hammer, he removed the locking pin that prevented the steering wheel from moving before going to work on the wiring. After a few moments, he raised his head and gave a thumbs-up to Amanda and Leon.

Jim touched the two wires together. They sparked and the motor cranked. It dragged on, agonizing turn after agonizing turn, before he let the wires fall apart and climbed into the seat. He reclined and closed his eyes.

A loud bang on the garage door made him leap from the van. "They're here." Leon cried.

Another crash against the door—Amanda backed away from the center of the garage to the back wall.

"We've got to do something, now!" Leon shrieked, panic washing over him. Jim was frantically searching the room for anything that could help them.

Darkness smothered them as the last rays of light began to disappear. "The light! The flashlight!" he yelled to Amanda.

Amanda pulled the flashlight from her bag and handed it to Jim as another crash shook the garage door, then another and another. Inside the house—the sound of glass shattering.

Milly began to bark again.

Jim pressed the button with his thumb and the flashlight's beam split the darkness. He shined it around until it met Leon's face. "Lock that door." He shined the light over to the door between the kitchen and the garage.

"What good will that do? It locks from the kitchen side."

"Yeah, but those things don't know that. It may take them a while to figure it out. It might give us the time we need."

"The time we need for what?" Leon cried. "Praying?"

"To get out of here—DO IT!"

Leon had barely locked and closed the door when a thud rattled it. He had been too close to one of them when he stuck his hand around the door to lock it. He backed away when the realization dawned on him.

Jim pulled the generator from under the table and checked it for fuel. It was half full, but the gas smelled old…stale. He replaced the cap and slid it closer to the van.

"Get me something to plug into this if it starts," he told no one in particular. "I need to drain some of the power this thing makes or it'll blow the battery sky high."

Jim grabbed an extension cord from the table and clipped one end off with a knife, then cut the rubber coating, exposing the copper wire inside.

Leon found a yellow light stand with two square lights attached and dragged it to where Jim squatted, rigging the cord. He flashed a look to Amanda and Leon, who stood over him. Amanda held the flashlight for him and the fear in both of their eyes was obvious. "God help us," he said as the pounding around them intensified. He pulled the start cord on the generator three times before it sputtered. It was the sign of life he was looking for, and a ray of hope.

On the fourth pull, the generator came to life. The crowd on the other side of the garage door had grown larger and their relentless hammering had buckled one side inward. Several arms thrust through the opening in an attempt to grab anyone nearby. It wouldn't be long before the whole door came down. The dead things sensed this and intensified their attack.

Jim plugged in the yellow lights and the room lit up. The ghouls' discolored faces could now be seen pressed against the garage door windows. Crazed eyes, glazed with death.

Jim picked up the extension cord and plugged the good end into the generator. He stood there in front of the van with the two stripped wires on the other end pulled apart, holding one of them in each hand.

"Leon, get in and touch those two wires together under the dash. I'll use this to give it the extra juice it needs. Amanda, grab that dog and get in the back of the van and lock the doors."

Amanda opened her mouth. "Jim—"

He cut her off with, "I'll get in, too, as soon as it starts."

Amanda grabbed Milly and reluctantly did as she was told.

Leon twisted the wires together and the engine cranked slowly.

On the other side of the door leading to the kitchen, one of the zombies fumbled around with the knob. The pressure of his hand moved the lock to the open position.

Jim touched the wire to the battery terminal just as the kitchen door came open and the gaggle of ghouls staggered into the garage.

Sparks flew—the battery began to smoke and the engine turned faster, as if supercharged.

The creatures moved toward Jim. Excited by the presence of living flesh, they quickened their pace. The van engine roared to life and the battery exploded, sending hot acid spewing toward Jim's face. He turned and most of it splattered across the side of his head. Some found its way into his eyes. In his blindness he felt the cold grip of one of the creatures as it grabbed his throat. With lightning speed, he sent an uppercut to where he thought its chin would be. His fist cut empty air. The pain from the burning acid was intensifying. Another ghoul bit at his shoulder and pulled away with a hunk of cloth from his shirt. Jim forced his eyes open long enough to see through clouded tears. Three creatures tugged at him as he thrashed and kicked at them. He slung the one at his throat to the floor and made a dash for the van, jumping in on the passenger side. "Gun it, Leon! Crash though the garage door and run right over them!" he shouted as he wiped his eyes.

Leon revved the engine and slammed the shifter into reverse. The wheels squealed as the van roared backward and smashed into the garage door.

The door collapsed into a V around the van as it bounced violently over the bodies of the reanimated corpses outside.

The neighborhood had become populated with hundreds of ghouls as the van sped backward toward the road at the end of the driveway.

Amanda took her last, small bottle of water from her backpack and handed it to Jim. He flushed his eyes as Amanda and Milly settled down in the backseat.

As long as the motor didn't stop running, they would be okay. The alternator would keep the van going, but if it stopped running for any reason, it would not start again.

Leon drove on, weaving the van around ghouls drawn by the commotion. "What now?" he asked, his voice cracking.

Jim did his best to see into the darkness beyond the headlights. "Seventeen. Find Route Seventeen. That'll take us home."

PART 3

PLANS OF POWER

37

Chris Smith eased the boat closer to the shoreline and dropped anchor a couple of hundred yards off Smith's Point. It was essential that he refuel and get some rest in the safety of the bay before his voyage in the morning.

The red gas can was heavy as he pulled it from its resting place behind where he was seated. He set it down in front of him and looked across the water into the night. His presence had not gone unnoticed by the indigenous population of Smith's Point. They moaned and howled in the darkness. Some cackled like hyenas while others yelped. It was a strange mix of chilling sounds.

His comrades were not exactly the type of people he would normally pal around with, but his survival was unlikely without them. The militia had saved his life a year before and for that, he was grateful. They had fed him and kept him safe, but he did not subscribe to their way of thinking. To each his own, he thought. What did it matter now? Like it or not, they were all he had left.

The gas flowed into the tank with a *glunk-glunk* as Chris held the can over the opening.

Hathaway had given him little information. He was only told to come to Smith's Point and find evidence of living people, then report back on his findings via the radio he'd been given. If he found no one alive at Smith's Point, he was to go across the bay to a string of islands and search there. At no time was he to tell anyone who he was or from where he had come. He was just a survivor out looking for food. He didn't like it, but he had no other choice except to do as told. It was true that they had saved his life, but they would have no qualms about taking it away should he prove himself a liability.

Chris threw the can into the back of the boat and leaned back for some sleep. He closed his eyes and listened to the ghoul-song echoing from shore. The sounds reverberated through his mind as he slept and made for some very disturbing dreams.

38

It was ten o'clock at night when the minivan arrived at the Mount Weather security gate. Jim stepped out of the van and listened intently to the night. Chirping crickets were music to his ears. There were no footsteps or cries from lurching ghouls to bristle the hair on the back of his neck. It was a calm, cool, country night on top of a mountain, away from the rotted remains of civilization.

Jim helped Amanda out of the van and took the gate key from her when she held it out to him.

"The chain's not locked," she said.

He offered her a warm smile and stroked her soft cheek with his hand. Even if she had not caught his subtle message, he had made a silent promise to never leave her again.

Amanda and Leon followed Jim as he walked to the gate and punched in the code on the keypad. He entered each number: eighteen, fifteen, thirteen, five, eighteen, and then finally, fifteen. Each time he pressed ENTER before going to the next number.

A soft chime rang inside the guardhouse. The lock clicked and the unchained gate opened.

Mick was walking to his room to meet Felicia when he noticed the blinking red light over the intersection of halls leading away from the main thoroughfare. He stopped and stared at it, then bolted down the hall to Griz's quarters. He pounded on the door until the burly man appeared.

"Something's on the compound grounds," Mick said. "The red light is blinking."

"Jim?" Griz said, then stepped back into his room and returned with two M16 rifles.

"I hope so," Mick said, "or Amanda."

***

Jim entered the second code to open the door to the lobby area. His hand found the light switch on the wall and the room glowed with florescence. "Home sweet home," he said with a smile and motioned them toward the elevator.

The elevator began its rapid descent and Leon's knees buckled. By the time he regained his wits and balance, the door opened and they were on the main level of the underground, more than three hundred feet below the surface. They stood face to face with Mick and Griz, who had their weapons raised and ready.

Mick quickly lowered his weapon and grinned at the welcome sight of Jim and Amanda. "Jim! Thank God it's you!"

Jim nodded wearily.

Mick's eyes blazed when he looked at Amanda. "Damn you, girl! You scared the hell out of me, tearing out of here like you did. I thought—" He stopped mid-sentence as his eyes settled on Leon. "Where's Matt?

39

Chris awoke with a start at dawn. He watched a seagull perched on the front edge of the boat until it took flight, then wiped the crust from his eyes and sat up.

The shore was visible now in the morning mist and it was unsettling to see what had been making the chilling sounds during the night.

A group of nearly one hundred creatures wailed and flailed their arms along the water's edge. Each time the waves crashed to shore, they backed away. When the water receded, they moved en masse back to the water's edge. It was a surreal water dance dictated by the rhythm of the sea.

Chris watched them for a while before taking the map from his pocket.

Tangier, the southernmost of a string of small islands in the bay, was the closest island to Smith's Point. Smith's Point was a departure point to the islands and part of the mainland. There were just too many walking dead there for anyone to survive. However, the islands would be a sound choice to put down roots. Once cleared of their ungodly inhabitants, their isolation would provide a safe and pleasant existence.

Chris refolded the map and put it back into his shirt pocket. He watched the creatures on shore for a while longer and decided that it would be a waste of time to further investigate Smith's Point.

It took almost thirty minutes to reach Tangier.

The fog here was much thicker than the fog surrounding the mainland and Chris leaned forward to identify movement through the haze.

A man was knee deep in the surf. He was holding a fishing pole. He could see it now as he drew closer. He was casting his line into the bay water with a swirling motion and reeling it back in to repeat the technique for another try. The man was wearing a baseball cap and khaki shorts just above the knees. When he noticed Chris, he raised his hand for a friendly greeting. Chris returned the welcoming gesture and continued on a course parallel with the coast and away from the fisherman. Soon, it would be time to contact Hathaway. Then he would better know why he was sent there.

40

Leon joined Jim, Amanda, Mick, and Felicia for breakfast in the main cafeteria at dawn. The excitement of Jim and Amanda returning safely was subdued by the news of Matt's death.

Leon thought the Mount Weather Underground to be quite drab with most of the walls painted dull gray. The concrete floors were already wreaking havoc on his legs and feet. The cafeteria was brighter, but it reminded him of the schools he'd attended in his youth. Most of the sleeping quarters were more of the same: Rows of bunk beds lined large rooms with metal lockers for personal belongings. Only the hierarchy's quarters, meant for the President and his staff were pleasing, but they were limited in number, and the current residents had already laid claim to all of them.

Mick pushed the powdered eggs on his plate into a tight pile, then scattered them again before finally pushing the plate aside. "Cardboard," he complained.

The others looked up from their plates.

"This crap tastes like cardboard," Mick repeated.

Jim swallowed his eggs. "What do you expect? It's probably at least two years old. All of the food is."

"I'm sick of it," Mick grumped. "I'm sick of this place, too. Sick of the isolation. What's out there, Jim? How bad is it?"

Jim put his fork down and pushed his own plate away. "I thought you were ready to wait this thing out right here. Wasn't that your thinking only days ago?"

Mick only shrugged.

"It's bad," Jim told him. "It's as bad as it's ever been. Those things are everywhere. To be in the open for an extended period of time means certain death."

"You said there were people on the islands," Mick said, shooting a glance at Leon. "It's safe *there*, isn't it?"

"Yeah, it's safe," Jim said, "and there are a lot of people there. If you mean to suggest that we move there, I'd love to, but I'm not sure how all the extra mouths to feed would impact their food supply."

"It's an island, for Christ's sake," Mick said. "We can fish. Besides, our food here won't last forever. You said that yourself. And what if the militia that killed Matt finds us?"

Jim looked to Leon for input.

"I think it would be fine," he said, taking the hint. "I don't think sixty people will make much of a difference on how much we get to eat. Like Mick said, you can fish. And we have plenty of fruit trees. Where the soil permits, we grow gardens." He grinned wryly. "Fresh tomatoes," he teased.

"Oh my god!" Felicia cried. "Fresh tomatoes?"

Still grinning, he said, "Apples, too."

Mick couldn't help but smile at the possibilities. Fresh food, sunlight…It was the chance for a normal life again. "Can we do it safely?"

Jim pondered Mick's question. It wasn't as though he hadn't already given it a lot of thought. "With time to prepare, I think we can. We have the weapons again. The warehouse up top has plenty of armored vehicles. Everything we need is here to make a move. There's only one problem. When we get to Smith's Point, we need to have a way to get everyone across to the islands quickly. The boats anchored there are small and we don't know how many of them will actually move. The ones that do may not hold all of us and we can't afford to hang around there for very long."

Leon ate the last morsel from his plate. "We have many boats on the islands," he said, still chewing. "There's a ferry too. It'll hold everyone. We've not used it in quite a while but it should be fine. If we send a party out ahead of the main group, we can get our boats over to The Point and be ready. Not a big deal."

"It *is* a big deal," Jim said. "It's a big move. We need to think this thing through first. And we should talk this over with everyone. Let them decide for themselves. Some of them may not want to go."

Sharon Darney approached their table. She opened her lab coat so that the long tails would hang comfortably at her sides and pulled up a seat beside Amanda. She smiled at the others, who only stared at her.

"Did I miss something?" Sharon asked.

Jim stood, and gathered his tray for disposal. "Nothing much. Just some talk about the possibility of moving to the islands."

"The islands?" An eyebrow shot up in surprise. "When?"

"We don't know. Soon maybe. We'll see. I'm going to call a meeting with everyone tomorrow night to discuss it."

"That sounds good," Sharon said. "I have so much to tell you. I can do it then."

"What, Sharon?" Jim asked.

Sharon's eyes twinkled, mischievously. "Everything."

41

Felicia tugged at the juicy red apple until it broke free from the branch and brought it to her mouth for a bite. Just as she was about to bite into it, a familiar voice from behind said, "There you go again. Are you back on that vegetarian kick?"

Felicia dropped the apple and spun around. "Where have you been?" she cried, throwing her arms around her brother.

"Easy, easy," he said. "You're choking me."

"Where have you been?" she asked again, and pulled away.

Her brother smiled and his sky blue eyes twinkled with laughter in the morning sun. "You know."

"No, I don't know."

"I couldn't just run up here. I had things to do first."

"That doesn't make a bit of sense," Felicia said. "Of course you could. It's so pretty here." Felicia twirled around in a circle, her arms outstretched. She smiled, and tilted her face up to the sun. After several turns she slowed to a stop. "Where is 'here'?" she asked, realizing that she was in a strange place.

He took her by the hand. "Come, I'll show you."

He pulled her up a hill and through some trees, into the clearing where their grandmother's house stood, and Felicia realized where she was. She was dreaming again.

"You see now?" he asked, pointing.

Felicia nodded, and followed him inside.

Once there, she turned to her brother again, but he had vanished. She called out for him, but there was no answer.

A panic rose in her throat as Felicia ran through the house hoping to find him again. She stopped in the living room and watched the flames in the fireplace lick the sides of the logs placed evenly there in rows of three.

"The fire keeps 'em out real good," a voice behind her said.

Felicia turned. "Grandma! Where did you come from?"

"I came from the kitchen, child."

Felicia glanced back at the fire. "Keeps who out, Grandma?"

"The wolves, child. We can't let them in or they'll ruin everything. They'll get into the pantry and eat all the supplies. Hateful animals, they are. No compassion, you know."

"I know, Grandma, but we got rid of the wolf already. He didn't fool us."

Isabelle Smith turned and hobbled back to the kitchen. "One of many, child. You know that. I told you before. Don't you remember?"

Felicia thought back to one of the dreams she had experienced a year before, "Yes, I remember," Felicia said, following her. "My brother was here just a minute ago, but he's gone now. Where did he go?"

Grandmother Isabelle poured two cups of tea and placed one in front of Felicia. "He didn't go anywhere, child. You brought him here—and you sent him away."

Felicia took a sip of the tea. It was good, sweetened just the way she liked it. "Then where did I send him?"

"He has his cross to bear, just as Jesus had his own tree to be impaled on, child. You've come a long way and fought many battles, but the time's coming when everything will make sense to you. You'll know the truth and it will set you free."

Felicia took another drink from her cup. When she looked up again, her grandmother was gone. Usually the dream ended at this point, but not this time. She sat there for a while, waiting.

She had just finished drinking her tea when there was a scratch at the door.

Felicia crept to the door and put her ear close to it. She listened for a moment, then there it was again…the scratching.

Felicia leaned in closer.

"Come," a voice whispered.

A foreboding feeling raced through her body as she whipped the door open wide and screamed.

Her brother stood at the door. Creatures, too many to count, standing in the darkness behind him, dragged him into a waiting crowd.

"NO!" Felicia screamed as she bolted upright in her bed.

42

The conference room began filling with the residents of Mount Weather. They filed in and took their seats in front of the podium while Jim, Mick, and Sharon stood at the front of the room and conversed.

Sharon, who was confident that she had solved the riddle, would speak first. After many months of study and dead ends, it all made sense to her now. It was a bit complicated for the layman mind, but she was prepared to explain in simple terms to everyone.

Sharon wheeled the chalkboard closer to the podium and then adjusted the microphone so she could talk and point out her findings on the board at the same time. The microphone squealed briefly as she adjusted it downward. Once everyone was seated, the chatter stopped and she had their attention.

"I think I've figured this all out," she said, and the chatter returned. She waited for it to subside before continuing.

"It's kind of complicated so you'll have to pay close attention to understand completely."

Sharon picked up a piece of chalk and drew everyone's attention to the chalkboard, where there were several drawings. To the left was a tadpole-shaped image labeled "EVOLUTIONARY ORGANISM." To its right were three oval-shaped images labeled "Healthy Blood Cells."

Sharon pointed to the tadpole image. "This single-celled organism is responsible and it was very difficult to isolate. In the human body there are roughly one hundred billion cells. In a reanimate's body I estimate there are approximately one million of these cell-sized organisms, ten of these cells per one million cells making up the body. I've also come to the conclusion that we all have the same number of this particular organism living in our own bodies. This organism alone causes the dead to walk."

The room exploded. Fear and shock hit the faces of many, while others paled and turned to those next to them.

"No, wait!" Sharon shouted, trying to calm them. "There's no reason for fear. It won't affect us. Not while we are alive, anyway. Let me explain."

The room quieted and she continued.

"First, let me say that although I have found some answers, I don't know everything. I don't know what suddenly triggered this dormant organism to make itself known which in turn enabled the dead to reanimate. With my limited facilities and resources, I simply don't have enough information to make that determination. I do believe, however, that I can explain it from this point forward.

"The process is twofold. One way for the condition to develop is at the point of death." Sharon pointed back to the tadpole drawing on the board. "This is the original carrier and like I said, I believe we all have this organism hiding in our bodies, but it is not designed to attack its host until death. The cell temperature must drop before it can carry out its function. Once the cell temperature is around ninety degrees or below, it will begin to mutate the cells that surround it. These cells in turn do the same thing in a swift chain reaction until the entire body is altered at the cellular level. The entire process happens very quickly. This I call the Assault Phase. Once complete, the body is recharged and reanimated. It is recharged through something that happens during this phase. Part of the process of altering the cells is to add something new to them. My study has shown that chloroplasts, or something very similar, are added to each dead cell as it's altered. A chloroplast is the part of a plant cell that allows it to gather energy from sunlight. It's something you may be familiar with and learned about in elementary school, called photosynthesis. That is why the hundred or so creatures that inhabited this facility were inactive upon our arrival. The people here were killed below ground and never saw the sun after reanimation. The organisms were able to draw enough energy from the host bodies to reanimate them for only a short period of time. When that energy was exhausted, they returned to a state of true death. The one specimen in my lab that survived had been exposed to a sunlamp sitting close to the gurney it was strapped to. It received what it needed from that lamp, but its lifespan was greatly shortened as well, though not as severely as those that received no sunlight at all."

Sharon pushed the chalkboard away and returned to the podium. She took a sip of water before continuing. She needed a moment to think.

"As everyone knows, this is not the only way to get infected and become one of them after death. A single bite that breaks the skin is deadly and will achieve the same result in the end. The mouths of these things are a breeding ground for bacteria and filth. Death occurs in a matter of days. The Komodo Dragon— I'm sure you all know what a Komodo Dragon is? It's a large lizard that kills its victim with an infectious bite. Its mouth contains four forms of deadly bacteria that no known antibiotics can cure. The bacteria causes blood poisoning, which results in death in a week even if the bitten animal gets away. The bacteria found in a reanimate's bite is not the same as what is found in a Komodo Dragon's. In rare cases, people have survived a Dragon's bite. No one has survived a bite from the living dead. Even the slightest break in the skin can allow these organisms to be introduced into the bloodstream. At first, we were certain that the bacteria found in living cadavers' bites could not be responsible for death, but after further study, I've come to the conclusion that it is the combination of the different forms of bacteria found in a living cadaver's saliva and not the work of one in particular. So far, I've discovered sixteen different organisms. Most of them were already known and catalogued. But one of them is something new, and was difficult to find."

Frank Thompson, a bald, portly man in his fifties, stood up. "Where'd this disease come from? I mean, if you say we all have this…this *thing* responsible for the plague in our bodies, why hasn't it happened before now?"

Sharon nodded thoughtfully. "It's new. I don't know where it came from."

"How about outer space?" someone in the audience yelled. "Maybe it came here on a meteorite or something."

Sharon smiled thinly at the notion. "I don't think so. From what I've seen through study, the Earth is its point of origin. It's true that it's different than anything we've seen before, but it still contains the basic makeup and structure of an earthbound organism and remember, the organism hiding in all of us, the one responsible for reanimation, is not the same as the bacteria found in their saliva. It is not bacteria at all. It is something else."

Alice Johnson stood and asked, "Why can't they reason like we do? They're mindless zombies, more or less. They seem to have no recollection of their former lives, or who they are…or once were."

"The period of time from death until the body is reanimated is now twenty minutes or more," Sharon explained. "Brain damage takes place in less than four minutes. By the time reactivation occurs, the brain is damaged beyond the ability to reason, not to mention the damage caused by an extremely high fever and infection as the individual becomes sick and dies. They *are*, in effect, mindless zombies."

"Zombies who want to eat us!" another voice cried out.

"Yes," Sharon answered. "I believe that is a product of basic instinct—their instinct to reproduce. We, as living beings, are nothing more than a collection of cells doing their best to thrive and survive. Evolution is simply the process of one-celled animals changing the way they interact with each other to improve their chances for survival. Scientifically, our existence comes down to that simple equation. These creatures cannot reproduce through sexual contact, so nature has given them an alternative course of action, reproduction through infection."

Sharon looked back at the chalkboard. "Of course, that is just my hypothesis. We have no way of knowing what motivates these creatures. It could be some latent instinct that this unknown organism has reawakened during the process."

"How long, doctor?" Frank blurted out. "How long before this all ends? Will it ever?"

"If you mean, how long will the disease cause the dead to come back?…I don't know. But on closing, I can tell you one thing. At first, I thought the creatures, and I use that term loosely, they're *not* human, you know, they don't function as such, would remain mobile for ten years, maybe more. But recent findings suggest that their lifespan may be much shorter."

"How much shorter?" another asked.

"As I mentioned before, sunlight powers them. It gives them their energy, not the consumption of flesh. But it's a double-edged sword. It could also be their undoing. Eventually, the sun and other elements will take its toll on the reanimates' dead flesh. I think it's possible that we might be seeing the last months of their existence. Hot weather is on the way so we must wait and see. That doesn't mean more can't be produced through infection; it's just that the ones presently walking our planet could quite possibly be burning out."

The chatter commenced again and Sharon took the opportunity to move aside and give Jim the podium.

Jim smiled at Sharon as he moved toward the podium. "Nice work, Doc."

"Nice work, hell," she smirked. "I have yet to find a cure for the bite."

Jim leaned forward and surveyed the crowd. They had become a family. Two years of surviving had made it so. In the front row sat Bob Deavers, a farmer-turned-floor-sweeper (the latter of which was his chore at the facility). Behind him was Shelly Sage. In her early fifties, Shelly still pined for her husband who was lost in the plague. Several families had made it through the living-dead onslaught intact. One such family corrected their unruly children in the back row. Others made new families once they had settled in. Brenda Welch was seven months pregnant. Her new husband held her hand as they both watched and waited for him to speak. Jim knew all of their names, but he wasn't sure that the next step was right for all of them.

"As most of you know," Jim began, "I just got back from Tangier Island, and I'm pleased to say that we are not alone. There are many more who have survived this horror."

Applause broke the silence of the crowd. Some stood and whistled. Jim waited for them to fully express their pleasure before continuing.

"Tangier Island is located between Virginia and Maryland, in the Chesapeake Bay, part of a string of inhabited islands. The people there are happy, content, and would welcome us. There's plenty of food available by way of the bay. We could fish and do a bit of farming, too. There are plenty of houses for anyone who would like to take up residency for a nearly-normal life."

A wave of chatter swept the gathering. He expected another round of applause at that point, but they waited, unsure. They had been safe where they were for more than a year, but they had all learned the hard way that safety in this new world was a tentative thing.

"I don't want to worry anyone," Jim continued, "but there's something else you all need to know. I encountered more survivors than those on Tangier Island." Jim glanced at Leon. "I encountered a group of militia members, a particularly nasty group at that. This militia is well-armed and from what I could gather, large in numbers. They are some of the worst our old civilization had to offer—racists, militants, white supremacists—Nazis. However you want to categorize them. They were once a small part of our world's population, but things have changed." He scanned the room, subconsciously making eye contact with the minorities on hand. "They are the ones who were responsible for Matt's death. They shot him in cold blood."

There were six blacks (not counting Leon), two Mexicans, an Asian, and a Pakistani out of sixty-three survivors. The rest were white. To the people of Mount Weather, they were part of the family, but the militia would not see it that way.

"They killed Matt because of the color of his skin. Their idea of the New World Order is racial purity. If you're not white, they will kill you. I don't know if they are aware of our little hideaway, but when they captured me, my map fell into their hands."

The room erupted again. "They know we're here?" Kelly Carley cried from the back. "They're coming here?"

"I don't know," Jim answered. "The map doesn't show this place as my starting point but it does come close."

"How close?"

"Route Seven."

"Jesus Christ, Jim. Are you saying that we aren't safe here anymore?" asked Bubby Wright, a short, plump black man known for his past job as the local weatherman. "Do we *have* to make the move to the islands?"

"No, I don't think so. For one thing, the map also shows the other end of my journey, so the islands may be unsafe as well."

Jim stepped out from behind the podium to address them on a more personal level: "I'm not here to tell you that we've got to move again, just to inform you of our options and our situation. I don't think we are in any immediate danger. Even if the militia should opt to storm this facility, they will need to plan carefully before doing it, and that means scouting the site and our numbers. It would be difficult for them to gain entrance, but enough of them could. It is my intention to uncover their plans and make preparations accordingly. To pick up and move at this time would be a bit premature."

Jim studied the anxious face of Sharon Darney. "Doctor Darney says those things are burning out, that they may be nearing the end of their lifespan. From what I've seen out there, that may be true, but we can't be sure. We have to operate and base our decisions on what we know, and right now that isn't much. So like it or not, some of us will have to leave the safety of this place again and go find answers."

He scanned the room. Things hadn't changed all that much. They were still the same downtrodden refugees from two years before. They were better fed and better housed, but fear still filled their hearts and minds, fear of the unknown and of what waited beyond the steel doors of the underground. He didn't see a room full of people; he saw a room full of ducks—sitting ducks.

"Tomorrow morning at nine o'clock, we want all of the men to attend a mandatory gun class. Should the need arise we need each and every one of you to know your way around an automatic weapon. Any of you ladies who wish to do the same are encouraged to do likewise. The class will be held on the firing range in C-section. As most of you know, that's just down the hall from here, through the double doors." Jim looked around the room once more. "That's it for tonight. Thanks for attending."

As the crowd dispersed, some nodded their thanks to Jim. Kelly Carley stopped to say to Jim, "I didn't mean to insinuate that you led them to us, you know? I didn't mean that," she said, worry lining her forehead.

"I know, Kelly. It's okay."

"If it weren't for you—"She looked past Jim to Mick. "If it weren't for all of you, we would all be dead now," she shuddered. "Dead or undead."

"We'll be fine. Don't let it worry you. We're safe here."

43

Turnout for target practice was better than Jim had anticipated. Thirty-three people arrived to better their firearm skills. Ten of them were women, who to Jim's surprise, held their own with most of the men. It was a comfort to know that so many were willing to defend their turf.

Two years earlier they had been scared sheep waiting for a leader, unable and unwilling to stick their heads out into the sunlight for fear of the unthinkable horrors awaiting them. Their sudden change did wonders to ease the tension that had been pulling at the back of his neck for the last few days.

***

Members of Jim's team were waiting when he entered the small conference chamber connected to the war room. Griz tagged along behind and plopped down in an empty seat.

These people were the heart and soul of their survival. They were the ones who risked their lives and forged ahead so that the others could follow. Jim's worry eased as he surveyed his comrades. He trusted them. He could count on them for anything. They were an impressive group, a collection of intelligent, heroic, determined people who were unwilling to give up.

Pete Wells chewed on a piece of jerky as he rocked back and forth in his chair close to the rectangular oak table. Jim noticed that Pete's hair had grayed a great deal in the past two years. Obviously, this had been a difficult transition for him. Pete knew his way around radio equipment, but that knowledge couldn't help him fully repair the communications equipment at Mount

Weather, not without the needed parts. Eventually, they had lost all capacity for outside contact.

Pete had spent hours listening to the endless stream of pink noise spewing from the prison radio when they were holed up there. After the move to Mount Weather, he had searched for live feeds, which in the end, led to dead air. They had finally come to the conclusion that they might indeed be the only survivors until the signal came from Tangier Island.

Sandwiched between Amanda and Felicia, Sharon Darney studied her notes. Mick chatted with Leon. When Jim entered the room, they all turned to face him, waiting for his next move—his plan.

Jim wasn't sure he liked the idea of so many depending on him for so much, not to mention trusting him with their lives. He was only human, and being human, he was just as apt to make a mistake as any one of them. Even Mick, who in Jim's opinion was every bit as competent as himself, leaned heavily on him for the final decision on most matters. They were Captain Kirk and Mister Spock, flawless in the execution of every plan and able to get them out of trouble, no matter what. But in truth, they had been lucky.

Jim pulled the chair out next to Amanda. "We've talked it over. Some of us will be going back to Tangier to pave the way for anyone wanting to relocate. I'd like to take volunteers. No one is required to go, but I'd like to have Mick, Griz, Amanda, and, of course, Leon, make the trip with me. Felicia, you need to stay. There's no way I'm going to take Izzy with us. She'll need you here. Pete, I want you here as well, to keep an eye on things."

Pete nodded, and swallowed the last of his jerky. "No problem, Jim. I can do that," he said, chewing like a cow with a mouthful of cud. "If that militia shows up to make trouble, they'll find more than they bargained for."

"No," Jim said. "If they show up, there'll be no resistance."

Pete blinked. "But you said those people were dangerous, racist, murderers. They will pose a definite danger to some of our people. Isn't that why we have everyone learning to handle a weapon?"

"Yes, it is," Jim answered, "but you can bet your ass that if they come here to attack, they'll be prepared. There's no point in risking all the lives down here. If they show up, you're to take the people they would target up top and evacuate them to another location. I don't think they will want to kill us all. They're looking for a world to rule. They'll want people in that world. We're training everyone to use a weapon in case I'm wrong. Should they *need* to defend themselves, they'll know how."

Amanda fought to remain silent, but failed. "And what about the people we so thoughtlessly relocate, Jim? What about them? Where will they go? Where can we take them to ensure their safety?"

Jim didn't like the solution any more than he figured anyone else would. He didn't have all the answers; he wished they understood that. "There's no other way right now," he said. "We've just got to work as fast as we can to remedy the situation. Hopefully, it won't come to that. If we can get things settled quickly, we'll have the support of a lot of people, but if it does come to that, Pete, those people will rely on you to keep them safe. You'll need to use one of the armored vehicles to get them out of here and to Tangier Island. If the militia shows up here, I think it will be a good bet that it will be safer there."

44

Chris Smith covered the radio Hathaway had given him with some rocks by the beach and scanned the area.

There was a small house on stilts close to him that appeared to be abandoned, but livable. The yellow, weathered, board siding was loose in spots and a little worse from wear in the salt air.

The town was just on the other side of a knoll of sandy soil sparse with grassy vegetation. The knoll would protect the structures on the other side in bad weather by absorbing the impact of lashing waves. The house would be a good place to set up his base of operations until he could learn more about what he was to do.

Chris started his walk toward the little town.

He would try to blend in first, take in every detail of the inhabitants' daily lives and defensive capabilities. In the back of his mind he hoped they were too well armed to attack with any hope for an easy victory. Even if that was true, it may not be enough to stop Hathaway from carrying out whatever plan he had in store for these people. And knowing Hathaway as he did, he was certain that his plan would not be to their benefit.

The midday sun warmed his broad shoulders as he stood atop the knoll looking across the village. A moderate breeze blew his blond hair and pelted the side of his face with grains of sand. As he squinted to keep the sand from blowing into his eyes, he could hear the gentle tide as it licked the shoreline behind him. A man worked on the roof of a house, hammering away to fix some shingles that had blown loose. Two more rode bicycles on the paved street. A woman stood at her front door, shaking a rug as dust particles flew in every direction.

This could be home, he thought as he watched the scenes play out before him, a normal life free of the desolation around it; the breeze, the blue skies over him, the people simply living a simple life.

In this secret place there was life again.

45

Jim slid the doors open and walked into the large warehouse as Mick flipped the light switch back and forth. "No lights," he said. Mick looked up at the darkened, dish-shaped lights in the ceiling.

"There's no power on out here," Jim said. "I guess there's a breaker around somewhere. It's a good idea to find it so we can see everything we have in here. We're going to need a little more than a motorcycle this time."

Mick searched the walls for the breaker box. He found it halfway to the back of the expansive room.

"I found it, Jim. Are you ready to power it up?"

Jim moved to where Mick had been standing by the switch and could see that the main power feed had simply been turned off. "Yeah, flip it."

Mick flipped the main breaker and Jim hit the switch. The lights crackled as they illuminated the large room and Mick was spellbound by what he saw.

"Don't pick out anything," Jim said, noticing his surprise by what he was seeing. "I've already decided what we need."

Jim walked through the line of armored vehicles and Mick followed. They stopped in front of a large green tank-like vehicle with six wheels. A large gun was mounted on top, with a smaller, less menacing machine gun next to it.

"This is the one," Jim said, patting the angled front end. "It's heavy, fast, and will plow through just about anything." He climbed up next to the hatch. "It's called a Grizzly. It'll go almost sixty miles an hour." He moved behind the big gun. "It's a fifty caliber, with two banks of smoke grenade dischargers and a diesel motor pushing two hundred and seventy-five horsepower. There's enough room for all of us to fit inside for the ride to Tangier."

"You know your military trucks, don't you?" Mick said.

"I've had some experience with it," Jim said, sliding down. "It went into service in the mid-seventies. It's still in service today. At least it was."

Mick patted Jim on the back. "It still is, Jim, at least for us. How about fuel? Will we need to take extra for the trip?"

"We should. It'll go a little over three hundred miles on one tank of fuel. The round trip is a little more than that. There's plenty here. We need to fill a few containers and strap them on." Jim walked back to the door. "We will essentially only have one thing to worry about in this thing: If it conks out, we're on foot."

Mick gave him a disapproving look. "Now why'd ya have to bring that up?"

Jim smiled. "Don't worry. I'll give it a good going over before we leave."

46

Robert Hathaway was sitting under a large oak tree as he watched Jake approach.

He walked slew-footed, his feet pointing outward with each step. It was the opposite of pigeon-toed where the toes point in as a person walks. It gave the impression that Jake was a clumsy hulk, that at any moment he would trip over his own feet and fall face-first to the gravel. But nothing was further from the truth. Jake was a powerful man and a champion wrestler in high school. Slew-footed or not, he could hold his own.

Hathaway shifted his attention from Jake to Ben, who was talking to an assemblage of men. The ignorant, uninformed bastard couldn't command a kindergarten class, Hathaway thought. He wasn't fit. He had no real training, no real combat experience. If he thought doing battle with those rotting piles of garbage was anything to be proud of, he was wrong, dead wrong.

"Talk on, you ignorant bastard," Hathaway mumbled. "They won't follow you." His jaw had started to ache from gritting his teeth and he opened his mouth to relax the muscles.

Jake, who now stood at Hathaway's side, spit and wiped his mouth. He never strayed too far from his friend. He felt secure when he was close to him, as if Hathaway was an older brother or father figure, even though there was only an eight-year difference in their ages.

"I've got almost a hundred men willing to make the trip, Bobby," Jake told him.

Hathaway stood. "I want more. We should have no less than twice that to do the job properly."

"It may be tough to get that many, Bobby. A lot of them are pretty pissed off at us right now, but these men are loyal to you."

"I know they're mad," Hathaway said, brushing the dirt from his trousers. "Colby's been trying to stir them up and turn them against me with his speculations and lies."

Jake followed as Hathaway walked down the gravel walk toward one of the small shelters. He watched Colby from the corner of his eye until he and Jake entered one of the small, unused rustic cabins.

Hathaway ran a finger through the dust on a wooden table beside the door and scanned the darkened room.

Many of the larger buildings had gone up in flames when the explosion rocked the camp. He had not anticipated such destruction. How could he have forgotten about the gas tanks beside Bates' office? It was an amateurish oversight.

Jake watched Hathaway pace the room. He looked apprehensive, afraid even, but that couldn't be true. Bobby Hathaway was fearless. He's in deep thought, that's all. He's devising a plan of some kind, making sure every detail is just right. That was it.

Hathaway moved to a small window and wiped away the layers of filth. Outside, Ben Colby was still talking to his men, bobbing his head as he patted one of them on the back. "Treacherous," Hathaway whispered. "Build your alliances, weasel. They can die with you." He turned to Jake. "Why do they listen to him? He's not really one of us. He's from the north; he's not a Freedom Fighter. College puke, that's what he is. He knows nothing. They're plotting against me. I know it."

Hathaway went to the table and pulled the map from his pocket, the one with the yellow tracings. The one *The Man* had been in possession of the day he was captured. He spread it out across the table and studied it.

"Have you decided where we're going yet?" Jake asked.

"I'm waiting to hear from someone before I know for sure," Hathaway grumbled. "I'll make contact with him in two days. I'll know more then."

"That's that fella's map that we killed on the ship, ain't it?" Jake said. "Too bad he didn't tell us something before he died."

"That man wasn't going to tell us shit," Hathaway said. "He had plenty to hide, but he wasn't talking, goddamned FEMA man. I'll know his secrets."

"FEMA man?"

Hathaway refolded the map. "Federals…Federals with way too much power. They're gone now with the rest of those federal pieces of shit, or so I thought. I just can't figure out what he was doing down in Fredericksburg. FEMA Headquarters is in Washington, D.C. I figure that he came from an island. I'd say he was a bleeding-heart, nigger-lover out looking for survivors. He was obviously a nigger-lover, but that son of a bitch was no bleeding heart." Hathaway shook the folded map in Jake's face. "You keep this shit under your hat, soldier. I don't want anyone else to know anything about this."

Suddenly the gnawing feeling Hathaway had struggled with for days revealed its message to him. Of course! There *was* another place! He remembered now. There was a FEMA center in Virginia as well.

He unfolded the map on the table again and stared at the yellow line. The southern end stopped at a place called Smith's Point. He was sure it wasn't there. No, it was in a secluded place, away from major population centers, much more secure than the Washington offices.

"It's here!" he pointed to the end of the line for Jake to see. "If memory serves me, there's a government compound of some kind right there in Bluemont."

Jake listened and studied the map as best he could. "That's Mount Weather. It used to be a government weather station. It's something else now."

"How do you know this?"

"I've been there, a long time ago. It's right along the road that goes over the mountain. I don't think it's a weather station anymore, though."

"Why's that?"

"Because, there's a lot of buildings on top of that mountain right there in one spot. It looks like a little town all fenced in and well protected. It's called the ERC or EAC. Something like that."

"EAC? Emergency Assistance Commission?" Hathaway thought for a moment. "That sounds a lot like FEMA to me."

47

"See here," Pete showed Jim, "the Grizzly has communication equipment we can use. It'll be on a military frequency."

"I know, but we have no relays or stations to carry the signal. It won't work."

"Oh, but we do!" Pete proclaimed. "We still have the one satellite working. We can bounce the signal off that. I just have to aim the dish and find the frequency."

"But the equipment in the war room isn't sending."

"I'll cut through the storage door with a torch," Pete said. "I'll get the needed parts and get it going."

Jim worked to strap two diesel canisters to the side of the Grizzly. "We don't even know that it's storage behind that door for sure. And even if it is, how do you know it'll have what we need?"

"It's in the war room. We've not found the parts anywhere else. It has to be. They wouldn't put themselves in the position of not having replacement parts. Even if it's not, I'll strip one of the Grizzlies for the parts I need."

Jim shrugged. "I want the radio working, but we don't have much time. We leave in the morning, regardless of whether that radio works or not. I'll move the Grizzly up close to the gate so we can get it properly equipped."

Pete climbed out of the vehicle and wiped his greasy hands on a rag, then tossed it on the floor. He studied Jim as he finished his task. "Jim, don't you think you're rushing things a bit? I mean, this has all happened so fast. Maybe if we wait a—"

"Wait for what?" Jim said. "For those maniacs to come up here and force themselves on us? No, I don't think so. Besides, we're not risking everyone. Only a few of us are going. If all goes well, we'll have a better life soon."

"Well, it was a thought. I had to say it, you know," he said with a grin. "Now I can say I *tried* to stop you if something goes wrong."

***

Amanda did her best to hide her excitement. She was excited to be going with Jim this time. She couldn't help but feel their search for a normal life was almost over. If they made the move to Tangier, things would be different. They could actually live the way people were meant to live, in the daylight and in a real home again.

Home…how long had it been since the word had heart, or real meaning? Home was a place you built your life around. Home was a place you lived with the people you loved, a place full of dreams for the future. For so long she had known no such place. She closed her eyes and dared to dream. It would be good to have that again.

On one hand, tomorrow could not come fast enough for her. On the other, it brought danger, maybe even death. "Not tomorrow," she whispered before reopening her eyes. They would not die tomorrow.

Amanda continued stuffing a bag with essentials for their journey until the zipper barely closed, then tossed it in the pile with the others. Mick entered just then and placed two more weapons on the heap. They would be well-armed, more than enough for their needs. Boxes of ammunition were stacked with the weapons and bags.

Mick's hair was hanging into his eyes. It had grown long since their stay at the prison last year. It touched his shoulders in the back and over his ears. He brushed it away as he looked over the stack of guns, taking count in his head. Amanda walked over to the pile and picked up a rather nasty-looking little weapon. It was heavy in her hand. "What is it?" she asked, turning it over and inspecting each side.

Mick took it from her and placed it back in the pile. "It's a Micro Uzi. It takes a clip, fully automatic. We're bringing six."

Amanda reached into the pile again, this time not for a gun, but for something else—eyewear, weighty with protruding lenses.

"I've never seen these for real before. Night vision?" She placed them to her face.

"Yes."

Amanda pushed the button on the side and the apparatus gently hummed. She suddenly tore them from her face, turned it off, and rubbed her eyes. Mick took them and returned them to the pile with the other equipment. "Sorry. I should've told you not to turn them on in here while you were wearing them."

Amanda squinted and blinked as though she'd just been caught in a camera's flash. "What *was* that?"

"They take what little available light there is at night and magnify it. It allows you to see in almost total darkness. Using them in a lit room isn't advised," he said with a laugh.

Amanda blinked again, "I'll remember that."

Pete dropped the dark cover on the welding mask and continued to burn away at the door's hinges. Sparks danced in every direction as bits of the metal fell to the floor in the form of glowing red particles. Jim watched from behind, wearing a mask of his own. He held a large crowbar and waited for Pete's signal to try again. The last hinge burned through and fizzled on the floor.

"Try it now," Pete told him.

Jim placed the end of the crowbar into the crack. "What if we open this thing up and there's a horde of hungry ghouls on the other side, Pete?"

"Then we're fucked."

Jim applied pressure again. The door creaked, then broke free from its frame, hanging only by the locking system on the latch side.

Jim and Pete stared in amazement.

"I'll be damned," Jim exclaimed, splitting the darkness with his flashlight. It was not a storage room as they had previously thought.

"This is a whole new section." Jim said.

The door opened to a corridor. Twenty feet in, there were two more doors, one on the left and one straight ahead. Jim eased himself in first and pulled his .44 from its holster as Pete followed.

They approached the door on the left first and opened it.

The room was small, with floor-to-ceiling shelves on the left and right. Some of the shelves held locked compartments. Pete rummaged through several containers before finding what he needed. He held out a circuit board and strained to read the small print on its bottom edge. "Not the one I need," he said, and placed it back in the box.

"How do you know?" Jim asked.

Pete continued his search. "Because that was a motherboard. I need a frequency processing board if I'm going to get the communications working properly. Got it here!" he said, holding the prized item high.

Jim walked back into the hall again and Pete closed the door to the stockroom behind them. "What's behind door number two?" Jim asked, pointing at it with the .44. "You ready to take a look-see?"

"Might as well while we're here."

Jim turned the knob and to his surprise this door opened too.

This was not simply a room. Directly ahead of them was a loading platform. A small blue and white train resembling a subway train was parked at the platform, the Presidential emblem emblazoned on the side. "I'll be damned," Pete said, "so it *is* true?"

Jim moved to the edge of the platform and peered down the tracks. "What's true?"

"The rumors. This place was supposed to be secret, but everyone knew it was here. One of the rumors was that there was an underground tunnel all the way to the White House. Once we got here, I never saw anything like that so I figured it wasn't true after all, but here it is, bigger than life."

"You mean to tell me this thing goes all the way to Washington, D.C.?"

"Yep, to the White House, rumor has it."

"To the White House," Jim muttered. "Are you sure?"

"What's sure these days?" Pete answered.

"It could be of use to us, but I want to know where it goes, with no doubts," Jim said. "Until we do, weld the door shut again. At the very least it may be a good escape route if the militia finds this place."

48

Chris Smith wrapped the radio in a burlap blanket and carried it into the small yellow house. He placed it on a nightstand in the front bedroom and covered it with the blanket.

The radio had batteries. They were big, bulky, and square, awkward things, reminiscent of World War II equipment. Hathaway would be expecting him to make contact soon. He was still unsure exactly what Hathaway's plans were. All he knew was what he'd been told. He was to blend in and simply report what he saw. So far, what he'd seen were people living their lives as best they could under the circumstances. They were regular people—young and old, sick and healthy, black and white, all sharing the island. It was a melting pot of nationalities. It was something to be preserved, not destroyed.

Chris stood by the window facing east and watched the gentle waves of the Bay lick the shoreline behind the house. The sight soothed his tired eyes in a hypnotic way. His vision blurred until only the blue of the Bay touching the blue of the sky filled his sight, a soft flow of blue movement. Unwillingly, he refocused. He didn't like the possibilities of what might happen should a well-armed militia move in and have its way. He was also constantly troubled with worry for his family, his mother and sisters. Where were they now? Alive? He hoped so. It had been years since he'd seen them. He had waited too long and then the dead came and there was no chance to seek them out. Instead, the Freedom Fighters had saved his life and now he was indebted to them. He was a part of them and whatever plans they might have.

But he was on the island now. He no longer needed the rogues to survive. He was safe from the murder across the water, safe as long as the militia stayed on that side of the bay. But he knew they'd eventually come, and that would be his undoing. One day he would fail to live up to their standards. It was just a matter of time. But what could he do to prevent that outcome? He was just one man. Certainly, he would die at their hands if he tried.

Chris left the house on stilts and made his way back to where he'd stashed his belongings. He would get the batteries for the radio and then have a better look around the island. Maybe he would go fishing too before his scheduled appointment with Robert Hathaway. Fishing would clear his troubled thoughts and calm his nerves.

As he fixed his gaze across the water, he dreamed.

Yes, the bay was very blue this evening.

49

At five A.M. the alarm clock rang and Jim Workman fumbled in the darkness to put an end to the noise it was making. Amanda stirred next to him and he placed his hand on the curve of her hip and pulled her closer. The responsibilities of the day ahead played through his mind as he gently caressed her, the dangers, and the steps they would need to take to avoid them. They were about to embark on an undertaking unmatched since they'd left the prison. It was a major move, and they'd go right through the heart of hell to get there. Everything had to be thought through, every possible contingency prepared for if they were to survive. A single bad judgment call could cost lives.

Jim had reconsidered his decision to make the move more than once. Staying was the smarter thing to do, a bird in the hand kind of thing. They were safe at Mount Weather, but in a year the food would run out and what would happen if the militia showed up? They'd be on the run again and fighting to survive. The move was undeniably the right thing to do, but this would be the last time. Once on Tangier, they'd have a home until the world was safe again.

Amanda stirred and rolled over toward him. She kissed his neck with soft, hot breaths, then moved down to his chest, where she lingered just long enough to make sure she had his attention before moving on.

A moan of pleasure rose in his throat.

***

Pete barely had time to install the computer board before Jim entered the war room. He grabbed the computer unit by the handles on each side and pushed it back into its rack mount, then flipped on the switch. The readouts lit up and made three beeping sounds before settling into a quiet hum made by the cooling fan.

Pete moved to the center of the room, took a seat in front of one of the computer screens, and typed in several commands. Jim quietly observed his actions as he reset the system and allowed the new hardware to install. When that was finished, Pete went to the setup screen and programmed it to do a frequency search. Numbers flashed endlessly on the screen as the system searched for a signal.

Pete turned to Jim. "Is it on?"

Jim nodded. "Mick's up there now in the Grizzly. He's keying the microphone. If this thing works, you'll hear him."

Pete returned his attention to the screen. It had stopped scanning and static spewed from the speakers. A voice was barely audible within the pink noise. Jim moved closer. "Is that Mick?"

"I don't think so. That signal is very weak. It could be coming from anywhere on the planet."

"Can't you zero in on where it's coming from?"

Pete studied the screen. He was good with electronics, but he'd never used a system like this. He moved the curser to the top of the screen and clicked several command links before finding the LOCATE command. A small box appeared that read: LOCATING PLEASE WAIT.

The caption started to blink. When it stopped, a new caption said: UNABLE TO LOCATE.

"It must be too faint to lock in on," Pete said.

They listened a while longer until the signal faded and the computer automatically began scanning again, only to stop on a clear signal. "Mick to Base. Do you read?" He then repeated the message.

Jim pulled a walkie-talkie from his belt. "Mick, we're reading you. Can you can hear us." He was calling Mick who also had a walkie talkie with him. If the war room radio did not work it would ensure communication while testing.

"Five by five, Jim," his voice came over the war room speakers again.

Pete spoke into the microphone attached to the console in front of him. "Mick, this is Pete. You getting all this clearly—no static?"

"Ten-four. Loud and clear. Looks like you did it."

"That's a big ten-four. You're ready to go. Over and out." Pete switched off the microphone and swiveled his chair around to face Jim. "Is that clear enough for you?"

Jim nodded. "How far will it reach?"

"Your guess is as good as mine. I'm not that familiar with this kinda gear, but it should serve you well for your trip to Tangier. It's being bounced off our satellite. The grizzly is updated with satellite communications. As long as that bird in space can see you, you should have signal...as long as your transmitter is up to speed. But don't take my word for it. I'm old, long in the tooth and outta touch."

"Yeah, me too, but not quite as old as you, ole man."

Pete frowned. "I guess you're right about that one, but not so old to have outlived my usefulness—yet."

Jim smiled.

50

Chris walked into the bar with the bright blue sign overhead and tried to adjust his eyes to the darkened room. As the room slowly revealed itself, he found his way to the bar and took a seat.

A short, scrawny, Hispanic man came from the kitchen and rambled on in his native tongue as he placed clean wine glasses in an overhead rack. After he hung the last glass he noticed Chris and raised a finger at him: "You are new here. I've not seen you before. Where are you from?"

"That's right. I just got here yesterday," Chris told him.

Julio made his way back to the kitchen, stopping halfway there. He turned to face Chris. "You want something? I get you something to drink."

Chris smiled. "A drink would be nice, but I've got no money."

"No money needed."

Chris said, "How about a beer?"

"No beer."

"Okay, a shot of tequila, then."

"No tequila."

Chris raised an eyebrow. "Okay, what *do* you have?"

"We have wine."

"Fine. Give me a chardonnay."

"No chardonnay."

"Any kind of wine is fine," Chris said with a smile.

Julio pulled the cork and poured until the glass filled to the halfway point. "Apple wine—All we got."

"It'll do," Chris mumbled, taking a sip.

The wine was surprisingly good and it showed on his face as he savored the flavor. "So who's in charge around here?"

"That would be me," Julio answered.

"No, I mean the islands."

"Ahh, that would be Carolyn Mayes. She makes the decisions for the islands. It was her husband who did it before, but he was killed shortly after the islands were made safe. Sad, sad, so sad. He was a good man. He was the one who put it all together."

"What do you have here in the way of protection?"

"What do you mean? Protection from what? The islands are safe from those demonios across the water."

"Invaders."

Julio laughed out loud. "Invaders? There is no one left to invade us."

He chuckled on his way back to the kitchen.

51

Jim placed the last of the weapons in the rack and connected the buckles on the straps to secure them. Mick made sure the passengers were in their seats and then stepped out to where Felicia stood with Izzy.

Leon grabbed Milly by the collar and made her sit next to him. The dog's movement irritated Griz.

"Does that damned dog have to go with us? It smells."

Leon gave Griz a bothered look. "Have you taken a whiff of yourself lately?"

Griz raised his arm, sniffed, and made a face. "Well what do you expect? There ain't no Right Guard around anymore."

Felicia's eyes filled with tears and her lip quivered as Mick approached her. "I want to go, too," she said.

Mick smiled, and wiped away the lone tear that rolled down her cheek. "I'll be back soon. Remember, it may take as long as a week. We have a lot to do once we get there. We'll be able to talk over the radio, but don't get worried if we lose communication. There's no guarantee the radios will work once we get away from here, or that they won't just stop working because they are held together with chicken wire and chewing gum."

"I understand." Felicia pouted.

Mick's attention was drawn to Izzy, who held out several strings of beads. He took them from her, five necklaces in all, each with an assortment of colored beads made from shiny plastic.

Felicia forced herself to smile. "You're supposed to wear them," she said.

Izzy pulled Felicia down to her and whispered in her ear, stomping her foot to make her point.

"She says you are to wear them always and never take them off, ever."

Mick stared at Izzy in wonderment as he put the necklaces on and tucked them inside his shirt.

"No!" Izzy said, reaching up. Mick bent over and Izzy pulled the beads out from beneath his shirt so they hung freely around his neck. "They have to be out, like this. It's important, very important," she said, patting them with her hand.

"You'd better do as she says," Felicia said.

Mick smiled, and lifted the child up in his arms. At first he simply stared at Izzy, bewildered.

"Don't worry, Izzy. I will wear the beads always, out like this."

Izzy smiled and kissed his cheek.

***

Jim drove past the spot where he and Matt had cut the tree out of the road, past the small town of Marshall, and then south on to Route 17. Except for small viewing slots, there were no windows for the passengers to see the desolate world outside.

Creatures dotted the landscape, but Jim was the only one who could see them clearly. He watched them as they performed their mindless waltz, the new residents of a dead world. They were darker now and more horrible than before. No longer were they the gray faces of the recently dead in business suits, blue jeans, or uniforms. They were grotesque, awful things, rotting piles of blackened skin and teeth, propped up by bony carcasses that moved about with quick jerks and thrashes. They were slack-jawed, sunken faces stinking of death, walking masses of disease and evil.

Mick kept an eye on all the gauges as Jim maneuvered the machine to avoid debris in the road. Tree branches and roof shingles littered the stretch of highway they were on now, no longer removed by road crews and chain gangs.

This part of the trip would not take them into heavily-populated areas, but after Fredericksburg, the trip would get more perilous.

It would take more than a flat tire to stop the Grizzly. The six wheels and all three axles were active parts of the drive train; it could easily operate on five, or four for that matter. This knowledge helped ease Jim's mind as he did his best to steer clear of danger.

Milly sat between Leon's legs and watched Amanda, who sat on the opposite side. Little more than metal benches built into the tank-like vehicle, the seats ran along each side, facing each other. They were uncomfortable and made for a very bumpy ride. Leon fidgeted in an effort to get comfortable.

Milly stretched out and fell asleep.

52

Later that day, the Grizzly moved slowly into Smith's Point.

The trip had been uneventful, a pleasant change that suited Jim just fine. He had been tempted to take his previous route to see if Matt was still there by the Humvee, mindlessly roaming the area around it. But today was not the day for that, and so they avoided Fredericksburg by taking the highway to the north, bypassing the city altogether.

Jim stopped the Grizzly before entering the harbor and grabbed his rifle, then moved to the center of the passenger area where he pulled down the locking mechanism to the overhead hatch.

"What are you doing?" Amanda asked.

Jim pushed on the hatch. "It's hard to see what's out there through the ports. I wanna see what we're up against before we spill out of this thing."

Mick grabbed his weapon and moved to the viewing ports on each side and opened all of them. He peered through the one on the driver's side, while Griz and Leon took positions at the other two.

Mick pressed his face against the small window. As Jim had said, it was indeed hard to see at an angle. "I think it's clear on this side, Jim," he said, and moved away from the port.

Jim shot a glance to Leon, who shrugged, then shook his head, unsure. Griz was peering through the port in the rear. He stepped away suddenly and tripped over Milly, who squealed in pain as the heel of his boot came down on her foot. Griz's head bounced off the hard floor when he went down. "An ass-load of deadheads!" he cried, as he scrambled back to his feet, pointing to the rear of the vehicle.

There were two groups, one on each side of the road. They approached from around the corners of buildings and abandoned cars.

"Fifty—maybe more," Jim said, as he moved back to the driver's seat to check the situation in front.

"We need to back off for a while," Mick said.

"Leon, what does it take to close the gate?" Jim asked.

Leon came up and sandwiched in between Jim and Mick. "What gate?"

Jim moved out of the way to give Leon the chance to look through the opening.

"I never even noticed it was there," Leon said. "If I'd known that, I would've kept it shut."

Jim moved to the hatch and Amanda grabbed his arm. "I don't think you should be doing this. There's too many. We can come back later."

Jim gently pulled her hand from his arm. "I'll be fine."

Jim flipped the hatch and sunlight streamed through the opening. "Get us through the gate, Mick!" he shouted, and handed his rifle to Amanda, then pulled himself through the opening. When he reached down, she handed the rifle up to him.

Mick moved the vehicle forward until they were twenty feet inside the gate and then stopped. He slung his own weapon over his shoulder and climbed up to join Jim.

Jim stuck his head back through the hole. "If something happens, Amanda, go back to the mountain. Is that understood?"

Amanda nodded, her eyes fearful.

The creatures lumbered forward, lurching, stumbling, walking dead that reeled and swayed in unison. A ghoul in front was a hideous-looking thing with shredded clothes and a left leg that was chewed to the bone from the ankle to the knee. It favored the bone leg as if it was made of wood and hobbled on, determined to reach his prey.

The rest of the rabble hadn't fared much better. Darker and more frightening now due to decomposition and exposure to the elements, most were nothing more than walking skeletons with stretched skin and sunken, blackened eyes.

Entrance to the harbor was achieved via a two-lane road, surrounded by a ten-foot chain-link fence that separated it from a residential area around it. There was a large warehouse close to the docks. Six bay doors faced the water where shipments were unloaded, stored, and then later distributed.

Jim and Mick ran to the gate in a race against the approaching horde.

The gate was in two parts that slid on a track from each side of the fence. As the men pulled the gate closed, Jim grabbed the rusted U-shaped lock hanging on his side and gripped it in his hand. When the gate slammed shut, Jim slipped the lock into place and pushed it closed.

Mick said, "We don't have a key to open that lock, you know?"

Jim brushed the hair from his eyes. "We'll cross that bridge when we get to it. If we're in that big of a hurry, the Grizzly will get through, locked or not."

They backed away as the crowd began to paw at the fence in front of them.

53

Inside the fence, several rotting corpses littered the ground. Missing from them was the usual gunshot wound, or trauma to the head. It appeared as if they had simply ceased to function. It was difficult to tell how long they had been that way. Even the ones still moving around were showing late stages of decay, propped up skeletons animated by an unknown force and sent on their way to do the bidding of some dark and evil god. But the ones on the ground were even more than that. They had been picked at by buzzards and small animals, missing eyes and much of their outer flesh.

The chain link fence surrounded the warehouse completely. With the gate closed, it was safe from further occupation of the walking dead unless the crowd grew too large. Already, a growing number of them were streaming down the road to fill the area around the gate. As the crowd grew, Milly started to bark, and raced toward them, voicing her displeasure with a torrent of yaps and growls.

Leon pulled the dog whistle from under his shirt and blew the silent order for her to return.

The effect was unmistakable as the dog stopped and the ghouls exploded into a chorus of agitated cries. They rattled the fence as their dead eyes focused fully on Leon, who stood bewildered, the whistle still hanging loosely from his parted lips.

"Jesus Christ!" Jim shouted, and took the whistle from around Leon's neck. He studied it first and then focused his stare on the horrid mob. "They can hear this thing. What's more, they're attracted to it, even riled by it."

Jim trotted a few yards away from the others and blew on the whistle again.

Just as he expected, every rotted face turned toward him, their rage stoked once more. They moved down the fence line until they were directly in front of him. There was no doubt. They could hear the dog whistle—and they didn't like it.

Also inside the fence, and to the rear of the warehouse was a fire department, a two-story structure with a siren in an enclosed bell tower on the roof. On the opposite side of the fire station, and outside the fence, there was a police station and a convenience store, and both were in ruins. The police station had burned, not to the ground, but a sizable portion of it had been gutted by fire, likely in the early days of the plague. Police stations became hot zones as people flooded to them in hopes that they would be protected. Usually the reverse was true. Jim had seen proof of it before. Hospitals, police stations, churches…Wherever people congregated, so did the living dead. It escalated the phenomenon and quickened the end of human civilization.

Jim stuffed the dog whistle into his pocket, and said, "It looks like we're okay for now, but we'd better move fast. We're attracting too much attention. Mick, you need to stay with Amanda and Griz while Leon and I find a boat."

Leon grabbed a toolkit from the Grizzly and ran with Jim to the docks. Milly followed, more interested in the safety and companionship of her master than yelping at the ghouls at the gate.

They ran past several boats that were either damaged by storms or in a state of disrepair until they came to a blue and white Stingray tied to a pier. It was close to the fence which ran all the way to the water's edge. Jim stepped on board and swung open the motor cover.

The battery terminals were covered with corrosion and a gritty white powder until Jim sprayed them with a cleaner and most of it disappeared. Then, without a word, he moved to the cockpit and began cutting wires under the dash. Leon knelt on the deck and watched through the windshield as Jim held two wires inches apart.

"Which one is gonna cause this thing not to start?—The battery, or the old fuel?" Jim asked.

Leon cracked a grin. "You gotta have faith, my friend."

Jim touched the wires together. The motor sputtered and came alive as he twisted the wires together.

Leon jumped into the seat next to Jim as he revved the engine "See? Ya gotta have faith!"

54

The canvas-covered personnel carriers were almost loaded with the supplies Hathaway and his men would need. Five trucks were required to transport the ninety-six men to their destination.

They would leave in two days.

Hathaway had hoped for more men. Less than one hundred was cutting it close for a job of this magnitude, but that was all he could muster under the circumstances. The camp had split into two factions. Ben Colby had publicly accused Hathaway of the bombing. There was no proof to support Colby's accusation, but somehow he had garnered the support of most of the camp. He had underestimated Ben Colby's desire to take command and his ability to achieve that goal through support.

Hathaway was checking off items from his list when Ben Colby and several men approached him.

Robert Hathaway gritted his teeth as Colby walked up to him with a confident swagger. He had the numbers on his side. He was in control, and he knew it.

Colby stopped a few feet short of coming face to face with Hathaway and watched the men loading the trucks for a moment, before saying, "I'm not going to let you take our supplies and run out of here, Bobby Boy."

Hathaway planted his feet and folded his arms across his chest. "And just what do you plan to do about it?"

"I don't know what you have in mind, but I can tell you that it's not in the group's best interest," Colby said, taking a step closer. "These supplies belong to the force as a whole, not to a select few."

"These supplies go where I want them to go. It's you who's out of line. You're the one who circumvented normal protocol by assuming command here."

"You did it to yourself. You made your bed and now you don't want to sleep in it. I won't let you take those supplies, or the men."

Hathaway grinned. "You have no proof. What gives you the right? These are *my* men and they'll follow *me*. They recognize proper procedure. Are you willing to have our people shoot each other over this? The casualties will be high."

Colby stood his ground. "Are you? They're your people, too."

"Not anymore. I have my men. The others are *your* people now, aren't they?" Hathaway stiffened. "I'll do it, and so will my men."

Colby searched Hathaway's face for signs of a bluff. Was it possible that he was willing to carry out such threats? His determination was unmistakable. He had blown up half the camp already. Why wouldn't he be willing to go to war with his own people? No, this was no bluff.

"If you leave, you're out. There will be no coming back."

Hathaway smiled. "It'll be you that's out of the loop once we leave."

55

The nose of the Stingray bumped against the pier on Tangier Island.

Jim throttled down and let the motor sputter into silence and Leon tied the boat so the starboard side was against the pier.

Amanda stepped out of the bobbing boat first and turned to help the others. Jim was the last one out of the boat as Amanda breathed in the clean sea air.

A flock of seagulls swooped low over the water, calling raucously to each other. One of the gulls took a hard dive into the bay with a loud splash. The sudden splash made Amanda turn quickly, pistol in hand.

Jim took the gun from her. "I don't think you'll need this here."

"Let me be the judge of that," she said, and snatched it from his hand and returned it to her side holster. "Even if I don't, it feels good just to know I have it there."

Leon led them to Julio's bar first. It was his turn to show *them* a little hospitality and he couldn't think of a better way to do so than to have Julio serve them a glass of apple wine and allow them a moment to relax.

Jim resisted the idea at first. He was always thinking of what had to be done, how fast he could do it, and how the alcohol might affect his judgment. Amanda had insisted though and so he caved in. She, more than anyone, wanted a glass of wine (or two) to adjust to her new surroundings and she was not drinking alone.

The five of them entered the dark room and made their way to the bar. Jim took a seat and the rest followed suit. Leon smiled as he waited for Julio to serve them. It was his favorite place to be. He'd always liked the bars, but this bar wasn't like those of years past. Julio's was more laid back. The jukebox in the corner was always playing, never too loudly, and only what Julio wanted to hear.

Julio was a Credence Clearwater Revival fan and to Leon, that was fine. They were one of those groups whose music never failed to make him want to sing along. It wasn't flashy or crisp like the new stuff, but it had soul and heart. Leon appreciated that. He had never been one for the new stuff anyway, Motown…now that was 'the shit.'

Julio finally made his way over to them. "I'm thinking you make lots of friends, Leon, but these are people I've not seen here before—more mainlanders?" He looked at Jim. "Except for you. I remember you. You are new to the islands and from the mainland. They are friends of yours I assume."

Leon smiled. "They sure are. How about hooking all of them up with a glass of wine?"

"For you, I do it," Julio said, "and for you too, pretty lady," he said to Amanda with a wink.

Jim scanned the dimly-lit room. Two people sat at a high table in front of a small window and sipped from their glasses and ate cracked peanuts, letting the shells fall to the floor. An old man with the tiniest bit of hair on top of his head, read an old magazine in the center of the room, aided only by the light of an oil lamp. In the shadows of a far corner, a young man sat by himself.

Julio placed the glasses in front of them. Mick took the first taste and his face puckered at the tart flavor.

Julio noticed his wrinkled nose. "That is from my newest batch. It's not as sweet as the other wine. If you don't like it, I can—"

"No," Mick said. "It's fine." He took another sip. "I'm afraid we don't have anything to give you for it, though."

"That's not a problem here," Julio said. "Money's no good anymore. What would I do with it?"

Mick nodded, taking in the surroundings. "Is this all you do?—work here in this place and serve people free wine? Why?"

Julio smiled thinly, and said with a shrug, "Why not?"

"He does *his* part," Leon added. "Everyone here does. We see to it that everyone has what he or she needs. Julio's job is vital, maybe the most important on the island. This place gives us a chance to unwind, relax—try to forget all that has happened."

"What about the other islands? Is it the same there?"

"More or less."

Jim stood and walked over to Leon. "Who's in charge of the islands? We should be seeing them soon to pave the way for us to move the others who want to come."

Leon thought for a moment. There were several who *thought* they were in charge, but when it came down to it, there was only one who *was*. "That would be Carolyn Mayes. She's the one you want to talk to. Her husband's the one who led the invasion. I guess you could call it an invasion. He's the one who came up with the plan to clear the island of danger and evacuate those who still survived on the mainland to safety here. He was killed making sure we all got here safely. His wife Carolyn finished the job. She's a strong woman. She'll help you."

"Is she here on Tangier or on one of the other islands?"

"She's here. There are a lot of people here on Tangier. It seems everyone wanted to be on this one. It has a real tourist feel to it. You kind of feel like you're on permanent vacation and that's a good thing, considering what's across the bay. Know what I mean?"

Jim nodded and went back to his barstool. He subtly watched the young man in the corner. He wished he could get a better look at him, but his face was in shadows. There was something he thought he recognized. He watched from the corner of his eye as he sipped his wine and it wasn't long before the young man stood and his face was revealed.

Jim reached over and grabbed Mick's arm. "Cover my back."

"What?"

"We've got trouble. Watch my back."

Mick's hand went to the grip of his pistol. He stood up, but remained at the bar as Jim moved toward the man in the corner.

"What are you doing here?" Jim asked, now face to face with the young man.

The question must have startled him. He stepped backward and stumbled over the chair behind him. On impulse, Jim drew his weapon and trained it at the man's head.

"You know me, don't you?" Jim said. "I know you, too. I saw you on the *Nimitz*."

Chris tried to speak, but his throat had tightened. Only his lips moved.

"Where's Hathaway? Is he here, too?"

"No," Chris finally managed. "Not yet."

"When?"

"I'm not sure. I'm supposed to radio him tomorrow. I don't even know why I'm here yet."

"I know why you're here," Jim said. "Who else is here with you?"

"No one. Just me, I swear."

Mick moved close to Jim, but kept a vigilant eye on the room for unseen trouble. "What's going on, Jim? Who is this guy?"

"He's part of the militia who killed Matt and tried to kill me. I saw him on the aircraft carrier when I was there."

"Why is he here?"

"That's obvious. He's a scout."

Jim held out his hand to Chris. "Give me your weapons. All of them."

Chris removed his holster and handed it to Jim, then took his hunting knife from his pocket and tossed it at Jim's feet.

Jim bent down and picked it up, all the while maintaining eye contact.

"Where are you staying?"

"In a little house down by the water," Chris said.

"I assume you have a radio. Is it there?"

"Yes."

"Good. Take us there."

56

Chris entered first and the others followed.

Jim kept the gun trained on him as they moved through the small beach house. When they got to a bedroom, Chris removed a wool blanket to reveal the radio equipment.

"That's it," he said, pointing.

The radio was standard Army issue, enclosed in a self containing gray metal box that unlatched on one side and hinged on the other.

"Where are your other weapons?" Jim asked.

"There's a rifle over there." Chris pointed to a corner of the room. "But that's all. He thought it might be a bad idea for me to bring too much firepower. For some reason he didn't want me to draw attention to myself."

Jim motioned for Mick to get the rifle.

Chris wiped away the sweat that had beaded on his brow. "What now?"

Jim pointed to a chair by the bed. "Sit down."

Chris did as he was told, slowly, and without any sudden moves.

"I want you to tell us everything you know. Why are you here? What are your plans for this island?"

Chris thought hard. This was a definite crossroads for him. He could give them his name, rank, and serial number, so to say, like a good soldier, which might get him killed, or he could tell them what they wanted to know. They weren't going to like his answers because he had no answers. Hathaway was a dangerous, ambitious man who would stop at nothing to get what he wanted, including killing every last person, himself included, on the island if he felt the need. Chris prayed silently for guidance—a sign, anything.

"I don't know anything other than I was told to come here to check things out and we'd make contact at a specific time."

"He told you to come to Tangier?"

"Not exactly. I was told to go to Smith's Point first. If there were living people there, I was to blend in. If not, then I was to come here, to the islands."

"To blend in?"

"Yes."

Jim studied Chris. He was twenty-five, maybe twenty-six, but no older than that. "What's your name?" Jim asked.

"Christopher Smith."

"How long have you been with the Freedom Fighters, Chris?"

Chris shifted in his chair. "Only a while. I didn't meet up with them until after those things started showing up and everything went to hell. They saved my life."

"So you felt it necessary to share in their dirty deeds in return for them saving you?"

"Yes—I mean, no—there were no dirty deeds that I was aware of, at least not that I saw. Yes, I saw you on the *Nimitz* but I didn't know anything about you other than you were a prisoner."

"But you had to know what they stood for."

"Now how the hell would I know that? I knew they were militiamen. But being in a militia doesn't necessarily make you a bad person. For all I knew they were the only ones left alive. I didn't have much of a choice."

Maybe the boy wasn't privy to Hathaway's plans after all, Jim thought. It did seem unlikely that everyone associated with the militia would share Hathaway's views and hatreds, especially if they were made up of plague survivors. Still, he was spying for him.

Jim holstered his weapon. "Where are you from?"

"From the mountains, a little place called Browntown. It's in the Shenandoah Valley."

The reaction was unmistakable. Chris saw recognition in their faces. "You know where it is?"

"What did you say your last name was again?" Jim asked.

"Smith. Why?"

"Felicia's last name is Smith," Mick told Jim.

Mick came closer. "And she grew up in Browntown," he added, looking at Chris. "You're not *that* Chris?"

Chris snapped to his feet and Jim's hand tightened on his weapon.

"My sister's name is Felicia. Do you know her? Is she alive? Will you take me to her?" Chris demanded; his questions came fast, one after the other.

"Wait a minute. Slow down," Jim cautioned. "This could be a trick."

Chris became frantic. "No—I'm not lying. My sister's name is Felicia. I also have another sister. Her name is Rebecca. We call her Becky. Do you know her, too? My mother...is she okay?"

"Felicia is okay," Mick said. "She's been with us throughout this nightmare. We don't know about your mother or Becky."

"Where is she? Is she here? Can I see her?"

Jim pushed Chris back into his chair. "She's not here, but you'll see her soon, assuming you're telling the truth. This seems like quite the coincidence. A bit too much of one for my liking."

"I swear to you: I'm not lying. Ask me anything."

"Tell us a little about Felicia," Jim told him. "What's she look like? What is special about her?"

Chris covered his face with his hands to hide his emotional state. Unable to speak, he slumped back into the chair and struggled to regain his composure. This was so unexpected, so unreal. Were they playing a trick on him instead? Maybe Hathaway had sent them to the island to test his loyalty to the troop. But that couldn't be. He had never shared his personal life with them. They did not know his sister's name or where he was raised as a child. It seemed too much a coincidence, too good to be true.

"She's tall, blonde. Thirty-one, I believe, and, yes, she is special. She has a gift. She sees things that others don't. She's very special—a gentle soul. Growing up, it was difficult for her to make friends because of her special nature. They called her names...made fun of her. She would come home after school, crying her eyes out because someone had called her a freak, or devil girl." Then Chris fell silent for a moment as a tear escaped the corner of his left eye. "Please...let me see her."

"I believe him," Jim said.

"So what do we do now?" Mick asked.

Jim paced the floor, his hands in his pockets. He felt the metallic shape of the dog whistle there and pulled it out. He stared at it and in that moment it all became clear to him, as though God himself had shown him the way.

He turned his radiant face to them. "I know what we do next."

57

The radio crackled with static as Hathaway tried to find the proper frequency. Jake watched from over his shoulder, his face inches from Robert's left ear. He was breathing through his nose as he chewed his tobacco.

Hathaway tensed. Jake was breathing down his neck. He disliked having someone's hot breath on him, and he was chewing his cud right into his ear. For a moment, he considered pushing him away, or at least telling him to back off, but he said nothing and continued to fine tune the radio.

It was almost time for the call from Chris Smith if he had made it to his destination alive. But dead or alive, he would make the move to Smith's Point. The information he would get from Chris was important. It would give him a definite course of action and cut down on the number of casualties, but not necessary for his plan.

Robert Hathaway was confident of his men's abilities. In his opinion, they were the best of the best. They believed what he believed, not what the others had ultimately grown to believe. The others had become soft in their thinking. His men were strong—pure.

Hathaway glanced at his watch for the third time. Chris was ten minutes late and his anger grew. He hated incompetence and it was incompetent to be late. Having the proper information now was vital. Maybe he was dead. Better dead than incompetent. At least dead was a valid excuse. Or maybe the radio wasn't working properly. But that couldn't be the reason. He'd checked it himself. It was more than adequate to do the job, even at this distance. No, Chris was dead and now they would need to make the trip blind, with no recon.

Suddenly, there was a voice and Hathaway jumped for the microphone. He listened again before answering, careful to be sure it was Smith and not another location, or worse yet, someone from their own camp. But this was a secure frequency, not one the Freedom Fighters used and unlikely that anyone else did either. It was the reason he had chosen it. The only reason someone would be on this channel is if they were scanning for survivors, and other than their own people, the Freedom Fighters did not care who was left alive or who was walking around dead.

Hathaway turned to Jake. "Watch the door. Let me know if anyone comes near."

Jake moved to the window beside the door and spread the filthy red and blue checked curtains just enough to see outside.

The voice came again. "This is Smith to Lieutenant Hathaway. Come in. Do you read me?"

Hathaway keyed the mic. "Go ahead, Smith. I read you."

"Sir, I'm here. What is it that you need to know?"

"First things first. Where are you?"

"I went to Smith's Point just like you told me. It was overrun with those things so I went to the islands. I found people here."

"How many?"

"It's hard to tell, but I'd say several hundred. Mostly women and children."

"Are the men armed?"

"They have weapons. Hunting rifles and handguns, but most of them don't carry them around."

Hathaway could hardly keep his widening smile from unleashing full-blown laughter. "What island are you on?"

The radio was silent for a moment, then—"Tangier."

"Do they have boats on the island?"

"Yes, sir. They have fishing boats. Most of their food is brought in from the bay."

Hathaway leaned his head against the microphone as he thought. "Are there enough boats to carry a hundred men?"

Again there was silence. Hathaway reasoned it was because Chris was calculating the numbers in his head.

"Yes, sir. There's a big fishing boat anchored here. It should carry that many, if I throw any unneeded items overboard."

Hathaway grinned. "Okay, now listen carefully. I want you to get the guy who captains that boat, at gunpoint if necessary, and the two of you take it over to Smith's Point on Thursday. That's two days from now. I want you to have it there at exactly fifteen hundred hours. Do you understand?"

"Yes, sir, but that won't work."

"Why not?"

"There are too many people around at that time. They take the boats out during the day to fish. They don't return until around six o'clock. It's too risky."

Hathaway snorted. "Too risky. Too risky for us?" he mused to himself. He keyed the mic again. "Can you have it there by eighteen-thirty?"

"Yes, sir. I can do that, I'm sure of it."

"You'd better be sure, mister! This is going to run us late in the evening. It doesn't give us a lot of time to work before it starts to get dark. If you're late, it's really going to piss me off and let me tell you…that's not something you want. Is it?"

"No, sir, it isn't. Don't worry, I'll be there."

Hathaway was secure in the belief that his plan was coming together. "That's it, then. I'll see you at Smith's Point at eighteen-thirty on Thursday. It's thirteen-hundred now. Synchronize your watch."

Hathaway turned off the radio and focused his attention on Jake who was still standing guard at the window. His plan was coming together perfectly. It would be easy.

***

Jim patted Chris on the back. "You did that very well. Even I believed you."

Chris released the breath he'd been holding. "I hope so."

Jim tossed the dog whistle to Mick. "Don't lose that. I hope to hell you can do what you say you can do."

Mick pocketed the whistle. "If it can be done, we'll do it."

"The fading light will be to our advantage," Jim said. "We'll need every little bit we can get."

"You know that if we fail, he will kill us all, don't you?" Chris said.

Jim said, "It'll work."

58

"The sun will be setting soon," Jim said. "I'd rather wait till tomorrow to do this, but we just don't have the time to spare."

Mick set down the toolbox and raised his binoculars to his eyes. He studied the area around the gate just up the hill. There were two creatures roaming about, but they had not taken notice of them yet.

He lowered the field glasses and turned around to face the bay. "The Militia will most likely assemble there by the water where we came in," Mick said, pointing to an open area of the parking lot close to the docks. "They'll be able to see the gate from there. We need to do something to block their view of it."

Jim drew Mick's attention to the warehouse. In a grassy area at the far end, he counted nine temporary construction office trailers ranging from twenty feet to over thirty feet in length. "If we place those trailers on the crest of that hill, they'll hide that gate from sight once the militia gets down here."

Mick considered his plan. "Yeah, but once they get down here, won't they realize that and either set up lookouts or move the trailers?"

"I'm betting that they'll think it's unnecessary. In their minds, Chris will be on the way with the boat."

Mick nodded. "This has to go just right, doesn't it?"

"It does," Jim replied. "Let's go check out the firehouse."

***

The firehouse was wrapped in red brick with four large doors to garage the trucks. Jim stood on his toes and peered through the window of the door closest to a smaller one. It was hard to see past the trucks with only ten or twelve feet between each one parked inside, and impossible to see directly behind the smaller door through which they would be entering.

Jim dropped down so his feet were flat on the ground. "It looks okay," he said, pulling a crowbar from the bag he'd been carrying.

"It looks okay?" Mick asked.

"Yes, it looks okay…from what I could see through that little window," Jim said with a sly grin. "What's wrong, Mick? Not in the mood for a little excitement?"

Mick could only frown and grunt as he stepped forward to take position behind Jim.

The smaller door was made of steel, one with a metal frame and no window to see inside. Jim braced himself and slid the crooked end of the crowbar into the doorjamb and pulled.

First the knob broke free and dangled loosely from the hole. Then without warning the door gave away and flew open.

Before Jim could react, a body was on him and he was on the ground.

The creature's hands grabbed him by the shirt collar as its rotting face leaked a thick, toxic fluid from an open wound in his left cheek. Jim shifted his face to prevent the vile liquid from making contact with his nose, mouth or eyes.

Its weight was incredible; the heavy brown jumpsuit and oxygen tanks strapped to the dead fireman's back added more than seventy pounds to the load crushing down on him.

Jim brought the crowbar up and placed it crossways into the creature's mouth as it moved in closer. With a final hard thrust, he sent the ghoul up and off to the left. Shattered teeth showered down like brown Chiclets as Jim scrambled to his feet.

The creature wore a fireman's helmet held in place by a chinstrap. With his first swing, the strap broke and the helmet went flying. Jim swung again and brought the creature to its knees. On the third swing, the impact cracked the fireman's head like a ripe melon and it collapsed facedown on the asphalt. Brain pulp spilled from the open cavity. Now partially liquefied, the air became polluted with its odor.

"That one's past its goddamned sell date," Mick coughed out as he swatted at the air in front of his face.

The stench didn't appear to faze Jim as he walked through the open doorway.

Once inside, they searched the building for more danger. On the second floor they found it.

It stagger-stepped in a circular motion, unaware of their presence as they watched from the doorway. It was tall and lanky with a bald head. This one also wore the jumpsuit and jacket of a fireman.

It continued to walk its loopy circle; its face tilted downward, watching the concrete floor at its feet, placing one step in front of the other as if it would stumble and fall if it didn't chart every move carefully. The name emblazoned on the back of its jacket simply read: LURCH. Jim gripped the crowbar with both hands and moved in as it continued its loopy dance and brought it down with the first swing.

First, they would need to find a generator. Every firehouse had one in case of a power failure and they found it in a back room on the second floor. It was a diesel-powered monster and it started as if it had been used only yesterday and hummed evenly.

Outside, the noise was barely audible, almost silent, over the small breeze that blew their hair.

"The militia won't hear it where they'll be waiting for Chris," Jim said.

"Yeah, as long as they don't come over here to the firehouse."

"They won't. They won't have the time."

"Now for the easy stuff." Mick said. "I get to invent a new fire siren." Mick grabbed the toolbox and headed inside and up the steps as Jim followed.

They passed through a door behind the kitchen and into a small storage area. To their right, a metal ladder hung against the wall. Eighteen inches in front of the ladder, a ventilation shaft ran down from the ceiling and disappeared into the wall on the other side of the small room.

Mick studied the trapdoor at the top. "It's gonna be tight," he said, as he gave the toolbox to Jim and started his climb up the ladder.

Three rungs up, he had to shift to one side to get past the ventilation shaft. He placed his feet on the side of the rungs and continued unsteadily. Near the top, he stopped. Jim climbed up as far as he could and handed the toolbox up to him. Mick turned around and placed it on top of the shaft and flipped open the trapdoor. Sunlight filtered down as he climbed up to the roof. Once there, Jim handed the tools up to him.

From the rooftop they could see the entire harbor. Outside of their gated refuge, the bodies of the dead roamed in scattered groups of three and four. They plodded slowly, like winos who'd had too much to drink, they swayed and held on to things for support, conserving their strength for more profitable gains.

The siren was six feet high and positioned in the center area of the roof. Twelve horns adorned its cap. Mick twisted his head upward from beneath and located the bolts to remove it. Just under the horns, a heavy fan rotor pushed air up into them when it was activated. The fan was his horseshoe. It would tweak his mistakes. Close was good in horseshoes, hand grenades, and sirens.

With a little effort, and half a can of spray lubricant, he had the horn assembly loose and Jim helped him get it down.

Mick rubbed at his chin. "I've got to remove all these. They won't work," he said, pointing to the horns. "It'll be too hard to modify them. I'll create four new ones to replace the twelve."

Jim looked at the contraption. "You're sure this will work?"

"Yes, if I do it right."

"That is the question, isn't it?" Jim said.

"I did research at the library on Tangier. It needs to be 5800 Hertz to 12400 Hertz to work properly. If I get it close, we can change the speed of the fan to get it right. But I've got to get it above 5800 Hz. That's important."

"Good. You and Griz work on getting that right tonight. In the morning, I'll get Amanda and Leon to help me do the rest. We have till Thursday."

59

Griz and Mick were at the airport hangar the following morning. Notes and books taken from the library were scattered across a table for reference. They had spent most of the night reworking the firehouse horns to suit their needs. Mick had split the dog whistle in half and was getting exact measurements of the cavities inside when Jim and Leon walked in. Griz flipped up the brim on his welding shield and turned off the torch.

Jim handed them each a cup of coffee. "There's more over at Chris's house if you want it."

Mick took a sip. "You left Chris up there with the radio all by himself?"

Jim reached into his pocket and pulled out a small vacuum tube. "It won't work without this. I want to trust him, but I won't risk our lives on it."

"My thoughts exactly," Mick said.

"What do you have so far?"

From the table, Mick picked up a metal cylinder that was six inches long and an inch in diameter. He tilted it so the open end faced Jim. The inside was split into two compartments. Mick picked up a small piece of metal from the table and fitted it inside, against the piece that separated it in half, and held it there. "Three of these will get welded into each one of the four horns."

He threw the small piece of metal back onto the table and picked up one of the old horns that had been cut just below where it started to flare. An adapter had been welded at the small end and Mick slid it over the cylinder to create the new siren.

"We should be ready for a test around noon," Mick said, putting the invention back on the table. "We'll know then if it works. Are you going over to the harbor now?"

"Yeah, shortly."

Reign Of The Dead

"Where's Amanda?"

"At Carolyn Mayes' house, explaining our situation to her. If this doesn't work, we're hoping to get enough men to thwart the militia's attack here on the island. Once we do what we're going to do tomorrow the secret will be out and we'll lose the element of surprise. If it works, we'll save some lives. If not…" He shook his head.

Mick said, "do me a favor when you get over on the mainland, will you?"

"Sure."

"Call Felicia on the Grizzly radio and tell her we're okay."

"I have to check in with Pete anyway. I'll do it then"

"One other thing, Jim. Don't tell her about Chris quite yet. If something happens to him, I'm not sure we should say anything to her about his being here."

***

Amanda sat at the kitchen table with Carolyn Mayes.

A heavyset black woman in her early fifties, Carolyn had a strong, but kind face, a trustworthy face. It was also the face of a person who had been to hell and back again. Her eyes masked an unknown turmoil.

Over the course of the morning, Amanda had relayed the story of how she and the others had survived for the past two years and what had brought them to Tangier. She also told Carolyn about the militia and the dangers it posed. Carolyn listened intently, weighing as she always did the information she was being given versus the greater good of the island community. When Amanda told her of the militia's wicked deeds, and what they had done to Matt, her eyes darkened. A hard expression replaced her countenance.

"Why didn't you just lie to them on the radio? Tell them there was no one here? Wouldn't that have made things easier? Maybe they wouldn't have come at all."

"No," Amanda said. "Jim is convinced they would come regardless. If not here, then back at Mount Weather, probably both. Eventually, we'd have to deal with them. This way, we have the element of surprise. The only way to be truly secure is to eliminate the problem."

"I don't know," Carolyn said. "More killing. It seems so…avoidable."

Amanda leaned in closer. "History has shown us the outcome time and again. Think about it. Raiders, conquerors, slavers. Did you hear about or encounter gangs of criminals who terrorized communities when this thing started?"

Carolyn nodded, "Yes."

"The horrible things they did? The gang rapes, the religious maniacs? How about the soldiers, stripped of friends and family with little hope of survival themselves? Do you remember their desperation and the terrible, terrible things some of them did?"

"Yes."

"Imagine that, only in greater numbers. Now *add* to that. These people were programmed with hatred even before the plague. That hatred has become a building block for their new religion, one driven by hate and led by dictators. They will lay to waste your tranquil community and replace it with their version of how things should be. If there's no other way, then there's nothing wrong with killing to preserve our own lives and freedoms. And believe me, there *is* no other way."

Carolyn stood. "All right. I'll call an emergency meeting. We'll get the men you need, but I won't send them off the island. We will make our stand here."

Amanda blew out a sigh of relief. "That's all I ask."

60

Jim switched off the radio and climbed out of the Grizzly. He slid down to the ground and Amanda reached out to catch him.

Leon held two metal boxes in his arms and placed them on the asphalt, then flipped the latches on one of them to open it. Inside were radio-controlled detonators taken from the highway department on Tangier. The other box contained dynamite. Chris pushed a cart filled with oxygen tanks from the firehouse, the wheels squeaking as it rolled.

"How is everything at home, Jim?" Amanda asked.

"Pete followed the tunnel we found the other day. It doesn't lead to the White House like he thought. It only goes a few miles, and then comes out in the sub-basement of a barn on a back road just off Route 50. I thought it sounded a bit far-fetched that it went sixty miles to the White House. At least they'll have an escape route should the militia show up there. He's coordinating the movement of some vehicles to the inside of that barn, in case an escape becomes necessary."

Chris rolled the oxygen tanks to the middle of the open area of the parking lot and started randomly placing them in stacks four wide and three high. When he was finished, he walked to where Leon squatted with the metal boxes.

"You'd better make sure those things are set to a frequency we won't be using," Chris said.

Leon held up a detonator. "Do you know how to do it?"

Chris took the detonator. "Yes."

"Good. I don't like fooling with this stuff."

"I don't mind," Chris said. "I used it all the time when I was on a bridge crew; I was certified. I'll try to set this up to detonate on a frequency the militia won't use either. We don't want anything going off before we're ready."

"No, we don't," Jim said, "and be careful with it. It's old and sweaty, and it's been in humid conditions. When you get that done, move that one stack of oxygen tanks. It's out in the open too much. We don't want to draw attention to them."

Chris nodded and went to work bundling dynamite.

Jim and Amanda used the Grizzly to move the office trailers. It had a hitch on the back and plenty of power to pull them up the hill in front of the gate. One by one, he placed them in such a way as to obstruct the militia's view from the area below. The road from the gate came down the hill and snaked to the left. Once the trailers were in place, the militia would not be able to see anything happening there. The gate and a two hundred-foot section of fence would be concealed. Buildings closed in the rest. This was vital to their plan.

There were four bundles of dynamite on the ground in front of Chris. He attached the devices to trigger the explosions and then placed a bundle in the middle of each of the four stacks of oxygen tanks to hide them.

Jim moved the last trailer into place. By now he had drawn unwanted attention. Twenty or so creatures had gathered at the gate to rake the chain link with their hands, leaving bits of flesh and clothing caked on the wire. Their cries were more like pleas than sounds of anger or lust.

They were pitiful things, with their blackened faces and rotted stumps. Ragged clothing barely covered their hideous bodies. They were weak, but still deadly in large numbers, and their numbers would grow at the gate very soon.

***

Mick watched as Griz welded the last horn into place. He had been precise with each modification. Tiny tools for tedious work had made the job possible. He had filed each piece so they were exact, but larger replicas of the original, but this whistle would be much more effective.

Mick poured a cup of water over the hot metal. Steam roiled up as the water cooled the newly-welded seams at the base of the horns.

Griz tossed the welding mask on the table and slicked the greasy strands of his unkempt beard back into place. They were ready to test it.

***

It was up to Jim and Mick to test the siren whistle. Power had to be rerouted directly to the fan in order to bypass the relays and switches that made the fan speed up or slow down. For their purpose, the pitch needed to remain constant.

When Jim turned on the power a high-pitched whine was produced that disappeared once the fan was up to full speed. The few creatures lingering by the gate became suddenly agitated. They flailed their arms and rattled the gate. They moaned and hissed as their determination grew. The affect was unmistakable. From the firehouse rooftop where Jim and Mick stood, the sounds the creatures made were barely audible. Tomorrow it would be different. There would be many more. This worried Jim. If the creatures created too much noise, it would alert the militia and upset the delicate balance of their plan. An alternate plan was in place should this one fail, but if successful, this plan would devastate the enemy.

That night, they all sat around Chris's table, rehearsing each detail of their responsibilities. Each had an important job to do. If one person failed, the entire plan could fail. It would be dangerous, six of them against an army, but they would have help from an unlikely source.

Chris nervously squirmed in his chair. "I'm not so sure this plan is going to work like you think it will," he said. "These men are well-armed and trained. You think we'll get the help we need from a bunch of deteriorating bone bags, but I'm not sold on that."

Jim understood his concern, but his own personal experience had given him the confidence to go forward with this bold plan.

"When we were at the prison, we had everything we thought was needed for safety. We had weapons, a secure location, and fences that were stronger and bigger than those that surround the harbor. We made one mistake though—we let those 'bone bags' know we existed. When we left the prison to find supplies, they saw us and followed. Just a few at first, but those few went on a seventeen-mile journey down the highway behind us. They lost sight of us, but they followed the road. Eventually it led them to us. By the time they made it to the prison, their numbers had snowballed. You see, they are creatures of instinct more than anything else. Creatures that saw the others making their way to us instinctively followed. Maybe they had nothing better to do. Who knows? The closer they got, the larger their numbers became. By the time they reached the prison, there were thousands. It was by accident, of course. We didn't intend to attract them, but tomorrow we intend to do just that. We'll have a lot less time, but we have a secret weapon. There are literally thousands of them around Smith's Point. I don't expect to draw in all of them, but I think we'll get enough. They will hear the whistle for nearly a mile, maybe more."

Chris leaned back in his chair. He finally understood, but now he had a new concern: "What happens if your secret weapon works too well, Jim, and there are too many even for us to make our escape?"

Jim shot a glance to Amanda. "Then we have to be very, very careful."

PART 4
APOCALYPSE END

61

It was five in the afternoon when they finished their preparations and everything was quiet.

Griz and Leon were stationed in a building close to the docks. They had barricaded themselves in a room with two windows that faced the parking lot that would give them a good view of the militia when they arrived.

Two gray bazookas were loaded and leaned against the wall by the two windows that faced the road leading into the enclosed harbor area and parking lot. Beside them, three refill shells. The men wore two holstered pistols and each carried a micro Uzi.

Griz chewed his fingernails as they waited, spitting bits of torn nail onto the floor. Leon held his walkie-talkie, ready for instructions.

Chris waited with Mick close to the gate, which was open to make the area appear abandoned. Several creatures had meandered inside the perimeter, completing the picture. The Grizzly was parked out of sight inside the firehouse.

Chris placed a radio detonation device on top of an old truck tire and extended the antennae. When the time came, he would use it to detonate the dynamite placed between the firemen's oxygen tanks.

Mick stooped behind a concrete wall and studied Chris, who was watching ghouls lumber mindlessly down the hill. Chris' hair was blonde like Felicia's. Their eyes were the same, too, bright blue and bottomless. Both had that faraway look, the look of a dreamer. For Felicia, he felt the need to ensure his safety. He was all the family she had left in the world.

Jim opened the hatch and climbed onto the firehouse roof. Amanda handed the weapons to him and then climbed up with him. They trotted across the roof and took up positions behind a two-foot wall that bordered the roof. The knee-high wall would give them some cover from enemy fire.

"When they show up, it's important that you stay out of sight," Jim said. "If you have to move, stay low."

Amanda gave him a harsh look and Jim could see that he had just told her something that was common sense knowledge. Unintentionally, he had just treated her like a naïve child. His need to protect her made him forget sometimes just how capable she truly was.

"I hope Carolyn has the island ready in case this doesn't work," Amanda said, "because if this doesn't work, they will really be pissed off."

"She will. It'll be tough for them to get over to the island anyway. Mick hid our boat and made the others inoperative. The harbor will be the end of the line for the militia. Even if we lose the battle, enough of their forces will be killed to prevent any kind of real offensive on the islands."

***

At six twenty-five, Jim heard the sound of approaching vehicles and scooted to the side of the roof for a better look.

A line of green, canvas-covered trucks pulled up to it and stopped. Jim raised his binoculars and watched as several men poured from the back of the lead truck and took up defensive positions. Four more trucks stopped in line behind it. Hathaway stepped out of the first truck.

Three creatures moved toward them. One man raised his weapon to shoot it, but Hathaway stopped him before he could fire. The man dropped his aim and instead, used the butt of his rifle to crush their skulls.

Jim couldn't hear what they were saying, but it looked as though Hathaway was giving orders. Several men ran through the gate and past the construction trailers. They walked briskly down the hill, their rifles raised, sighting down the barrels as they moved. After a quick evaluation, the point man waved the others through and the trucks inched forward. Hathaway walked up to the gate as the others moved through.

The original lock hung on the latch. Hathaway took the bait and used it to lock the gate once everyone was inside. The lock was easily picked and soon Mick would reopen it.

Just as they had hoped, the trucks stopped in the open area by the docks. It was the most convenient place to wait for the boat. It was the same spot where Jim had met Leon almost a week before. Two militiamen were stationed at the gate to keep watch.

The sun was low in the west. Dusk arrived around seven-fifteen and the dimming light would help add to the confusion should the battle be prolonged.

Jim scooted back to Amanda and picked up his walkie-talkie. "Mick, come in," he whispered.

"I'm here," Mick whispered back.

"As soon as you think they won't see you from below, use your gun with the silencer and take out the two guards at the gate. As soon as you've done that, I'll start the siren."

"Ten-four."

Jim watched as the two militiamen who were guarding the gate walked behind the trailers and out of his line of sight. A minute or two later, they returned. Jim raised his binoculars as one of the guards made a slight hand gesture toward him. Through the binoculars Jim saw that Mick and Chris wore the jackets and hats of the guards they had just dispatched. From a distance, no one would know the difference.

Jim turned to Amanda. "Okay, it's time. Start the whistle."

Amanda crept across the roof to where they had rerouted the power to the siren and plugged the two ends together. The fan turned faster and faster and the high-pitched whine squealed from the horns for an instant. Jim took a quick peek over the edge to see if anyone had noticed.

Soldiers continued to unload provisions and weapons from the trucks, oblivious to anything but their job. Three militiamen walked the parking lot, using the butts of their rifles to destroy the brains of the ghouls that had gained entry before their arrival.

Amanda returned to Jim's side. "Are you sure this will work? I can't hear a thing from that siren now."

"You're not supposed to, but the creatures will." Jim looked toward the gates. Ten or twelve creatures were there and others were approaching. "That siren will attract every vile monster within earshot of this place. In a short time, there will be too many to count."

Amanda pulled her jacket closed and sunk closer to the gravelly roof surface.

Jim gently touched her shoulder. "Don't worry. They can't get up here. We'll go down when it's safe."

"What about Mick and the others?"

"They know what to do."

62

Mick backed away from the gate, pulling Chris with him to a place out of sight of the approaching horde. They found cover in a place where they could see both the soldiers below and the dead walkers moving in. The soldiers were more spread out now, their provisions stacked close to an open dock.

Hathaway leaned against a wooden post at the end of the dock and watched the bay. It was six-forty and there was still no sign of a boat or of Chris Smith.

He despised tardiness. Even if he caught sight of the boat now, it would take it ten minutes to reach the shore. He wondered if Smith had run into trouble acquiring the boat. Maybe the boat's captain had put up a fight. Maybe he had been discovered. Those were good reasons for being late. Any other reason required disciplinary action.

Mick turned around in his crouched position to face the gate. The mob of creatures had swelled unbelievably in the last fifteen minutes. They pushed noisily against the fence and the meshed wire bulged with their combined weight. Mick feared they would burst through before it was time. The plan required precise timing. Everything had to fall into place just right for it to be a success.

Chris edged closer to Mick and peered out at the creatures from behind a concrete jersey wall. "Jesus, I've not seen that many things in one place for a while," he said.

"Neither have I," Mick said. "Let's just hope the fence holds. If it comes down, be ready to move fast."

Jim watched and waited.

From his position he could see only a small portion on either side of the fence, but he could see farther out behind it. A huge mob of ghouls crowded the landscape. For blocks on end there was a steady stream that stretched down the road like a line of ants on its way to a picnic.

The first wave hit the fence with a fury. The sudden addition of their weight stressed it even further.

Now even Jim could hear them as they cried out in frustration and hunger. It was only a matter of time before the militia took notice as their cries grew in strength and volume.

Another wave arrived at the gate and pushed against the ones already there. Some climbed the wire and hung over the top. Less capable ones were trampled and buried beneath the pressing mob.

Jim's radio crackled to life and he grabbed it.

"Jim, this is Mick," he whispered, his tone urgent. "They're going to come crashing through any minute. We need to move *now* and get this thing in gear."

Jim watched the militia for signs that they were aware of the coming danger. Hathaway ran from the dock into the crowd of men.

The jig was up.

"How many creatures are there, Mick? Can you give me an approximate head count?"

"Jesus, Jim, there's a shitload! And there's a shitload more on the way!" Mick said, not whispering anymore.

"Open the gate and get the hell out of there!" Jim said. "Don't linger!"

63

Hathaway was breathless and his eyes were wide as he ran to Jake.

For the first time in his life, Jake saw real fear in him.

"Something's wrong!" Hathaway cried.

"He's late, Bobby, that's all. He'll be here."

"No! No! *Listen*!"

Jake turned his ear into the light wind. He could hear a faint, rhythmic sound, like bees, but lighter, and higher-pitched. It came from the direction the wind was blowing, toward the gate.

"It's a trap, Jake! Goddamn it, it's a trap! Those trailers—they've been placed there in such a way to block our line of vision to the gate. I can hear them! It's a trap!"

"Hear who, Bobby?

"Can't you hear them?—The DEAD!"

And then Jake understood what he was listening to and almost swallowed his wad of tobacco.

Hathaway was spinning on his heels. His head felt light as the truth suddenly hit home: he'd been deceived, and he was not in command of the situation.

Hathaway clicked on his radio. "Billy Ray? What the hell's going on up there?" Only static answered him. "Billy Ray, goddamn it, you'd better answer me now!" When no answer was forthcoming, Hathaway belted the radio and turned to Jake. "Get some men and go up there and…" His words trailed off as he stared toward the gate, his mouth agape.

Jake turned, and watched as dead cannibals spilled out from around the trailers, a multitude of hideous apparitions that outnumbered the militia five to one. They shuffled with uncertain steps down the hill, crazed even more by the sight of their prey.

Jim watched from the roof as militiamen hurried to take defensive positions and with a wide grin he pressed the button on his radio. "All right, people, let's unleash hell!"

Two flashes erupted on the other side of the harbor as Griz and Leon sent their first barrage of bazooka fire. The explosions hit dead center of the militia's position, sending six men to the ground. They returned fire, momentarily ignoring the approaching mob of walking dead as Griz and Leon ducked for cover.

Jim and Amanda sent their own volley just as Chris detonated the dynamite.

The resulting explosions sent the oxygen tanks blasting out in all directions and the militia scattered for cover. A quarter of the enemy went down amid flying shrapnel from the mega firestorm. Hathaway dashed for cover behind a half-full water barrel by the dock. Jim saw him as he made his dash and hurried to load his own bazooka.

He took aim and fired at the barrel.

The explosion sent the barrel flying along with a cloud of smoke and fire. Chips of brick and mortar blasted Jim's face as enemy bullets nearly hit their mark. Jim threw himself on Amanda and the two went down behind the small ledge. Ricocheting fragments rained down on them as they laid facedown on the tarred surface.

Mick turned to wait for Chris. A second ago Chris had been right behind him; now he was nowhere to be seen. He backtracked and ran down a gravel walkway between the docks on the right and an eight-foot wooden fence on the left. The walkway turned to concrete and Mick ran up a ramp to a loading area with a locked gate to a dead end.

"Chris?" he yelled above the rapid gunfire. "Chris?"

Mick ran down the ramp and came face to face with the first creature coming around the corner of the walkway. It reached out with a swat and Mick's weapon was knocked from his hand and skidded away.

The creature lurched forward.

Mick stumbled backward until he was against the locked gate of the loading ramp. Eight more ghouls turned the corner of the narrow walkway and made their way to him.

Mick wheeled around and sent a devastating blow to the jaw of the one that was closest to him. It fell into the creature behind it and both went down. The remaining ghouls closed in and surrounded him with surprising speed as the two on the ground struggled to regain their footing.

A man with no nose reached for his collar. What it got was a handful of the necklaces Izzy had given him. It pulled, and the necklaces broke, causing a flood of little beads to bounce down the concrete. They rolled down the ramp and under the feet of the advancing reanimates.

The ghoul that had broken the necklace slipped on the beads first and fell into the one behind it. Without so much as an attempt to keep its footing, it fell into the next one and so on until they resembled a row of dominos falling, each into the other, until the last ghoul lay squirming on the ramp.

At first Mick was too shocked to move as he watched them squirm on the concrete ramp. Izzy's beaded necklaces, they had saved him. She had foreseen this.

Mick was still staring at the pile of bodies until one of them got to its knees, then he scooped up his weapon and ran down the corridor, skipping over them until he was safely past.

The gunfire stopped after two more explosions and Jim peered over the ledge. Griz and Leon had fired their bazookas and the militiamen scattered. The throng of walking dead advanced into the soldier's ranks. Many fought for their lives in hand-to-hand combat. They were no longer able to fight both the army of undead and the small band of attackers. Jim fired his Uzi, targeting only the living soldiers and the militia's numbers dwindled even more.

Leon lowered his weapon and watched from the window. Most of the enemy had been dispatched by either weapon fire or the horde of undead ravaging their bodies. The creatures attacked both the remaining soldiers and the freshly-wounded lying on the ground. The militia was no match for the enormously-growing undead crowd. Leon turned his face from the carnage.

Jim pulled Amanda across the roof and stopped under the siren. He jerked the power cord apart and sat down next to her.

"The dog whistle siren worked. It attracted every dead thing in the area. It's over, we did it," he said.

"It was horrible," Amanda said somberly. "I hope to God we never have to do anything like this again."

Jim got to his feet, "Go back to the ledge and start shooting the ghouls. I'm going to find the others and get the gate shut again. Keep an eye out for anyone who might shoot back at you."

Amanda said, "Be careful. There's a whole lot of those things down there."

"Don't worry," Jim said. "I will. You just make sure you stay here. Don't go down there until I come back for you."

64

Jim shimmied down the ladder, jumping the last six feet to the floor. At the far end of the room there was a door that opened to a balcony on the opposite side of the action. He would go down the stairs there. It would be the safest route to the others, remaining unseen for the better part.

When Jim opened the door he came face to face with Robert Hathaway.

"YOU!" Hathaway screamed.

A foot apart, they both raised their weapons to fire. Jim used his rifle to knock Hathaway's to the side, bulled forward and pushed him against the railing. Hathaway's rifle went flying over the edge and clanged to the asphalt below where it discharged.

Jim's weapon was now between them as each man wrestled to gain possession of it. Hathaway twisted the rifle until the butt was turned upward and under Jim's chin. "Where's your big oaf, Hathaway?" Jim spit. "There's no one here to fight your battle now!"

Several ghouls saw them and began climbing the stairs.

Hathaway gave a quick thrust and the butt slammed into Jim's chin. The impact caused him to lose his grip on the weapon, and his focus.

Hathaway took aim at Jim's head and pulled the trigger.

Click.

Hathaway flipped the weapon around and took it by the barrel end and swung it against the side of Jim's head.

Jim staggered back, teetering on the edge of the third step.

A cold hand grabbed Jim's arm and the blackened teeth of the closest ghoul bit into his left shoulder. Jim cried out and shoved the creature back down the steps behind him. Hathaway laughed manically as Jim pressed down on the injury and charged.

He grabbed Hathaway by the collar and drove an upward kick into his groin. Hathaway exhaled and bowed. Jim sent an uppercut to his chin and with newfound strength tossed him down the stairs.

As Hathaway fell, he took the ghouls with him.

Dazed and confused at the bottom of the stairs, he faced the awful truth as eight ghouls covered him. He was face to face with the same zombie that had bitten Jim in the shoulder.

As though bobbing for apples, the ghoul lowered its face and bit into Hathaway's nose. Warm blood flowed over his face as its teeth tightened their grip and it twisted its head back and forth. The fleshy part of Hathaway's nose ripped away with the monster's teeth, leaving the open nasal cavity to fill with blood.

Jim listened to Hathaway's screams and watched as the mob tore into him. He waited until Hathaway fell silent and the dead things turned their attention on him before making his way back into the building and locking the door.

65

Jim finally met up with Mick, Griz, and Leon by the docks, away from the dangerous feeding frenzy. Chris bounded out from under one of the docks drenched in blood.

"What happened?" Mick asked. He held Chris by his blood-soaked arm.

"I had to take cover. I got shot in the arm."

Mick pulled up Chris' sleeve and inspected the injury. "Hell, boy, it's only a flesh wound. You'll be fine." Then he noticed the torn shirt and the blood on Jim's shoulder. He thought if he waited to say something, maybe the explanation would be different than what he already knew it to be. Maybe Jim had been shot like Chris. But it was plainly not a gunshot wound. He had seen this kind of injury before and his heart sank. It was a bite.

Jim said, "Go close the gate and get the boat ready. I'll get Amanda." And without another word, he turned toward the firehouse and ran back through the ghastly feeding zone.

***

Amanda had not seen the fight between Jim and Robert Hathaway. She'd been too busy sending more than one hundred creatures to their final death. She was still plucking away at them when Jim stepped onto the roof.

Jim did his best to hide his wound, but the blood still flowed to soak the blue jacket he had found in the firehouse and he slung his rifle over that shoulder, hoping Amanda wouldn't notice.

"Come on!" he called to her from the trapdoor. "Let's go. We're going to make a run for the boat."

Amanda picked up her things and eagerly ran to him. "Are you okay?" She asked, once she was by his side.

"I'm fine."

Amanda swiped her hand across his shoulder. Her fingertips were red with blood. "No, you're not! What happened?"

"I'm fine," he assured her.

The look on his face told her a different story and she pulled the weapon from his shoulder.

Before he could react, Amanda pulled back his jacket and exposed the bite. Amanda gasped and the rifle slipped from her hand to the surface of the roof. "Oh my god, Jim! We've got to get you to a doctor."

"It's all right. It really is. There's only one thing left to do and that's get all of you back to the island."

"No, Jim, I won't let you go. You can't leave me." The tears flowed, and a knot formed in her throat. "You can beat this. Goddamn it, you can beat this!"

Jim pulled her close and held her tightly. "No, I can't."

66

The next day, Mick took a small group of men back to the Smith's Point, killed the rest of the creatures, and cleaned up the bodies. It gave him time to use the Grizzly's radio to contact Felicia and tell her what had happened. He told her about the necklace and how it had saved his life. He told her about her brother and let her speak to him.

Chris cried as he spoke to his sister and the fact hit home that they were the only family members known to survive the plague. They would be reunited in two days when Mick returned to the mountain with Chris. Soon after, they would make preparations to move everyone to Tangier.

Amanda was devastated. Unlike Felicia, who had found happiness in the post-plague world, Amanda was in danger of losing the love of her life. Jim was her soul mate. The wound would soon take him from her and she would be alone again. He had become distant, quiet, and standoffish for fear of transmitting the infection to her through his affections. The strain had been too much for her and now she slept at Chris's house. A mild sedative had been given to her and she was finally getting the rest she needed.

When she awoke, Jim was gone.

67

Something had changed as Jim drove into Fredericksburg.

As he made his way through town, he was noticing less activity. Most of the walking dead were motionless on the ground. Others were nothing more than writhing, crawling corpses, unable to find their footing enough to walk.

At one point, he had left the safety of the truck to advance on a creature he thought might be Matt when a bump from behind pushed him forward.

Jim turned to meet the menace, only to watch it slide down his chest and fall motionless at his feet. They were slower and weaker now. It was no trouble to pass large groups of them without much thought of a chase. The sudden change was all around him, as far as he could see down the long, wide avenue.

Jim leaned against the front of the Humvee. He had been waiting for Matt for more than an hour. It was the same spot where they had first encountered the militia. The wrecked plane was a hundred yards up the road. He was certain that Matt would return. His malfunctioning body had probably revisited this place many times already, not sure exactly why it was drawn to it. It was just something they were prone to do. This was an important place to him. It was where he died.

Jim wasn't one for long good-byes. Mick had understood that and had done his best to keep his emotions about Jim's dilemma to himself, but Amanda had been grief stricken. He missed her now and in a way, wished she was there with him. Her love would be of some comfort now that his ultimate fate was close at hand. With death so near, deep feelings gnawed at his sanity. His fear and the growing illness clouded his mind. But he had one last duty to perform before he could do what must be done for himself—before he could let go of reason.

As the sun faded and darkness came, Jim sat in the Humvee's driver's seat. The damaged Humvee afforded him better protection than the canvas-covered truck he had driven there, but that wasn't the only reason he had chosen it for the night's stay. Matt's body would still feel a connection to the vehicle, and surely be drawn back to it.

As Jim fought sleep, his shoulder burned like fire. The infection was taking its toll now. He was sweating. A fever was building and wild colors were dancing before his eyes even in the darkness of night. If he was a religious man, he would pray that he wouldn't die before morning.

A childhood prayer came to mind...

> *Now I lay me down to sleep,*
> *I pray the Lord my soul to keep;*
> *if I die before I wake,*
> *I pray for Lord my soul to...*

—And finally a restless sleep.

***

The scent of spring flowers wafted through the cracked window. Jim opened his eyes, yawned, and sat upright in his seat.

Matt stood in front of the vehicle. His glazed eyes stared into Jim and he leaned unsteadily to one side, the palm of his left hand resting on the hood of the Humvee. His mouth moved as if to speak, but no sound came. Then, he stood up straight and pulled his shirt down from its wrinkled position above his belt for a more respectable look.

The sight was a bit funny to Jim, as though there was still something of Matt remaining in this walking dead flesh and he was trying with all his might to find a bit of dignity.

Jim stepped out of the driver's seat. Matt only watched as he raised the .44.

"Hello, Matt," Jim said. "It's good to see you again. I took care of everything for you. We took care of the men who did this to you."

The undead-Matt simply groaned.

"Are you ready to go home now?"

Undead-Matt moaned again, then staggered toward Jim in an aggressive manner.

Jim pulled the trigger and fulfilled his promise.

***

Jim had brought a shovel with him from Tangier and he pulled it from the back of the covered truck.

Birds sang in the distance as large, black buzzards hovered overhead, waiting to pick at the multitude of unburied corpses littering the ground. They paid no mind to Jim as he dug Matt's grave.

In an hour the job was done and the last shovel of dirt was thrown on top. Thankfully, no creatures had interrupted him. Actually, there were none to be seen as Jim scanned the area. Certainly, there were more bodies on the ground now than there had been the night before, but no sign of cannibalistic walkers. During the night more had come to die.

For the first time that day Jim remembered his injury. It wasn't hurting as much now and the fever was gone. Less than twelve hours ago he had been worried that he wouldn't make it through the night. Now it barely bothered him. Was he beating it? The doctor on Tangier had shot him up with antibiotics before he left the Island. Had the penicillin done its job? This was the third day. By now he should be incoherent and too weak to walk. Instead, he felt good, alert, and even hungry. He touched the wound. It was tender to the touch, but certainly much better than the day before. He had not eaten in more than a day and now his stomach groaned. For the first time since leaving the island he thought of food. A nice thick, juicy steak would be nice, he thought—rare of course.

Yes, he was hungry. What did that mean? He leaned the shovel against a tree close to where he had buried Matt and stared at his hands. He turned them over, palms up. And then he held his arms outstretched, studying them for color and life. He was not pale. His thoughts were clear. He turned and looked at the ground around him and the countless bodies lying there. In yesterday's partial daze he had failed to completely understand what was happening. But for all intents and purposes, it appeared the plague was over or at least ending. The great rising of the dead was not going to last ten years. It would last only two. The dead were once again bound to the realm of Hades and the common grave.

—the end

Epilogue

Jim Workman did not understand that not only was the plague nearing its end, but his death and quick revival upon hitting the water when he was thrown from the aircraft carrier had affected his fate as well. The disease was a hidden plague in all of us and for thousands of years it had waited, lurking there in our genetic code from the dawn of recorded history for a time to explode upon the Earth. Each of us carried the invisible enemy that upon death wormed its way through the human body.

Like any good preventive booster shot, Jim Workman's temporary death acted as anti-venom. His death forced the devil's hand into action, prematurely activating and interrupting an evolutionally change. His revival upon hitting the icy waters of the bay allowed his system to become familiar enough with its terrible effects to combat it. Jim Workman had the upper hand in the fight for life and true death. He would not revive as billions had before him.

The unknown bacteria found in a living corpse's bite that once killed its victim in only days had run its course. Like algae deprived of moisture, this new organism dried up and was cast to the wind even before the last corpse fell, and before Jim Workman had been bitten. His infection and illness was normal, inflicted by the remaining normal bacteria living in his attacker's mouth. The dose of antibiotics given him when he left Mount Weather for Tangier

Island was enough to cure him of a bite no longer containing the new and deadly organism.

Jim would soon realize that not only did he live, but that he could return to Tangier and Amanda. His miraculous survival would result in the inevitable conclusion that his experience offered a remedy, a new approach to combating revival upon death. This treatment, administered to the population would prevent an explosion of their numbers. One would not become two. Two would not become four. Four would not become eight and so on. Should future outbreaks take place, humanity would not be slaves to the bite of living dead corpses. Their numbers could be kept in check and mankind would be free to once again become many and fill, or overfill, the Earth.

But the more things change, the more they stay the same. At least in the grand scheme of things, and certainly over the great span of time. Yes, it is true that the Earth will breathe easier for a while with its much smaller population. But soon, new boundaries and borders will take shape. History being bound to repeat itself, new nations will arise and new wars will be fought. The quest for riches and comforts, and improvements of every kind will continue, and again mankind will prove that his fate is not to be directed or planned out. For it is not in man's genetic code to govern himself. To that end, it seems a greater Being is needed.

So full circle we've come. And if we face a rock from space, or erupting super volcanoes from deep within, or our own misguided steps, our fate seems sealed. Our failures are met with a final abrupt solution that may not always benefit the food chain's temporary masters.

RESURRECTION
By Tim Curran
www.corpseking.com

The rain is falling and the dead are rising. It began at an ultra-secret government laboratory. Experiments in limb regeneration-an unspeakable union of Medieval alchemy and cutting edge genetics result in the very germ of horror itself: a gene trigger that will reanimate dead tissue...any dead tissue. Now it's loose. It's gone viral. It's in the rain. And the rain has not stopped falling for weeks. As the country floods and corpses float in the streets, as cities are submerged, the evil dead are rising. And they are hungry.

"I REALLY love this book...Curran is a wonderful storyteller who really should be unleashed upon the general horror reading public sooner rather than leter." – *DREAD CENTRAL*

THE DEVIL NEXT DOOR

Cannibalism. Murder. Rape. Absolute brutality. When civilizations ends...when the human race begins to revert to ancient, predatory savagery...when the world descends into a bloodthirsty hell...there is only survival. But for one man and one woman, survival means becoming something less than human. Something from the primeval dawn of the race.

Dead Bait

DEMONMACHY
Brant Danay

As the universe slowly dies, all demonkind is at war in a tournament of genocide. The prize? Nirvana. The Necrodelic, a death addict who smokes the flesh of his victims as a drug, is determined to win this afterlife for himself. His quest has taken him to the planet Grystiawa, and into a duel with a dream-devouring snake demon who is more than he seems. Grystiawa has also been chosen as the final battleground in the ancient spider-serpent wars. As armies of arachnid monstrosities and ophidian gladiators converge upon the planet, the Necrodelic is forced to choose sides in a cataclysmic combat that could well prove his demise. Beyond Grystiawa, a Siamese twin incubus and succubus, a brain-raping nightmare fetishist, a gargantuan insect queen, and an entire universe of genocidal demons are forming battle plans of their own. Observing the apocalyptic carnage all the while is Satan himself, watching voyeuristically from the very Hell in which all those who fail will be damned to eternal torment. Who will emerge victorious from this cosmic armageddon? And what awaits the victor beyond the blood-drenched end of time? The battle begins in Demonmachy. Twisting Satanic mythologies and Eastern religions into an ultraviolent grotesque nightmare, the Messiah of Death Saga will rip your eyeballs right out of your skull. Addicted to its psychedelic darkness, you'll immediately sew and screw and staple and weld them back into their sockets so you can read more. It's an intergalactic, interdimensional harrowing that you'll never forget...and may never recover from.

Available at www.severedpress.com, Amazon and most online bookstores

GREY DOGS
IAN SANDUSKY

WHEN GOD TURNS HIS BACK ON THE EARTH

Fires blaze out of control. Looters are run through with speeding lead. Children scream as their flesh is torn by broken teeth. Firearms insistently discharge in the night air. Over it all, the moans of the infected crowd out any pause for silence.

THE EPIDEMIC SHOWS NO MERCY

Men. Women. Fathers. Daughters. Wives. Brothers. All are susceptible, and the viral infection is a death sentence. One hundred percent communicable. One hundred percent untreatable. It's making people insane, turning them feral. *Zombies.* No end is in sight, and Carey Cardinal has run out of options.

ONE SHOT AT SEEING SUNRISE

Past lives, shadowed histories and long-kept secrets will emerge, making the twisted road ahead ever more difficult to navigate as Carey will discover a foe far more dangerous than the shattered grey dogs - himself.

Available at www.severedpress.com, Amazon and most online bookstores

The Official Zombie Handbook: Sean T Page

Since pre-history, the living dead have been among us, with documented outbreaks from ancient Babylon and Rome right up to the present day. But what if we were to suffer a zombie apocalypse in the UK today? Through meticulous research and field work, The Official Zombie Handbook (UK) is the only guide you need to make it through a major zombie outbreak in the UK, including: -Full analysis of the latest scientific information available on the zombie virus, the living dead creatures it creates and most importantly, how to take them down - UK style. Everything you need to implement a complete 90 Day Zombie Survival Plan for you and your family including home fortification, foraging for supplies and even surviving a ghoul siege. Detailed case studies and guidelines on how to battle the living dead, which weapons to use, where to hide out and how to survive in a country dominated by millions of bloodthirsty zombies. Packed with invaluable information, the genesis of this handbook was the realisation that our country is sleep walking towards a catastrophe - that is the day when an outbreak of zombies will reach critical mass and turn our green and pleasant land into a grey and shambling wasteland. Remember, don't become a cheap meat snack for the zombies!

BIOHAZARD

Tim Curran

The day after tomorrow: Nuclear fallout. Mutations. Deadly pandemics. Corpse wagons. Body pits. Empty cities. The human race trembling on the edge of extinction. Only the desperate survive. One of them is Rick Nash. But there is a price for survival: communion with a ravenous evil born from the furnace of radioactive waste. It demands sacrifice. Only it can keep Nash one step ahead of the nightmare that stalks him-a sentient, seething plague-entity that stalks its chosen prey: the last of the human race. To accept it is a living death. To defy it, a hell beyond imagining

"kick back and enjoy some the most violent and genuinely scary apocalyptic horror written by one of the finest dark fiction authors plying his trade today" HORRORWORLD

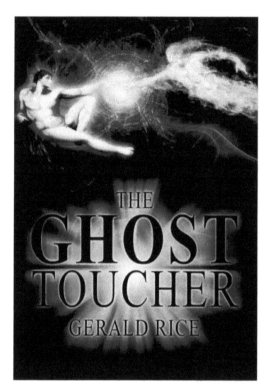

THE GHOST TOUCHER
Gerald Rice

"Haven't you ever picked up your keys for no reason and realized you had nowhere to go?" Israel asked. "Or picked up a pen and didn't have anything to write?"

"No," Kelly said.

"Sure you have. Everybody has. It's like having déjà vu about déjà vu."

"What?"

"You know-you remember remembering you've done a thing before, but you only remember remembering it when you're remembering it?"

"So when I'm not remembering it, I forget it?"

"You got it."

"No. No, I don't."

In a world where ghosts are an accepted reality, Stout Roost, reality star and host of the Network's The Ghost Toucher reality series has vanished. But Israel, the spiritual detective they hire, doesn't exactly have a plan to find him. Kelly Greene, a customer service rep, is tapped to assist the detective, but he quickly realizes that as far as unconventional methods go, Israel's are insane. He informs Kelly there is an afterworld and it was already populated by pesty ghosts. They also hate humans because they eventually become ghosts and are seeking a 'clean' way to exterminate us all. The two learn finding Stout is the least of their worries as they are pursued through metro-Detroit by obsessive compulsive wannabe warriors, mutants who worship an insane deity, weapons from the other side and a mysterious, perpetually pregnant, augmentative woman with a gender complex.

Available at www.severedpress.com, Amazon and most online bookstores